T0089100

Little Sister's Last Dose

LITTLE SISTER'S LAST DOSE

A NEW YORK MYSTERY

ALEX MINTER

POCKET BOOKS
New York London Toronto Sydney Singapore

This book is a work of fiction. Names, characters, places and incidents are products of the author's imagination or are used fictitiously. Any resemblance to actual events or locales or persons, living or dead, is entirely coincidental.

An Original Publication of POCKET BOOKS

POCKET BOOKS, a division of Simon & Schuster, Inc.
1230 Avenue of the Americas, New York, NY 10020

Produced by 17th Street Productions,
an Alloy company
151 West 26th Street
New York, NY 10001

ISBN: 978-0-7434-6331-7

First Pocket Books trade paperback printing May 2003

10 9 8 7 6 5 4 3 2 1

Printed in the U.S.A.

Little Sister's Last Dose

Prologue

Light flashed on the girl's eyes and Soraya knew her. She called out over the bass thump of revamped Supertramp.

"Penelope?"

The girl didn't respond. Everybody was dancing hard and Soraya Navarro wasn't about to stop. It couldn't be Penelope. Soraya shook her head and kept on—she was waiting for Gus Moravia to come out of one of his midnight meetings with Terrence Cheng. She danced with her arms up, and then she was enveloped by a loose circle of women she didn't know.

"We heard about you," one of them yelled.

Soraya nodded, like notoriety was familiar. Being with Eden-Roc's manager made her the queen, and that status gave her a primitive kind of pleasure. She wasn't ashamed: she allowed herself to indulge in nothing besides Gus. But then the girl she thought she knew sailed over the sea green lights embedded in the dance floor's perimeter. A beautiful girl who'd been a grubby playmate so long ago. Now it looked like she was a phantom in somebody else's entourage.

"Penelope?" Soraya called again.

But the girl was hearing nothing. She kept going, past the dance floor, toward the door in the back that led to the basement VIP lounge. She followed a young man in a flat-black suit made of what might've been boiled silk, who was laughing. He had one hand raised, his fingers spread out and waggling, like some crazy New York nightclub tour guide. His hair was cut conservatively and his collar was small and white. No earrings, no visible tattoo. Some kind of rich guy. Half a dozen people were behind him: several girls followed by an older man, who might have been anything, a bodyguard or business partner or worse, a dealer looking to trade expensive drugs for flesh.

Danny was working the lounge door. He stepped quickly to his right and waved the group in and down the stairs. He even smiled. Soraya knew then that the guy in the suit must be large. Nobody got that kind of quick and friendly entrance unless they were famous or they were friends with Gus's boss, Terrence Cheng.

Soraya grabbed the high-octane mojito her girl Kashmira had made for her and finished it, letting the ice bang against her teeth. Penelope would be her age, nineteen, or half a year younger. The discussion Soraya had led on Kristeva that morning up at Barnard slipped out of her head, the half-dozen calls from her mom, the people staring, whispering, well, yelling to one another that she was new with Gus and was to be envied *if* she was smart and hot enough to truly hold on to him—it all went. Couldn't be Penelope Novak. No way.

This was the weekly Orange Glow party, a Thursday in late November, and Eden-Roc felt crisp. At least, if you could stuff a thousand people into a space meant for three hundred and get them dancing hard to Swayzak beats and still feel fresh, then it was crisp. And Soraya could. She smiled and saw a white pin dot of light, and then somebody snapped a picture of her. She looked over to her left. It was that *New York Spectator* photo guy. Long-haired loser. And right next to him was Lanie Salisbury, the little reporter bitch. She wondered why Gus let them in—but of course it was promotions, just business.

She felt the things she kept hidden from back when she was a kid bumping around inside and she knew she had to look at that girl again. Just say hello. Tell her she looked like somebody she'd known from a long time ago. If it wasn't her, that'd kill the mystery right there and Soraya could get on with her night. She came fast, moved past Kashmira, who winked at her as she danced behind the rainbow-colored Lucite bar, while a dozen men watched her moves and forgot drink orders, fifty-dollar bills squeezed tight in their fists.

Soraya got over to Danny, who stood at the basement door. He was sipping a quart of iced coffee through a straw.

"Gus isn't down there," Danny said, impatient with her. Not so impressed with the manager's new girlfriend.

"So?" Soraya snapped. She stared at Danny. His head was shaved and he was huge. He stood like a cop manning the Do Not Cross line at the crime scene, pumped up on his bullshit authority. He let a couple of models in before her and then he smirked, stepped aside slow, and she had to angle him out of the way to get down the stairs.

In the basement room the light was brighter, more yellow. Arno, who waited tables and ran drinks to the VIPs, was busy at the far end of the room, taking care of a table crowded with the members of some band—Spacehog—who'd lost their record deal but stayed cool because industry people and models liked to hang out with them. Candles burned behind glass bricks and the music was trance: Freescha. Several different groups massed around the low tables. They weren't older than the people dancing upstairs, but they were more serious, cooler.

Soraya looked down toward the end of the divan, where the young guy was sitting with his people. The girl who could be Penelope was sitting off to the side, her head flopped back on the green velvet, not paying attention to the conversation. She was in a tiny white T-shirt and a pair of what looked like Miss Sixty jeans, and her feet were up on the cushion next to her. Her shoes were from elsewhere—they were some kind of moccasin, the kind of thing a tall girl might wear to hide her height before she realized that height was legitimate currency in Manhattan. If that was Penelope, though, and she'd just come into town from whatever backwater her mother had dragged her off to all those years ago, then the wrong shoes made sense. Soraya watched the girl's head slip forward—her eyes bulged and her nostrils involuntarily flared like she'd taken a wrong hit. If it *was* Penelope, then she was royally fucked up.

"Penelope?" Soraya was right beside her, and now she was sure. Same pug nose and shaggy brown hair. Penelope looked up. Once they focused they were the same bright green don't-dare-me-twice eyes.

"Yeah?"

"It's me. Soraya. You remember?" Soraya sat down next to her. She glanced quickly around the group. But they weren't paying attention, were busy chopping up short lines of yellow-and-purple powder on the glass tabletop. Soraya knew the powder was a mix of OxyContin and cocaine. Snorting that stuff was as dangerous as mainlining and wildly expensive. She'd heard the high was finely tuned and built to last, like an eight ball but with better control. The ultimate high-low. Soraya made a note to tell Gus about that, how overt these new users were becoming. He'd told her he couldn't stop them and wouldn't try. But Soraya still thought they ought to at least act a little covert.

"You okay?" Soraya said to Penelope.

"Yeah," Penelope said. But her skin was pink and flushed, like she was trying to beat the young out of it.

"You just get to town?"

"No, I've been here," Penelope said. "I think it's been months. I'm not the one you should ask, actually."

And then she threw her arm around Soraya's neck, the same way she used to when they were kids in Brooklyn. She drummed her fingers on Soraya's cheek and giggled.

"Soraya Navarro," she said. "Hey there, sister."

But Soraya was remembering when she'd last seen Penelope. It was right after she'd lost her father and days and days had gone by with no one ever smiling. She remembered seeing Penelope in the back of Ellie Novak's car, Penelope staring at her, neither of them understanding why Soraya's father's death meant that Penelope and her big brother, Felix, had to disappear. And, in truth, nobody knew even now.

"What are you doing here?" Soraya asked. "Have you seen your father?"

"The old man? Fuck, no." Penelope's laughter was false courage. Her voice was too soft and too high. She stood up, her arm still around Soraya. She wobbled a little, but she looked straight ahead. Soraya followed her eyes and saw the back of the guy in the black suit. He disappeared up the stairs. A woman walked by and waved at the group, then slipped in among them. Soraya saw that it was Liza Pruitt, past twenty-five and old-school cool. She was supposed to be helping Terrence Cheng reopen Peppermint Lounge, a venerable club up in Chelsea.

Soraya looked back at the group. Liza Pruitt was watching her now and Soraya took a step back, knocked up against one of the big guys she'd seen upstairs. She recognized him, too: Max Udris, who worked on interiors for Terrence. He was staring around, looking for somebody, probably Terrence, ignoring the music, not even pretending to act like he fit in. And he didn't, Soraya thought. In his short leather jacket and black slacks he looked like a mobster waiting for his connection, and he didn't seem to care who knew it. Terrence liked to keep his people waiting and he was elusive. Soraya had never properly met him.

As she inched away from Udris she saw Penelope make a long line of purple Oxy disappear off the table. Soraya found that she had to look elsewhere. Then she felt air rush around her, and when she turned back, Penelope was already drifting up the stairs, following the guy in the good suit. Soraya looked down at the group, but they were tucked forward, bowed in toward one another, heads angled low as if in prayer. And Max Udris had already moved to the bar.

Soraya went quickly upstairs, but Penelope was gone. Lanie Salisbury was still around, prowling for anything interesting. Soraya tried to snub her, but Lanie wasn't the type to even notice.

"What's happening down there?" Lanie asked.

"Nothing," Soraya said. She turned to Danny, said, "Don't let this one downstairs."

"Knew that," Danny said.

1

Felix Novak crossed into Manhattan at about half-past one in the morning, on the last of what had been a succession of unusually hot March nights. He came off the George Washington Bridge and coasted down Broadway. He told himself again that he knew where he was headed and fought to keep cool against the great human surge of the city.

Within minutes he'd made eye contact with a man who told him to go the fuck on back home, with a woman who smiled and ran her hand over the sparkling purple paint on the hood of his car. Soon he was caught up in late night Times Square traffic. He found himself banging on his horn for what felt like the first time in his life. Then he eased back, remembered what he was here to do, turned down the old Nirvana that always helped him think. He looked away from the tourists who stared at his '70 Roadrunner, beaten down but still beautiful, Plum Crazy and powerful as any production ever built, by every standard Detroit ever set.

When he'd called Soraya Navarro that morning, she'd said to meet her at a place called Eden-Roc. He had the address. He'd been driving straight for a day and hadn't slept since Cleveland. But he couldn't stand the idea of waiting anymore.

He drove fast, one hand on the map he'd bought, and soon got down to the south edge of Chinatown. He slid along Chrystie Street and stared around him. He smelled the hard mix of hot oil and food and exhaust fumes. He looked out at Chinese men in white shirts, black pants, and sneakers, sitting on benches in front of something that looked like a garbage-strewn highway median. His map called it Roosevelt Park. Behind the men, he saw bunches of kids chasing one another through pools of yellow light.

He found Canal Street on his third try. He circled around, cut right onto Eldridge Street, and parked. Salsa music came pulsing out of the brightly lit store on the corner—Richie's Bodega. More men stood there, all Latin, drinking Coronitas poorly hidden in brown paper bags.

They ignored him. A low doorway across the street was marked by a black awning that had the street number written across it in dark blue script. That was all. Felix checked the address Soraya had given him. It matched. He leaned against his car, his tan suede cowboy hat pulled low over his dirty brown hair, blue jeans stiff from sitting, a rumpled white windbreaker covering his sweatshirt.

A doorman with a shaved head opened the mirrored door and a couple dressed in black came out and turned west, acknowledged no one. Felix waved at the doorman, who did not react. Felix came across the street. Still the doorman was unseeing.

"I'm looking for Soraya Navarro," Felix said. "She knows me."

Felix heard the steady bump of hand-scratched bass coming from inside the club. The doorman disappeared. Felix went back and stood by his car. The doorman came out with a pink-eyed albino pit bull on a short metal chain. He stepped into the street.

"She'll be along," the doorman said.

Felix said nothing. The dog pulled toward him and the man tugged hard on the chain. He saw the dog wince and cower. The man kicked the dog behind its rib cage. The dog whined and sat down on the curb.

"She likes you," the man said.

Felix squatted down and looked the dog in the eyes, said, "That makes one of us."

The man stopped smiling and got ready to kick the dog again. But he stopped when Soraya Navarro came fast through the doors and moved across the street. She was in low-cut black cords and a black gypsy tee, with her hair shooting out at all angles. She came up and hugged Felix hard. He felt the tension ease out of him, like breath released after cars don't collide. And then he was crying.

Soraya said, "I'm sorry we've got to say hello like this."

Felix crushed into her like there hadn't been a dozen years since he'd seen her, and then he knew he'd never hugged her before, certainly not when she was eight and he was eleven. But still, he didn't let her go. Then he felt the doorman's gaze and made himself stop.

"Walk with me," Soraya said. He saw her nod to the doorman. She was definitely grown. Just nineteen now and no more tomboy about her. She was as tall as him in her boots, with brown skin, long black hair. But there was the same dark scar below her left eye, in the shape of a crescent moon.

"Don't worry about your car," Soraya said. "Danny will look after it. My boyfriend, Gus Moravia, manages the place."

They walked east, toward the river. The sidewalk was slick with oil and the remains of the day's markets, fish scales and rotting vegetables. Felix let his steps grow careful. They were surrounded by redbrick tenements, with dozens of open windows. They heard a radio playing songs in Chinese. A squirrel-sized rat ran out of an open black garbage bag on the curb and disappeared between close-set iron bars over a restaurant. Felix looked at Soraya. She'd jerked back but then moved on without comment.

"Tell me about Penelope," Soraya said. "I'm sick about what happened to her and I know I can help you. But first—tell me good things about her."

He kept it brief, which wasn't hard. He hadn't seen his sister for over three months before she'd died. She'd been running away on and off for years before that, and in the last year, no matter what he'd said, he couldn't get her to come back home to Oregon and see their mother. Then she'd stopped talking to him. Now nothing was left but nightmares and the half hour of funeral that he'd had to run himself.

"I miss her," Felix said. "My mom keeps getting so frustrated with me. She says she feels like since we left this place, Penelope was the only person I ever trusted. And she's right. Then Penelope comes back here, and a few months later, she's gone."

Soraya put her arm around Felix's shoulders. He just kept shaking his head. To their left were acres of vast gray projects, which blotted out most of the eastern sky. Cars hurtled past them on Allen, turned hard on Delancey, and headed down to the Williamsburg Bridge.

Felix said, "All I know is what's long past. She was running with some serious users by the time she left Portland, I can tell you that for sure. Of what happened here, you probably know more than me."

"I saw her, back there at Eden-Roc, just one time, about a week before she passed." Soraya stopped. "One of the men she was with is called Max Udris. He does contracting for Gus's boss, Terrence Cheng."

"What kind of work?"

"Interiors, that kind of thing. Gus told me Max doesn't deal, but . . . he must've known the group she was with. There's always drugs around clubs. It's something you can't avoid, like drunks in a bar. Felix, I saw her using. And I asked Gus to bring me to Max, but he doesn't want to cross his boss."

"Max Udris. That's one more name than the police were able to give me."

"The police don't know anything about what goes on inside Terrence Cheng's clubs," Soraya said. "That much I know for sure. Pick me up tomorrow."

She wrote out information on an Eden-Roc card. Felix looked north, at the lights of Midtown, and felt the gas-heavy air blow around him. Then he looked at Soraya and saw that she'd grown beautiful. Her face was intense, and he imagined that her look was sought after, and further, that she probably knew it. He decided to say something before his own face betrayed his thoughts.

"You really turned out incredible looking, Soraya. Who'd have thought it, considering what a tough little tomboy you were."

She looked up at him, fast, searched his face.

"Liar," she said. "You always thought I was hot. Probably you think it less now and so you're talking to cover up. Here's my numbers. You have a cell phone with you?"

He shook his head.

She bit her lip and her face was suddenly open and young. "Don't think I'm not sorry," she said. "This has been bothering me for months. I feel like Penelope was my sister, too."

Felix breathed in, slow. He'd felt utterly alone since the funeral—

and he thought it was wrong to lose that feeling now. But Soraya was like family. And he needed somebody, that was for sure. He wouldn't go to the old man, and there was no way he could search the city alone.

"I know how to say goodbye to people," Felix said. "But her—I didn't think I'd have to say goodbye to her."

"Back when we were kids, you used to trust me, too."

"I've gotten harder since then," Felix said.

"You can still trust me. I promise. I know I can help."

Felix left her. He drove north and then west and parked on a quiet street next to some dark row houses. He pored over his five-borough map by a streetlight. He closed his eyes and thought, Horatio Street. He leaned forward to look up through his dirty windshield and the sign above showed him he was learning fast.

He fell asleep, cowboy hat pulled down low, head back. He rested his right hand on the steering wheel, his left on his money clip and the short aluminum billy club he kept tucked under his thigh. Everything else he'd brought was in the trunk. A few minutes before dawn, a patrol car stopped next to him. A policeman rapped on the window and woke him up.

"Welcome to New York, huh?" Felix said.

"That's right, genius. You want to sleep in this town, go get yourself a room with a bed in it," the cop said.

Felix nodded. He eased his hand off the club and started his engine.

The last phone call he'd gotten from Penelope had found him in his trailer on the land he shared with his mother outside of Washburn, in Oregon. He'd been fencing the property all day and was dead asleep. This time, she said she was in New York. In a hotel—some place called the Official.

She talked fast, said, "It's not trouble I'm in exactly—it's just, these aren't Portland street kids here, you know, these folks are way tougher than the space cowboys I used to hang with and I feel like I got brought up from the minor leagues and . . . I don't know. You know what?"

"What?" Felix asked. He got ready for her to ask for money.

"I'm scared."

"Scared of what?" Felix said.

"Ah, there's all this stuff here—they think I can run with them and the truth is I'm freaked out of my fucking mind. They're into volume like I've never seen before. Felix, I know you hate this stuff, but please, I need you to help me think of a way to get out of here."

And then Felix had made his mistake. She'd never said she was scared before, and she'd been on her own since she was fourteen. He was tired and angry at her for going to New York and he wanted to go back to bed. Because of all that, he read her voice wrong. He thought for sure she was fooling with him.

Felix said, "Come on, if you're so scared, then why don't you suck it up and call the old man? You're in his town now."

Penelope pulled in some air. Right at the moment where he was sure she would laugh, she said, "I left him a message. He didn't call back."

"Penelope, wait—"

But she hung up on him. There'd been some yelling in the background, people telling her to hurry up, it was time to go.

Neither of them had ever once called their father, and if she had, then she'd broken a pact, and only true fear could have made her break it. They hadn't seen or spoken to him since their mother had left him in New York, eleven years before.

"I wonder what our old man would say," they'd say to each other when they refused to do their chores. Ellie, their mother, grew furious at even this low allusion to Franklin Novak. She never mentioned his name, never acknowledged that he even existed.

Felix sat up in bed, in his trailer, and wondered how the hell Penelope had gone from hustling change on West Burnside in the Pearl District in Portland to charging calls to some hotel room in Manhattan. It bugged him, but he didn't tell Ellie or anybody.

So she'd made it to New York, apparently, and now the big time was freaking her silly. They'd never been further apart and he had no idea how to help her. He didn't even know where to begin. But he wouldn't call the old man. If she said she'd called and he hadn't called back, that was good enough for Felix. The bastard double-crossed everyone. No reason to think he'd turn straight now. The fact that Felix had idolized Franklin Novak right up to the moment he'd found out the truth about him made it all the worse. He felt nothing but humiliation at how much he'd loved his father and about how wrong he'd been.

A few days passed and then Ellie had gotten a call. The police had found Penelope, dead from an overdose of OxyContin at the Official Hotel in downtown Manhattan, Tribeca. She'd been dead only a few hours when somebody from room service went through the open door to her room and found her. Ellie refused to claim her, said she couldn't bear it. Though she confided to Felix that she'd been dreading this very thing for years.

So Felix flew to New York, accepted Penelope's body, and flew back to Oregon ten hours later. He didn't want to be there, wasn't curious, wouldn't see the old man, though the police had said that he'd asked to view the body, and Ellie had allowed his request. But Franklin's phone calls had gone unreturned. And that seemed right to Felix. He didn't believe he'd ever get past the last thing he heard her say: "He didn't call back."

After the funeral, things went on much as before. Except that when he was thinking about nothing, tending to the vineyard or mucking the horse stalls, he apologized to his sister. And he kept asking himself, How many times can you apologize while you sit and do nothing?

The police called his mother and explained that they'd found nothing to indicate that what had happened was more than a simple overdose. They'd checked in with the Portland police. They understood that Penelope had a history of minor drug arrests. She'd been found with a dozen bottles of OxyContin and no prescription. They figured she was holding with intent to deal, and she'd taken more than she could handle. Apparently she'd snorted over three hundred and twenty milligrams of straight OxyContin and drunk nearly twenty ounces of

Absolut over the course of four hours. They said a combination like that could take down a man twice her size. They'd sent scrapings from her fingernails, blood, tissue samples from vital organs, and specimens of everything found in her stomach to the state police lab. But they hadn't learned anything new. They concluded that she'd overdosed and ended the investigation.

Yes, they said when Ellie pressed them, they understood that Penelope was the daughter of Franklin Novak. But Franklin Novak had left the police force twelve long years ago. Beyond viewing the body, he had no legal right to review their investigation materials. Ellie was welcome to contact him, but they were unwilling to convey messages between an estranged wife and Franklin Novak. They had no more information and were sorry.

Felix wondered whether he should go to New York. He was in the middle of a none-too-good relationship with a girl called Iris who worked on a horse farm in Willamette, and she didn't want him to go back to New York, not even for a few days. She wanted to get married, didn't want him to get mixed up in whatever horrible thing had happened to his little sister. He kept saying they were too young to talk that way.

During the rainy evenings he sat outside his trailer and watched smoke dribble from his mother's chimney. He walked the muddy paths of their property with the dogs and checked the fences. He went to visit Iris and they argued about marriage. He'd been with three women in his life: He was shy and he knew it, and it didn't matter to him that girls found him handsome. Inside, he felt broken.

Finally he ended it with Iris. When he felt like crying he went out and chopped wood, swept the tears away with his chamois gloves, kept his eyes focused on the point of his ax.

And then one day he saw his mother coming fast over the hill from the big house. He'd been looking up at the Cascades and for a second he could swear he saw the range shaking behind her. She was in her overalls and green wellies. Her blond-and-gray hair was tied back so he could see her ears. Her eyes were red and her skin was windblown and coarse.

"I couldn't stand it if you went," Ellie said. "But I can't stand waiting here and not knowing the truth."

"Something went wrong before she died. I don't believe it was so simple," Felix said.

"Then go find out what happened," she said. "Go to New York. One of us has to, and I've got to stay here. You know I can't trust anyone else with this place. If you need money, see your grandfather. Just because I don't talk to him doesn't mean he won't talk to you."

"How do I find him?" Felix asked. He could barely remember his grandfather, Starling Furst. Starling had hated Felix's father and so they'd visited him rarely. Ellie's father was just another man she no longer spoke to, someone else she'd turned against when she left New York.

"Just go to the offices of the *New York Spectator.* They'll bring you to him."

That evening he got his Roadrunner and backed it up to his trailer. He packed clothes into a duffel bag, along with his billy club and several hundred dollars in cash.

He reached into a space he'd hollowed in the wall underneath one of the trailer's windows and pulled out the old Thompson 1911 that he'd found years before, forgotten along with some left-handed scissors and dried-out duct tape in the back of a kitchen drawer. He figured the old man had given the handgun to Ellie. Or maybe she took it when she left. Now he hefted it. At nearly four pounds of soot-colored steel, it was an ugly, dangerous weapon, loaded or not. He wrapped wool socks around it and dropped the bundle into an old saddlebag. When he'd packed everything tight, he slammed the trunk of his car and stretched. He saw his mother standing there, watching him.

"Promise me you'll come back," Ellie said.

"Of course I will," Felix said. "I'd never stay there."

She punched the door of the car. Then she reached in and kissed him on the forehead. He felt her dry lips, and then she turned and went into her house. He knew she wouldn't watch him go.

He took one last look down at the lights in the Willamette Valley and then out at the dark waters of the Pacific. Then he drove away. Out on the Wilson River Highway he ran his fingers along the outside of the door. Her knuckles had left dents.

2

Felix idled his Roadrunner at the corner of 116th and Broadway and watched the college girls. He rolled down his window. The good spring air of April Fools' Day came rushing in, along with exhaust and big-city street noise.

The street smelled of food. He looked at the row of restaurants, at El Viejo Yayo, Tinto, Socrates, Momoyama. All those tastes were strange to him. He rarely ate out, found himself in Portland no more than five or six times a year. He had no television in the trailer, didn't go to movies. He wondered what raw fish would taste like, how it might feel to be comfortable with America's pulsing, growing culture instead of always rubbing up against the wrong side of it.

He watched a girl with blue-and-white dreadlocks and black earrings the size of wine corks poked in her stretched lobes as she made her way up Broadway. Never was friendly with a girl like that. As she passed he looked at the tattoos creeping around her neck. All he had on his body was farming scars and one tattoo—a jumble of razor wire surrounding a heart at the top of his left shoulder. A souvenir from a night when he'd gotten drunk with his friends from the football team before high school graduation. His friends all chose armbands and told him he was nuts to get anything else. But drunk as he was, he knew what he wanted: a bruised heart and plenty of razor wire to protect it. Cliché or not, he didn't care. He'd always been contrary that way.

Soraya came around the corner and spotted the car. She gave a half smile and came forward. She was in a gauzy black shirt, black leather pants, and what looked like ankle boots, her black hair pushed back with a pair of tortoiseshell sunglasses. She stepped into the car. She smiled, reached forward, kissed him on the cheek.

"Where'd you sleep?" she asked.

"I just drove around," he said.

It was her lipstick that got him, the deep reddish brown of it, and her skin, and her smell filling the car—some kind of flowery perfume and the underneath smell that was something he couldn't name. He shook his head clear, told himself again that they were close enough to be related.

"You sure you're still in college?" he asked.

"Yeah, yeah," she said, and her voice was bored. "You want to be the thousandth guy to tell me I'm too sophisticated to be a college sophomore? Welcome to New York."

Felix nodded, motioned with his head: Where to?

"Go down Broadway," Soraya said.

"It's nice—you doing this for me," Felix said.

"For you?" Soraya asked. "I was way close to her back then, when you two were here. You forget all that? Before my father was killed and your family fell apart? When we were babies? And when I saw Pen that night at Eden-Roc . . . well, she wasn't remembering too much right then. I kept thinking your dad would swoop in, clean her up—but I heard nothing. Look."

She pulled a copy of the *New York Spectator* from her bag and turned back the pages.

"See this? Lanie Salisbury's column? That'd be a party for Bill Bratton at Elaine's," Soraya said. She made an ugly noise in her throat. The way Soraya said "Lanie" sounded like she was naming the girl who took her boyfriend into the bathroom at the senior prom and blew him.

"See the guest list? There's your dad, right next to Howard Safir and Bo Dietl and all the other corporate cops."

"How'd you know about it?" Felix asked. He traced a finger over the *Spectator*'s gaudy lettering. He wondered how old his grandfather was, whether he might still be involved in the day-to-day business of the paper.

"Elaine's is where all the big-time pricks go to get their mentions. It means they're looking for work. They want to stay on the low, they go to Rao's or even Umberto's in Brooklyn. New York is tighter than anybody realizes, and I've been watching Franklin Novak for a long time now."

"So the old man's not so hard to find," Felix said.

"You're talking through your teeth," Soraya said.

Felix said, "I—" but then he felt the set of his jaw and stopped. Franklin Novak had spoken through his teeth, back when Felix was growing up. His mom had hated the habit and now here was Felix, trying it out, doing something he used to do in the mirror when he was nine years old. He unclamped, smiled, and then whistled long and low, as if he were calling for an owl.

"Where are we going again?" Felix asked.

"Brooklyn. Make a left here; get us over to the FDR, on the East Side; go south."

Felix punched up Waylon Jennings on the iPod he'd hooked up to the car stereo. *New York Woman* got going and he sang along. Soraya reached into the backseat and grabbed his cowboy hat. She held it above her head like a cartoon thought bubble.

"If you're going to play that crap . . . you mind if I wear this?" she asked.

"Not at all," he said, "but you're so smart—it's probably too small."

"Didn't your girlfriend wear it back home?" Soraya asked. She sniffed the hat and then dropped it onto her head. She pulled it low over her forehead, till he could see only her blunt nose and perfect brown lips.

"Nobody ever wore that hat but me," Felix said.

"Well, you smell a lot sweeter than you talk."

They tooled along, barely speaking, and Felix thought of nothing but Penelope. She'd been down on pure country, too, and would never listen to Waylon. Now both she and Waylon were dead and the right thing to play was the new stuff from Beth Orton, which she would have loved. So he skipped over to that.

"Penelope's?" Soraya asked.

"Yeah," he said.

"Downstairs at Eden-Roc they play Luno Collision, other stuff that's stiffer than this; that's the logical step up. Maybe that's why I saw her there."

"Passing out to the stiffest beats?" Felix asked. He bit down on his lower lip, drove with both hands on the wheel.

"Something like that," Soraya said.

They pulled off the Williamsburg Bridge and turned onto Renwick Boulevard, just above the Navy Yards. Felix couldn't see a green thing anywhere—only variations on the color of metal. And that included the water that surrounded Manhattan, which lay to their right, beaten and angry, like the doorman's pit bull. The city impressed him, the way it stood so cold and clear, glittering on a cloudy April day. They coasted along a vast industrial stretch and then Soraya told Felix to park, just half a block down from Domsey's used clothing warehouse.

"You ought to get in there, find yourself a cheap dark suit," Soraya said. "Lose all that outdoorsy crap."

Felix looked down at his green Patagonia jacket.

"Yeah," Soraya said. "That."

They got out and looked for number 107. A typed card that said *Udris Stone* was the eighth in a row of twenty tin mailboxes. Below the mailbox was a printed note: *Deliverees go to the back,* with a black arrow taped underneath it. They followed it and came to a door that had a little sign above the window in the same handwriting: *U.S.*

Before Felix could hit the buzzer, a woman opened the door. Her hair was blond and kinky as steel wool, her eyes murky and brown. She wore a black down vest and jeans. She stared at them, said nothing.

"Liza?" Soraya said, surprised. "We're here to see Max."

"Did Terrence send you?" Liza sounded genuinely confused. Felix watched her. She looked awfully young to have such a tough face.

"Not exactly."

"Well." Liza shrugged, wiped at her cheek. "I was going over some stuff for Peppermint Lounge. The bathrooms are going to be all black granite. I'll go find Max for you."

"You don't need to explain anything," Soraya said.

"No. No, of course I don't," Liza said. But she wasn't looking at them anymore.

She turned and went back inside. They followed her into the warehouse. On either side of them were rows of stone slabs. The floor was gray with dust. On a platform at the far end of the space, five men were cutting and measuring stone, their faces covered in masks, their bodies zipped into white suits. The sound was sharp and loud, of huge water-cooled blades chewing through marble and granite.

"A lot of powder around here," Soraya whispered.

"Who's Liza?" Felix whispered back.

"Liza Pruitt. She works for Terrence Cheng, like Gus." Soraya frowned. "She was there the night I saw Penelope."

They followed Liza Pruitt into an office area and she motioned for them to wait. She passed through a door. Felix heard two men talking rapidly to each other in a language that he imagined to be Russian.

The inner door opened and a big man with veined red skin and a thick mustache came out at them, face first.

"I deliver in two weeks, Liza!" the man yelled over his shoulder. He wore black jeans, a bloodred turtleneck, and a green nylon jacket. A fine layer of powder seemed to follow him. Swirls of it were visible in the fluorescent office light.

"Hello, new people! What stone you like?" he said. He was a couple of inches shorter than Felix, but he was bigger everywhere else, and he had Felix's hand in his so fast that Felix was tugged forward, within inches of the thick man's face. Felix could hear Soraya's exhale—her obvious annoyance at his unwitting physical trust.

"For what? For kitchen counter? For bathroom? Terry send you? You investors in his clubs? Put your hand here—you feel that."

The man slammed Felix's hand down on a slab of cold black granite.

"No," Soraya said. "We just wanted to know about—"

"You're starting with me?" Udris asked Soraya. "Baby, that's not how we do it. What you want to do is look around for a while, then come back here and you can end yourself up with me—yeah, that's what I'm saying, we can make things real nice for you. . . ."

"I don't understand," Felix said.

"He thinks we want to renovate a kitchen," Soraya said, slowly. "We don't want stone. We have some questions. There was a girl, Penelope Novak, do you know her?"

"A girl? How I'm supposed to know a girl?" Max Udris said. He let go of Felix's hand. "She a designer? Who is she?"

"She's dead," Soraya said. She paused. "I saw you with her, one night at Eden-Roc. Maybe Liza knows her. Could you call her back in here?"

"Liza knows a girl?" the man said. "She knows plenty of girls, like everybody who works for Terry, but she just left, you know? Look who I am. I cut stone. Distribute high-end stone, to designers, people, couples like you, restaurant, hotel, the finest in the city—"

"We're not asking about stone," Felix said. The wet-saws in the warehouse whined through the office wall.

"Hey, you, come on now," Max Udris said. "All I know the answers to is questions about stone. Friends of Terry's, I don't know."

He knit his mouth together in a pout and brushed past them, as if the meeting was over. Soraya raised an eyebrow at Felix and followed Max. They went into the warehouse, into the clouds of powder and the noise from the saws and the grunting men.

Max walked up on the platform and spoke in Russian to a man who was covered in powder. His hair and beard were already milk white. He was taller than the other cutters and he wore jeans and a work shirt instead of coveralls. He turned and looked at them and laughed.

"Check out Kris Kringle," Soraya said. Felix nodded.

"Come back when you get your newlywed apartment, after you have your wedding at one of Terry's clubs," Max Udris called. "I get you a good deal—make all your countertops. I do the shower, red sandstone, get you happy, sexylike. Then we can be friends."

Felix turned to face a gigantic slab of white marble. He wiped the dust from the stone and it gleamed. Blue and green veins ran through it. The men up on the platform were all looking down at them now.

"Let's go," Soraya said. "Obviously we came here too soon."

She was already out the door, walking back toward the boulevard. They slapped the dust from their clothes.

"But we haven't learned anything yet," Felix said.

Soraya said, "Haven't we? It's just like he said. We only showed up, without thinking first. Why should he answer our questions?"

They drove in silence. When Felix looked over at Soraya, she was smiling, grinning wide.

"What's so funny?" Felix asked.

"He was waiting for us," she said. "I'm sure of it. He wasn't curious, you know? No need to be curious if you already know what's up. But that's not why I'm smiling. He had no idea who I am. He would know, if he were connected to Gus. So he's not and that's a huge relief. I don't know what he and Liza are up to and I don't even know if Terrence Cheng knows about it, but Gus definitely doesn't. Play that Waylon if you want. I feel so stupid that I'm ready to learn something new."

"I didn't realize you were so worried about your baby," Felix said. "Wanna tell me why?"

Soraya shrugged. "Coming from where Gus is from, with a mother like he had, there's no way he'd be dealing, but I did get afraid there for a minute. After Penelope died at the Official, nothing felt right. The truth is that I've been afraid since, but this is one good thing." She trailed off and turned fast, but then she saw Felix's face and dropped her smile. "I'm sorry," she said.

Soraya settled the cowboy hat back on her head and put her feet up on the dash. Felix flipped her the iPod. He drove and said nothing, only worked at trying to loosen his jaw. He looked at the back of his wrist, where Max Udris had gripped him, tried to memorize the man's touch.

"Let's think this through," Soraya said. "When I saw them that night, that guy was nervous for all the wrong reasons and Liza Pruitt didn't seem nervous at all. There was another guy Penelope was with that night, a young guy in a silk suit, and she seemed a lot more interested in him. I'd like to figure out who that other guy was. Look, Max

Udris is creepy, and I've tried to see how he plays into this, but it's not coming clear. Just now, the way he wasn't scared, it makes me wonder more about Liza Pruitt than him. Just now she was the nervous one, trying to explain to us why she was there."

Felix watched her. He realized that they'd come out to see this Max Udris in large part because Soraya was afraid her boyfriend was somehow connected to Penelope's death. And now she'd decided that he wasn't. Now she seemed relaxed, even more eager to help.

But Felix knew all too well that you can get mixed up when you love people and you can't think straight. You can't tell good people from bad people. Sometimes you can't even see what's right in front of you. That was what had happened, anyway, when his mother fell for Franklin Novak.

"I'd like to meet Gus," Felix said.

"He wants to meet you, too."

3

"So fill me in on your last decade," Soraya said.

Felix gave her his half grin and sighed. They were downstairs at Eden-Roc, in a back booth, underneath a gigantic painting of a naked mermaid on a lily pad, her hair turning to clouds above her. Though it was only ten, they'd been drinking for a while. Weak Dewar's and sodas for him, weaker Maker's Mark and ginger ale for her.

"Basically, my mom was so furious at my old man after your dad was killed that she left town and turned us all into farmers," Felix said.

Soraya laughed. "*My* mother was so furious at your old man that she got religion."

"To hear my mom tell it, you'd think my old man sleeps in a coffin," Felix said.

"I think my mom must have given her that idea," Soraya said. "After my father was killed, she was never with a man again."

They smiled at each other, and Felix felt good, like they were finally recognizing who they used to be. Though he had to admit that the feeling was cut with the idea that somebody had blasted out anything sweet that was left from their childhood. Or shot it out.

"What happened with Penelope?" Soraya asked. "How'd she totally go over? We used to write each other letters after you three left. I always knew she'd grow up wild—but not that kind of wild."

A waiter in a black T-shirt delivered a plate of shrimp dumplings. He set them down and wiped off the table. Then he stood, waiting. His body was built hard from weight lifting. But he had a florid, reddish face, with broken blood vessels in his nose and cheeks. To Felix it looked like his body was fighting the drinking his head liked too much.

"How've you been, Arno?" Soraya asked.

"Okay, Soraya," the waiter said. "Gus was looking for you before."

Soraya nodded and Arno walked away. She motioned for Felix to eat up.

Felix said, "Put it this way: What I'm not, Penelope was. She did things I couldn't understand—like she'd go hang out with the rodeo guys and drink with them, date them, even. Starting too early, when she was fourteen. She set fire to a barn down at the fairgrounds. This was—damn, this was only about two years ago, a little more, a year before she left."

"A big barn?" Soraya asked. "She was always egging me on to do wild shit—I'm not surprised." The screen of her cell phone lit up. "My mom's daily check-in. She gets up at five-thirty to work on her lesson plans and she has to speak to me before she goes to bed. It's not only religion. She's obsessive about everything."

Soraya text-messaged back an "Am ok" and sent it, ignored the "Please call me" she got back instantly, dropped the thing into her bag. She had her feet scrunched up underneath her on the leather banquette.

"So she was punky with the cowboys, that was the deal?"

"Don't make it a joke," Felix said. "That's a big event, burning down a country barn. She was out with the rodeo guys and somebody threw her up in the attic of this old barn. Like, they literally flung her up there and took away the ladder. They were laughing and I don't know who all was there—not me, that's for sure. And so she got this hay bale—she had a lighter, and she set fire to the bale, got it burning good. Then she threw it down on some yahoo's head."

Soraya said, "I guess she didn't lose the kick-ass part of her when she got older."

"So he gets upset and tries to throw it back at her and burns himself, and pretty soon everything's burning. She's still up there, flames all over the place, everybody screaming, and she's laughing her ass off. She had to wait for a fireman to come and get her down. She was hanging from the support beam in the middle of the place. They caught her in a trampoline, like the circus."

"She didn't just set fire to the barn. She set fire to a guy."

"I guess," Felix said. "Not afraid of a single thing."

"What about the drugs?" Soraya asked.

"Well, I know she was into the same stuff as all those cowboys—OxyContin."

"Yeah, that's what I saw her using. Oxy—the hillbilly heroin," Soraya said. "I knew it was headed this way. Users here cut it with coke. But it's like you say, she'd fight somebody who tried to hurt her?"

"I believe she'd fight, yes," Felix said. He sighed deep. "My mother taught her how to defend herself well enough. How to poke somebody in the windpipe or gouge an eye. She knew all that."

"Let's say it wasn't just an overdose, 'cause I don't want to believe she was that stupid. Say there was any kind of struggle . . . she'd have some cuts or bruises on her. We need a copy of the ME's report," Soraya said. "Otherwise we're just going to stay up all night telling stories."

Felix watched Soraya. She'd been staring away from him while she spoke.

"She had boyfriends?" Soraya asked.

"Always. The worst bunch of bastards I ever knew. If they hadn't been arrested, she didn't want to know them."

"Then she would have been with a guy here," Soraya said. Her voice was gentle. "If she had ugly taste in men—that wouldn't change. We need to find the guy I saw her with that night."

"You're telling me all you know?" Felix asked.

"Of course," Soraya said. "I see her with a guy, but I don't see her helpless. She was never that way, not even when I saw her, when she was all fucked up. We're a lot alike, me and her. She just seemed like she needed a real long rest."

Felix sipped his drink. He closed his eyes and found that he wanted time alone. He said, "Speaking of which—"

"It *is* late. I'll stay up in my dorm. You can sleep at the Official."

"'Cause of Gus you get rooms when you need them?" Felix asked.

"'Cause of Gus, yes. You got a problem with it? You jealous? Now why would that be? If she was the sister I never had, then that makes you—"

"Stop. I was waiting for that one. Okay. I've got nowhere else to sleep," Felix said, and yawned. "I've been here twenty hours. I'd like a bed, and if being happy for you and this Gus character is going to get me into one, then fair enough."

Soraya dug around in her bag and found a white plastic card with two orange stripes down the middle.

"Room 603," she said. "Don't have anybody visit whose services you have to charge to the room."

Felix raised an eyebrow. "Don't worry. Out in the country we learn to pay for hookers with cash."

Soraya covered what Felix thought might resemble a blush.

"Okay, sorry. Call me when you're rested and ready for more," she said.

"One more thing," Felix said. "Tell me it's a coincidence that Penelope died at the Official and that's where I'm going to spend the night."

Soraya yawned. Her mouth went wide and she brought her fist up to it. Through it all, Felix watched her.

"No," she said. "I can't tell you that. There's a lot more here that bothers me than just that me and her used to play cops and robbers under our dads' precinct desk. But finding out Gus isn't tight with Max Udris, that was one good thing."

Felix watched Soraya gather herself up, one hand clutching her bag, motioning to the waiter she'd called Arno to put the check on Gus's tab, to let Felix order whatever else he wanted because they were a kind of kin. And then she was gone, headed down the corridor and up the stairs out of the back room.

The waiter stayed after she left. He stared at Felix.

"Could I get a steak?" Felix asked.

"We'll put something together," the waiter said.

"And I bet if I asked you a question about Gus, you'd know the answer," Felix said.

The waiter picked up Soraya's half-full glass. He wiped nonexistent crumbs from the shiny glass table.

"I know answers about Gus?" the waiter said. "Steak I give you, yes.

'Cause of Soraya. Answers to questions, I don't give you, Soraya or no. Where you from, anyway?"

"West Coast," Felix said.

"Figures," the waiter said, and disappeared.

Felix watched women come dancing down the stairs. He wondered how many favors you had to exchange when you managed nightclubs and hotels. He wondered about all the different kinds of people that kind of manager might get to know.

4

Felix sat barefoot, cowboy hat pulled down low over his forehead. He was in jeans and no shirt, sunk down in a white leather club chair. He didn't move at all. She'd died downstairs, on the second floor, room 216.

Three in the morning and nobody to talk to. Penelope used to call him around now—West Coast time—and found him wanting nothing but sleep, halfway to getting up at five for chores, just as she was coming in from her night. She'd never been specific about what she was doing. She'd only said she was having fun learning about everything that made New York City go round. Then she'd ask after Ellie but refuse to speak to her. She'd never sounded scared until that last call.

He tipped back his hat and wondered how close the old man was. A block? A mile? He had no idea where Franklin Novak slept, where he worked, where he could be found, except at Elaine's or in the *Spectator.* Then he tried to think what he'd been saying to himself since he was ten, which was, Fuck him, anyway. Nobody needs an old man who would walk away from his partner, leave him lying facedown in the street. Nobody looks up to a man like that. He felt that same sense of craven humiliation, of having admired someone so much and then having watched as that man destroyed a family, forced a woman to take her children across the country and cut off all contact, all to leave the devil behind. Even now he felt stupid for having loved and trusted anybody that much. It would not happen again. Felix watched the door, as if the man would react, would come rushing in to defend himself.

And then a few soft raps did sound on the suite's door. Felix watched the doorknob, said nothing, stood up.

"Felix?" A man's voice—eager-sounding.

Felix got up and looked through the peephole. A young man stood there, jiggling, as if he were listening to a Walkman. The man was smaller than Felix, and wiry. Felix opened the door. The first thing Felix saw was his eyes, which were glinting and black—either his pupils were totally dilated or his eyes were dark as granite. The man had on a black suit over an untucked white shirt that was unbuttoned, with a green T-shirt underneath. His cheekbones were high, his jaw square and lightly stubbled. Kind of a Hollywood look, except that his skin was a powdery white, as if he never saw the sun. Either he was hearing music in his head or he just had some kind of innate sway to his step.

"Soraya said you were here and I thought I'd give you a personal greeting, you know? I'm Gus. Nice hat."

Gus slid around Felix and went and sat in the white club chair. He picked up the remote control and turned the television on without looking at it. He pressed another button and the sea foam green blinds slid down. The TV was tuned to an infomercial, a woman with a face painted like a Raggedy Ann doll saying that too much makeup was always a bad idea. Then Gus was flipping channels, his right leg bouncing up and down.

"You liking the city?" Gus asked. He didn't look at Felix, who went and sat on the bed, facing him. "First couple of months here I was freaked out of my head at all the shit to see, but now I'm cool with how it's overwhelming, and if it's too much I'm quick on a jet to Paris or somewhere, Antigua or Ixtapa, just like my boy Mike Bloomberg. I get hyped up and I dig that, but then I'm out if it's too much. Soraya, though, she's all together with the studying and I'm mad with respect but I'm . . ."

Gus went on. Felix said nothing. These New York boys, he thought, they're fast talkers. Real chatterboxes. Felix slipped the hat off his head and brushed his hair back. He'd barely touched a thing in the room and now it felt like he was visiting Gus, not the other way around. Gus did seem to fit much better into the sea green–and-gray room than he did.

Felix said, "You manage Eden-Roc, you manage this hotel. Tell me, what else do you do?"

"Huh—oh, you're slow with the friendship 'cause of the little sister. I get that. I run some operations—you know, keep ice in the icebox. But there's lots of managers. We all work for Terrence Cheng."

"And Max Udris works for Terrence?"

Gus stopped bouncing. He mashed his hair around on his head so it stood up at all angles, like grass.

"Yeah, I heard about your visit to Max. Fuck're you, Deputy Dog? Your sister OD'd. Not much mystery there. No offense, but nobody's going to talk to you about your little sister. There's nothing to say. Max Udris? That guy cuts stone for Terrence's bathrooms. Go check your sink, buddy boy—we used Carrara, 'cause this is a class place. You two called that totally wrong."

"What do you care?"

"Because I work for Terrence and he doesn't need aggravation," Gus said, and he got up and stood by the window, peered through the curtain at the city. "Look, nobody is going to talk to you and you're just going to make me look like I can't control my woman. Forget the Clint Eastwood routine, Mr. Cowboy Hat."

Felix said, "Who—"

But Gus was talking fast. "Clint Eastwood? Your overwrought squint is what reminds me. Look, everybody who could possibly have dealt the shit to your sister knows that they get found and Franklin Novak will come down on their ass but hard. I mean, your dad's old school. Punks think De Niro or Keitel when they see that bastard and they're gonna get a shank in the face if they blabber—"

"Hey, now," Felix said. "You're thinking too quick for me. Nobody here knows who I am. I'm just checking out the city, and then I've got to bring back some good memories of my sister for my mom, like how she was happy before she died, that kind of thing."

"Well, now you put it that way, that's real sweet of you," Gus said. "But take it from somebody who knows, heavy users don't leave a scrapbook of nice memories for the loved ones."

He turned to the TV, flipped by old movies, ads for phone sex, another infomercial, back to the phone sex ads, muted the set, and then turned back to Felix. He was chewing on the insides of his mouth.

"Dude, you want a cheeseburger or something? All of a sudden I'm crazy hungry. You want to head over to Florent and grab some dessert? Mocha-rum chocolate cake? Boysenberry milk shake?"

"Actually, I think I better get some sleep," Felix said. "I've been sitting up for two or three days now."

"Oh yeah," Gus said. He stood up, dropped the remote. "Well, sweet dreams. But dig on what I said. Nobody's going to talk to you about that girl. And you wouldn't want to hear the stories, anyway."

"Come on. You dig on what *I* said," Felix said, and smiled. He opened the door and felt cool air rush down the hall. "That girl was my sister."

"That's what I'm saying, friend: It's a tragedy. A sad thing. But Soraya can't help you more than she already has," Gus said. He went through the door.

"That's up to her," Felix said quietly. "And you're not making a ton of sense."

Gus didn't respond, didn't seem to hear. He said, "You sure you don't want something? Chicken burrito? Croque monsieur? Jamaican beef patty? I'm fucking famished."

Felix shook his head. He closed the door. He went and sat where Gus had been sitting, sniffed the air. Some kind of chemical smell he didn't recognize and then a high school smell. A Chiclet. The guy chewed Chiclets.

He watched the television for a moment, a young girl on a black bed rubbing at her purple panties and beckoning to him with her pointer finger: Pick up the phone.

He turned away and raised the curtains, looked out at the same red dawn he saw come up every morning over the Cascades. And for the first time in his life, he got into bed just as the sun came up. But—and it was an unsettling thing to feel—he didn't long to be back in his trailer in the valley, listening to the sheep and the chickens squawk in the pens. These sheets were white satin—that or something like it. He rubbed his calloused hand over the pillows. He didn't miss where he'd come from. Before he fell asleep, he admitted that.

5

"Your boyfriend sure is one jumpy guy," Felix said. "He's got a real narcotic bounce to his step."

"Don't say that," Soraya said. "He's just nervous about work. Terry Cheng runs him ragged."

They were on the steps in front of Low Library, in the middle of Columbia's campus. It was Wednesday morning and whipping cold, which made no sense to Felix, since it had been warm downtown.

"What exactly does Gus do for Terry?"

Soraya turned and pointed at Felix. She pressed her finger against the tip of his nose.

"Didn't he tell you? He runs all sorts of operations for him. Look, I know Terry's got a shit reputation, people think he's running all kinds of shit through his places, but Gus isn't involved with that end of what Terry does, which assumes the rumors about Terry are true, and they might not be. Anyway, leave Gus alone. He's sweet to me," Soraya said.

Felix didn't say more. He didn't want to make Soraya more defensive. And maybe he was just jealous of Gus. Maybe Gus wasn't involved at all. He did seem more worried about his job than anything else. And he wouldn't want to lose Soraya. Felix didn't believe that anybody would want to lose Soraya.

While Felix stroked his cowboy hat and tried to figure out how to hide the fact that he didn't like Gus, a light-skinned black girl with flowing dreadlocks came toward them. Her tan coat was open and several inches of her stomach showed between her jeans and the bottom of her T-shirt. She seemed familiar somehow, and it took Felix a moment to realize that he couldn't know her, so he must have seen her somewhere, in a movie or a magazine. And then he knew she must be really famous, because he didn't see many magazines or movies. She carried her books in a huge white canvas bag. A loose group of admirers flowed after her, as if the bag was a flag and she was leading a tour.

"Hi, Soraya," the girl said. "Tremendous party the other night."

"Thanks, Edwige," Soraya said. "It was great because of you."

Felix stared. The girl smiled down at him, and he looked away, tugged his hat low over his eyes.

"Come by my room later and we'll hang out. Bring your cowboy friend, too." The girl laughed and went on, admirers trailing.

"What's the matter?" Soraya asked. "Never seen a pretty little movie star like Edwige Jamison in person before?"

"Sorry," Felix muttered. "It's been a while."

"Come on. Don't tell me you were living up on that farm all these years and doing nothing but yanking weeds and playing checkers with Ellie."

"My mom . . . ," Felix said. "Wait, that reminds me—Edwige—is her father Sidney Jamison, the director?"

"Wow, you spend more time reading *Entertainment Weekly* than I would've thought."

"No, my mom always talks about Sidney Jamison. They went to school together. Here, actually."

"Well, I'll tell Edwige."

"Nah," Felix said. "I think my mom and him had a falling-out a long time ago. She hates his movies is why she talks about him. She thought *Sad Faces in the Morning* was dumber than hell."

"She sure has a lot of those falling-outs," Soraya said. "Do you think that's partly why Penelope ran?"

"I guess," Felix said. "Maybe me and my mother weren't the happiest people to live with."

"And no happy times now, either," Soraya said.

"That's right," Felix said. "Did I mention that Gus said you wouldn't be helping me for much longer?"

"He's just a nervous talker. Look, don't push me about him. Anyway, we won't need him just now," Soraya said. "I've got the police file."

Felix kept looking straight ahead. He didn't want to look up and see the same expression that had made him howl when he was a little kid, when she knew the meaning to a dirty word and he didn't, and she wouldn't say what the meaning was or how she knew.

"Where'd you get it?"

"Ex-boyfriend who's a cop. I put out that I was looking for it. When I checked my e-mail this morning, there it was."

"The old man sent it to you," Felix said.

"Did you not hear me? It was Paul Montoya, who I used to call Pally. Do me a favor and don't forget again that I'm not speaking to your father, either, got that, sheriff?"

"Don't call me that," Felix said.

They were already walking toward her dorm room.

"Okay, but lose the brooding look, would you? It might work with girls who don't know you, but I'm not one of them."

"Jee-zus, Soraya," Felix said. "I'm all tough and shit, ready to bang down doors in the big city and I get around you and I feel like I'm eight years old."

"You're not the first boy to say that."

"I don't want to hear about any of that, either," Felix said. And then his face did turn red.

"That's why I'm not telling you about my exes. You get jealous in the weirdest way."

"I'd call it protective."

"Protective and jealous—two gigantic steps on the road to friendship hell," Soraya said. "There's no time for any of that. I've got no allegiance to anybody except my mom—and you and your sister, and that's it. That's why I'm letting you take all my time."

"That and the fact that something else is bothering you. Like this is all hitting way too close to where you spend your nights."

"Fine," Soraya said. She glanced away. "Let's go check out the report. Then I've got to get to class."

The police file had everything in it and they had to open it carefully, with an Adobe Decipher program, because it was handwritten by the handling detective on the case, Rodney Paquette. The overseeing detective for the Fifth Precinct was named Mike Sharpman. He'd scribbled his initials on the bottom of each of the pages. They stood in front of the screen and tried to figure out the handwriting, clarifying each thing as it appeared on its appointed line.

"That's wrong," Felix said. He pointed at the spelling of Penelope's name.

"That's wrong," Soraya said. They'd put down an incorrect address for the Official.

"That can't be right," Felix said when he saw that Penelope's weight was one-ten. She'd been a tall girl—five feet, nine inches when she was barefoot, and she was strong enough to shear a sheep on her own—so he knew for sure that she weighed far more than that.

"Actually, if she was using, that may be right," Soraya said. But the rest of it was factually wrong.

They ended up focusing on one paragraph. It was the description of the room as it had been when she was found. Then there was a list of those who had viewed the scene. This list included half a dozen people from the hotel staff, several beat cops, the two detectives—Rodney Paquette and Mike Sharpman—the medical examiner, and the photographer. Each of these people and their approximate time of arrival were listed on the report. The other name that mattered was Lanie Salisbury's. Paul Montoya had written a note across the top of the first page saying that Lanie Salisbury had been assigned to the story. She'd been covering it from the start and probably knew as much as anybody.

"Lanie Salisbury," Soraya said. "Oh, Lord."

"What about her?"

"That little idiot reporter girl who does the Page Eight beat for the *Spectator.* I mentioned her before. She's been looking to take down Terrence Cheng forever. I'm not a fan."

"You remember my family connection?"

"That your grandfather owns the *Spectator*? What of it? It's still a crummy paper. And you won't see him, will you?"

"Probably not," Felix said. He stared at her. He thought of when he used to watch the old man on the phone. Franklin Novak could listen to anything and betray no reaction whatsoever. Years later, in spite of himself, Felix had practiced the old man's poker face during livestock auctions. It worked now. He wasn't sure if he'd need to see his grandfather. But his face had betrayed nothing. And that pleased him.

Soraya said, "Great. Many, many people in the room within a few hours of the time of death. Three empty bottles of Evian. American Spirit and Gitane cigarette butts in the ashtray. A black canvas bag containing clothes that belonged to your sister. A box of Uneeda toothpicks. Glass bottles. There's even a log of phone numbers called from that room. I wonder which call was to the boyfriend or if he was there. . . ."

"Who was the room registered to?" Felix asked. He sat on her single mattress and looked around. The dorm room was small, eight by eleven at best, with dozens of philosophy and history and feminist theory books neatly arranged on a bookshelf, a squat Bose radio, a halogen lamp, and a closet that was shut, with a poster of one of Mapplethorpe's naked black males stuck to its door with thumbtacks. On Soraya's desk was a picture of Billy Navarro, Soraya's father. His hair was long and it shot out from under his cap. He was smiling wide, wearing Ray-Bans and his patrolman's uniform. Which meant the picture must've been taken at least ten years before he was killed. Right at the beginning of his partnership with Franklin Novak, when Billy and Nancy and Franklin and Ellie had been two happy couples and the four of them were all the best of friends.

"That's odd," Soraya said. "There's no information about who paid for the room. It wouldn't just be open."

"Would Gus know why that would be?"

"He might," Soraya said. "And I'm sure that if he does he'll give me the answer. But right now I've got class."

Soraya sat next to Felix on the bed. She slipped her boots on. "Judith Butler guest lecturing on Katherine MacKinnon and snuff films. I don't want to miss it. Stay here if you like and keep looking this over. See you in an hour or so."

Soraya pushed Felix's shoulder and went to the door. She smiled. "I'll assume you won't go through my stuff."

Felix nodded, and the door closed. He took his time reading through the report on the screen again. After a while, he eased back in the chair. He stood up and then sat down lightly on the bed. He put his hand on the jade-colored bedspread, breathed in the girlish scent of the room. The phone rang.

Soraya's voice on the message machine, saying, "What you leave is up to you."

"Hey, baby. Missed you last night but checked out your boy's action. He's a little bit of a country bitch is what it looked like to me. Anyways, I'll see you tomorrow night at Orange Glow. Twelve-thirty, baby."

You're the bitch, Felix thought. Drug-addled wonder boy. Soraya was like his Penelope in one way, that was for sure—she had the same crap taste in men. He shook his head clear and went and read the report once through yet again. No evidence of foul play. But then, the ME's report hadn't been released. Two or even three other people in that room when his sister died. Tell me who you are, he thought. Let me talk to you. Whoever it was had left little droppings, hints, like any animal. You were close to her, and now you want to let me know you.

He dialed the first number on the phone log and a recording said it was no longer in service. The next number connected him to a Duane Reade pharmacy on Broadway. The list was long. He shook his head. He checked a clock and realized that he'd already lost nearly forty minutes. Soraya would be coming back and he hadn't accomplished anything.

There was a knock on the door, and he looked up. He'd made no noise, so he knew he could've played it as if there were nobody home, but he was curious. He opened the door and looked at a small girl, pixielike in stature, with brown curly hair, a pointed chin, and black-framed glasses. She carried a big black leather bag that was shaped like a bowling ball.

"Um, is Soraya around?" she asked. Her voice was lower than he would've thought. Older.

"No, but I could tell her—"

"Well, I'm Lisee Ettlinger and I'm in her . . . in her philosophy class and she said she left the homework here for me. So I'll just come in and look around and find it."

The girl was already past Felix into the room, looking through Soraya's things. Felix watched her movements. She was quickly flipping through papers, looking under things, edging toward the open iBook.

"You mean her big philosophy class?" Felix said. "The one where Judith Butler is lecturing on . . ."

"Yeah, that's the one I need notes for."

The girl's face was turned away from Felix. Her hands were like mower blades. Papers were literally in the air.

Felix blocked the doorway. He said, "Sit down on the bed with your hands spread flat over your knees."

The girl sat down and crossed her legs. She smiled at Felix and raised her eyebrows, without opening her mouth.

"That class is right now," Felix said. He picked her bag up off the floor and dumped its contents onto the foot of the bed.

"That's what I meant—I need to get the notes to—"

"You said homework."

"I think I said both. Who are you?" she said. She sounded strangely relaxed, more grown up, the play in her voice completely gone.

"First let's find out who *you* really are," Felix said.

Felix quickly tossed through the stuff in her bag: lipstick, press pass, wallet filled with IDs . . . Lanie Salisbury. He didn't look up.

"Where you from, anyway?" she asked.

He checked through her things again.

"West Coast."

"Figures," she said.

He kept going. Her press credentials were clear. And the fact that she was a liar was clear, too. He began to push her stuff back into her bag.

"Let me do that," she said. "You're cute with the tough guy bit, but you don't know how to pack a purse. I know who Soraya is. Now you know who I am. Who are you?"

"I'm Felix Novak. How'd you find Soraya's room?"

"Maybe I'm not taking philosophy, but I'm pretty good with the phone book," she said.

She finished with her bag and stood, facing Felix. He watched her eyes twitch behind her glasses. He said nothing. He felt like he could see her heart beating fast under her black sweater. Then he pushed his eyes in another direction.

"Felix Novak," Lanie said. "That means your father is—"

"Nobody knows I'm here," Felix said, fast, and then he knew he'd sounded like a little kid and had completely revealed himself. He kicked Soraya's desk, dented it like it was tinfoil.

The door opened. Soraya walked in.

"Shoot, Felix," Soraya said. "I go to one lecture and you drag in the worst piece of trash." She shook her head and laughed. "Get out of here, Lanie. I'm sick of you chasing me and Gus. Whatever you're looking for, Gus has nothing to do with it."

"She knows who I am," Felix said.

"Then you better call your old man before she files for tomorrow's first edition."

Felix stared fixedly at Lanie, gave her his angry squint. She smiled back at him.

"I'm serious, Felix," Soraya said. "You better let Franklin Novak know you're here before anybody else does."

"Wait a second. Soraya, why don't you and me and Wild Wes have a drink first," Lanie said, "and we can talk about everything that Gus has nothing to do with."

6

"Don't be an ass, Lanie," Soraya said. "We're not going anywhere with you."

"What about young Mr. Novak?" Lanie asked. "Want to let him have his say?"

"He knows when he's being blackmailed."

"Does he?" Lanie asked.

Then it was quiet. Felix went and leaned against the windowsill. He got out a toothpick and chewed on it.

"I could have you arrested," Soraya said.

"Call P. J. McKenna at the 24th and have him bring me in. I haven't seen him in a while. Or forget the cops—call your boyfriend's boss. There's a fella who knows how to take a girl for a ride she won't forget."

Lanie was smiling. Soraya had her phone in her hand. It started ringing. The three of them looked at the ringing phone. Soraya pressed talk, said, "I'm busy," and threw the phone on the floor, where it popped open and the battery fell out and lay there like useless information.

Soraya said, "Nobody but murder junkies and gossip fiends reads the *Spectator* anymore."

"I know," Lanie said. "I'm the woolly mammoth of the media."

"More like the fuckin' cockroach—"

"Okay, ladies," Felix said. "That's enough. I'm going downtown. Lanie, you need a ride?"

"Felix?" Soraya said. He ran his hand behind his back where she could see it, palm down, waist high. *Cool it. I'm thinking straight.*

Lanie said, "Normally I prefer the IRT. But for a cute country boy, I'll make an exception."

Felix went to hug Soraya goodbye. He whispered, "I'll call you later. She'll tell me a thing or two."

"Don't you tell her one thing in return," Soraya said out loud. She was already hustling the two of them out of her dorm room, slamming the door. They found themselves in McBain's noisy hallway, where the sound of Bright Eyes nearly drowned out their conversation.

"What'd you do to her?" Felix asked.

"Not her—I disrespected Gus, in print. Why shouldn't I? He works for one of the biggest crooks in Manhattan. Soraya might have been in the piece, too. Wasn't my fault. I was on assignment."

"Use that line a lot?" They walked out of the dorm and onto 113th Street.

"I'm just covering the scene. If I dump a piece to Jimmy Tzatziki, the metro editor, over the phone and it ends up reading nasty in rewrite, whose fault is that?"

"You don't even write the stuff?"

"Nope, I recite it—welcome to the wonderful world of tabloid journalism."

"So you're not to blame?"

"You got it," Lanie said. She swung her black bag from her hand as if it were a gigantic yo-yo. Undergraduates scuttled out of the way. They came up onto Broadway.

"Wow," Lanie said when she saw the purple Roadrunner. "Honey, I blew up the Hot Wheels!"

Felix went around to the passenger side and opened the door for her. She looked at him twice.

"Gentleman, huh? This city'll help you lose that pose in a jiffy."

Felix got them over to Central Park West and then he coasted. He'd grown a map in his head by then, his second full day in town. He understood that for New Yorkers, southwest was south, east was northeast, and so on. He'd adjusted his internal compass to fit the city.

"So you're the long lost son. That'd make you and Soraya leaders of the new breed. With your dad cutting deals with high and low players, all based on his desire to clean up one of the messiest reputations the police force ever saw, and Soraya carrying a Hudson River full of tearful memories . . . Well, you and her have just the sort of legendary genealogy—"

"You New York people aren't afraid to prattle on, huh?" Felix asked. He tapped the brakes at an intersection and the car rocked. It occurred to him that he didn't know his destination, hadn't thought through to a next move. Penelope's boyfriend. That had to be next. The guy who Soraya had glimpsed that night. A boyfriend was an ugly thing to learn more about, but he knew he had to do it. He glanced over at the pixie in the passenger seat. She was whispering into what looked like a digital tape recorder. Apparently if she wasn't going to talk to him, she was still going to talk.

"Want a drink?" Felix said.

"Thank goodness—I was worried I'd have to do all the advance work myself. There's a bar I like on eighteenth—Old Town. Let's go there—and speed it up a little, huh?"

They were seated in a high wooden booth at Old Town and they were hugging the east wall, so they could see nothing but each other. Felix had a cold glass of Pabst Blue Ribbon and a roast beef sandwich on white bread with mayo in front of him. An untouched glass of cheap merlot stood in front of Lanie. She was too busy talking to drink. Felix hung back and listened and worked hard to separate the wheat from the chaff, as his mother would say.

"I never talk about myself this much," she said. "I don't know what you're doing to me." She blinked and fanned herself with her hand.

"Come on," Felix said. "I bet you talk about yourself all the time. And everybody listens."

"I wish," Lanie said. She asked for water and downed a glass while the waitress waited. Felix felt himself slump a little in the booth, his head falling a few inches to his left. And then he smiled at her before he knew what he was doing. Forget dreadlocked college girls. He'd never so much as imagined anything like Lanie before. If she was going to milk him for information on Gus Moravia, then he realized that soon enough that was just what he'd be—milked.

"I'm from Long Island—Manhasset," she said. "I never imagined all the sordid stuff that goes on here till I was assigned the Page Eight beat. I kind of hate it, but man! Do you know what goes on in places like Eden-Roc?"

"Innocent young girls from small towns are plied with strange drugs till they don't know friends from enemies?"

"Well . . . that, yes," Lanie said. "Don't think I've forgotten about your sister."

Felix drank long from his beer and looked to Lanie's left, at the men in suits who filed into the bar, laughing, getting ready to blow the ugly day away with mindless drink. The old Irish guys behind the bar were the only types in the room who were familiar to him—they looked like the men he'd met on those nights after he'd broken up with Iris and gone drinking at the Smuggler's Notch, around the corner from the post office in Washburn. He knew what he was doing, floating his head away from the painful thoughts, from his helplessness.

"Listen," Lanie said. "I'd bet my job that nobody who works for Terrence Cheng can keep from being involved with all the drugs that run through his places. Cheng is going to come down hard and soon, and I'll be there to report on it, and if I can help you out in the process, what's the harm?"

"Don't start thinking I need any help from you," he said, but his voice was soft. Even though he liked looking at Lanie, there was every reason not to trust her.

Lanie stared across at him without blinking. He realized she hadn't spoken for over a minute, the first minute of its kind since he'd met her.

"I'm not trying to be mean or anything. It's just I never sat across from a big-time New York reporter before. It's confusing me."

"Damn," she said. "You're making me feel all soft and weepy like the girl I forgot I ever was."

"Ha," Felix said. "That's cynical, right?"

"No."

Felix waited a second. When she didn't follow up he said, "If you're not being cynical, then you're sure coming on strong."

Then Lanie didn't say anything all over again and Felix felt himself redden for the second or third time that day. He wished he could focus on something else, do something with his hands instead of grip the wooden bench. Fight his growing fascination with the girl across from him.

The waitress delivered the check and Felix grabbed it.

"I imagine my mother wouldn't want to see me let a woman pay a check."

"And then there's your father—"

"Don't write about that, Lanie," Felix said. "I haven't spoken to my old man in a good dozen years. There's nothing between me and him. No story. Please."

"I don't know that I'd write anything. There's a story in your sister, but it hasn't broken clear yet, that's for sure. If you want me to keep a lid on what I know about you, I will."

Felix slipped a twenty-dollar bill off his brass clip and put it over the check. That left him with four hundred and ten dollars. Not much in New York. He wondered where more might come from.

"I don't want you to write anything about anything," he said.

"Then I won't," Lanie said. "For now. Anyway, it'll be a much better story when you and your dad are known to each other."

"Don't call him that."

"Boy, you're really all torn up on the inside, aren't you?"

They stood on the curb outside Old Town, with the after-work crowd streaming around them. The street was dark and Felix suddenly felt lonesome. He realized he had nowhere to go but back to his car.

"When will I see you again, cowboy?" Lanie asked. She reached up and brushed imaginary dirt from his cheek. He looked down at her and felt how close she was. He could have picked her up and walked off with her. And then he knew that the only reason he didn't was that he had promised Soraya he wouldn't.

"Maybe you could give me your number," he said. "Maybe I could give you a call."

She slipped a card into his T-shirt pocket, reached in under his denim shirt. She left her hand there. He didn't move. Her eyes glittered and her hair was curly and he didn't feel familiar with any of it.

She came up closer and said, "I better get away from you before I do something we both enjoy."

He watched from the corner as she melted into the crowd headed down Broadway. Then a bike messenger nearly sideswiped him and for a hot second he thought his money clip had been lifted. When he sought her out again she was gone.

He knew that he ought to let Franklin Novak know he was in town before somebody beat him to it. No matter what, he wanted to be one up on the old man, and that wasn't going to be easy because it was the old man's city, not his. It was like the hide-and-go-seek they'd played in their backyard in Brooklyn. The difference was that back then, Franklin Novak had liked to let the kids think they could win. But he didn't want to just call him up and talk to him. He wasn't ready for that, not yet. He needed to see Soraya again. After looking around for twenty minutes, he found a working phone booth on Irving Place, where it was quiet. Felix called Soraya's cell.

"Lanie bring you up-to-date on how she's been terrorizing Gus and how she's never gotten a damn thing on Terrence?"

"Sort of. I think I got her to not write about me and my old man. Look, I'll get to him, but I want to see you again and talk through some things."

They arranged to meet the next night at Sanction, the lounge on the ground floor of the Official.

7

Franklin Novak had a two-room office that he shared with his partner, Chris Gennardi, in the back of the seventh floor of a building in what had once been the Flower District, on 27th and Seventh. He also employed another guy, Philip Moyo, who did the bulk of their computer work because Franklin didn't trust machines that could remember more than he did. Philip Moyo and Gennardi handled most of the corporate accounts. Franklin did the tougher stuff that kept the corporate guys excited and willing to pay high fees. The CEOs liked to go to dinner and bask in the glamour of Franklin's violent stories. But their own security needs were hardly ever physical.

There was one other tenant on the floor—a photographer called Ivan Bulgarov who took pictures of models and actresses for *Vogue* and *W.* Franklin got along okay with him. Ivan had had a stalker who'd come from his hometown a few years back—a bartender who envied the success of the one gay guy from their West Virginia high school—and Franklin had sent the guy home with a tremble that ran straight through his body every few seconds. Franklin had promised the bartender that if he ever bothered old Ivan again, he'd give him a permanent tremble and his days pouring drinks would be nothing but a memory. So Ivan was grateful and made sure that his assistant, Jenny Hurly, screened Franklin's visitors and gave him leftover brie-and-apple sandwiches from photo shoots every now and again. And Jenny Hurly had fallen for Franklin a little, which wasn't a bad thing, either.

Franklin had one big room with a steel desk in it, a couch, and two chairs facing the desk. There was a reception room in front of the big room that Gennardi used when he was around. Franklin sat with his back to a wall that was three layers of prewar brick. Made him feel safe, leaning against that wall. He was built stocky, and he wasn't more than five and a half feet tall, so from the back he looked like a coffin built for a child, and he knew that.

He shaved his head so only black-and-gray stubble ran around the sides of his skull and there was nothing on top but fuzz. His eyebrows were that same black and gray and they were often knit together, like caterpillars in love. He sat in his office, feeling safe, bored, and angry, ready to kill somebody. It was his reputation that made him feel safe, that and the ten-inch-long Raging Bull 480 he kept slung over the back of his chair. He hefted it now and laughed. The handgun was so damn big that people just looked at it and got talkative. He'd only shot it a few times. Blown some doors open, that sort of thing. Nah, for the street he liked a Glock or the S&Ws—he had half a dozen .357s and .44 mags that he'd taken off a variety of jerks over the years.

A hidden pop-out drawer that ran the length of his desk held some cheap shotguns—mostly Mossbergs, the Persuader and a few 500s. Then there was the pretty Beretta Trident he'd hung on the wall—the room's only ornament. If he was feeling uninspired and wanted to speed up a Q&A, he'd wave a gun around, but he didn't usually have to bother. Guns were funny—folks thought they didn't make you powerful. They were wrong.

He put his feet up on his desk and sighed. Took a sip of takeout cappuccino. But guns didn't work real well as threats. You had to kill people with them. Otherwise what the fuck was the point? He sat back and wished he knew of somebody who would listen to him rant. The phone rang. Gennardi.

"Funny thing—a guy came up in conversation today who could be a boyfriend," Gennardi said.

"Diane'll be relieved to know the truth," Franklin said. "After all these years."

"Yeah," Gennardi said. "But I'm not ready to talk about my newfound sexuality with my wife yet. Anyway, this is Penelope we're talking about. Guy's name is Lem Dawes. Rich kid. Parties with the Mets and some actors down at Big Jar, FUN, and Suite 16. New clubs is what they are. Terry Cheng's involved in these ventures. But we knew that."

"He came up how?"

"You remember how Philip went through all the calls to that room Penelope was in at the Official? Well, some of them checked out to this fuck's cell. Now, I know she was an OD, but you said if anybody near her came up, we want to talk to them. So today I'm listening in on this lawyer Richard Dawes, for the thing we're doing for Silverstein, and he's on the phone with his son and it's this kid. He didn't mention her precisely, but he did say somebody he knew overdosed and it had to do with this club where he was going to a party. He's broke, apparently, so he was telling his daddy about his tough life."

"What about the party?"

"It's tomorrow night. Something . . . tomato, banana . . . Orange Glow. I know where."

"Let's meet for late dinner then, at Elaine's," Franklin said. He hung up the phone.

He put Johnny Cash on the little Nakamichi CD player Ivan had given him for Christmas. Johnny was covering Neil Diamond's "Solitary Man." So here he was—Franklin Novak. His only friends in the world were a fashion photographer and some ex-cops with personalities they'd bought in the back of *Soldier of Fortune* magazine along with their home safes. Now he was going to go have a talk with his daughter's boyfriend. At a fucking party. His daughter was dead and he could feel the hate tiptoe around, prod at him like the last woman he'd been romantic with, creeping through the night, when she'd stolen his wallet and his fake Rolex and walked out his door, five or so years ago. Or . . . shit. It was more like seven.

Now when the subject was sex, there was Ivan Bulgarov's assistant, Jenny Hurly. They slept together sometimes when she had a free late night. He liked to leave her two or three hundred dollars afterward. Not that she was a prostitute or anything. She was just a young girl who needed extra money to get around the city and she liked holding Franklin's old bald head in her arms for a few minutes after they were done. He liked to give her the money and he believed she liked the sex. If it disgusted Gennardi and Philip, so what? He'd never yet made a dime giving a shit what anybody else thought.

His desk phone rang again. He watched it. Caller ID came up *New York Spectator.* Brilliant. He tapped the phone with the butt of the Bull for a while. Then he picked it up.

He said, "What?"

The voice of a guy who sounded like he'd been trying to raise crops in a dust bowl for the last thirty years said, "Novak? Listen up, shit heel. It's your father-in-law."

"Oh, for Pete's sake, Starling, don't call up to threaten me and call yourself that. It's embarrassing."

"The truth often is. Tell me what you've got."

"I've got a gun pointed at the phone with a timer on it. How's business? I heard you bought another office tower, or was it three?"

"I'll have a press kit on the Furst organization messengered over. It's thirty-eight buildings under management now, a newspaper, a television station, seven boutique magazines, including *New York Informed.* All that and one daughter lost to you, you bastard, one Ellie Furst, and now one grandchild lost to drugs, on your watch, no less."

"My watch . . . How do you figure, Bird?"

"Don't call me—"

The line went to hold and Franklin sat there. His ex–father-in-law seemed angrier than usual, which meant he knew something. Franklin made a fist and punched himself lightly on the forehead. How was he supposed to know Ellie's daddy was rich when he picked her up during a Neil Young concert so many years back? He'd been working the barrier with a bunch of other off-duty cops and she was a VIP who'd literally fallen off the side of the stage and into his arms. Now he had nothing to show for the single great love of his life but unending loss, mixed up with one furious Starling Furst, one of the fifty richest men in the city—and certainly top ten in the psychopath rankings, maybe top eight, which was saying something. Now Starling's only living relatives were Ellie and his grandson, Felix. And the old bastard hadn't seen Felix since he was ten. Which makes two of us, Franklin thought, and he flicked something out of his eye until the room around him was tinged with red.

The line came alive again. "Point being, you bastard, if I hear you making any more mess about trying to find out who killed her, I'll find out who kills you. We both know it's an OD and I want it kept that way. Otherwise the *Post* and the *News* will use her death to smear the *Spectator* and I can't afford that."

"You're saying all that on a phone line?"

"I don't repeat myself, you dime-store rent-a-cop. You muscle-bound, Jewish, peephole-staring maggot. You heard me. Now, you keep quiet, or I'll pull the right judge out of my pocket and I'll yank your—"

"Don't repeat yourself," Franklin said. He sighed deep in his chest. He reached into the pocket of the jacket that hung on his chair and pulled out a Romeo y Julieta Bully, a thick, short cigar that produced a surprising quantity of white ash. It had a mellow taste, but Franklin liked it because it tasted good when he chewed it. He'd taken up the nasty habit again when he'd gotten the news. Though nearly four months had passed, it still felt like he'd gotten the call five minutes ago, like he was about to get it again. If he didn't have Starling Furst for comic relief he figured he would've offed himself back at the holidays, right after the Christmas Eve he'd spent with Gennardi and his family and the moment he got back to his apartment and realized that Jenny Hurly was home in Wisconsin until after New Year's.

Franklin said, "Look, three months ago I wouldn't have agreed with you. But now I see it's an overdose. We checked it every which way and found nothing to the contrary. There's nobody to point a finger at. Nobody to kill. We both know that. Me, I'm just taking a look at who knew her, drawing a picture to keep myself busy."

"Keep poking around and I'll have you poked right off this island."

"Your daughter know you talk like this? That you and me are phone buddies?"

The line clicked off and Franklin dropped the handset on the desk. It wasn't funny. None of it was. But Franklin took a pull on his unlit smoke and laughed, anyway. He pointed the Raging Bull at the opened door to his office.

Would that her killer would come and visit him, try to make things right. Would that she even had a killer, instead of what he knew well enough had been a simple overdose. Barring suicide, it was the ultimate stupid, tragic death. If only there really were somebody to blame. Franklin would fix things all up then. The nasty ball of undigested guilt would disappear then, too. Blast away.

Felix walked into New York Ironworks on Centre Street, near the 5th Precinct. It was lunchtime on Thursday and half a dozen cops milled around, looking at batons, laser sights, belts, holsters, and enough pins, hats, and NYPD and DOC gear to outfit a small army. The place smelled of cop, too, of blue polyester and dirty Hi-Tec boots, of body odor and righteous indignation.

Felix approached a glass counter and looked down at a shelf full of Leatherman tools and flashlights. The radio was playing Dion, "The Wanderer." A fat man with a walrus mustache came over. He wore a dirty red plaid shirt with overstrained buttons and a Sam Browne belt that must've been four inches wide.

Felix said, "I need some bullets and cleaning fluid for a rusted-out Thompson 1911."

The fat man started laughing. Then he said, "This store is for police officers. We don't sell bullets to wackos."

A few of the cops glanced over, but they went back to playing with their gear.

"I need to take care of this now," Felix said. "I'm not a wacko."

The fat man spread his thick fingers over the top of the glass case. He drew himself up and got right into Felix's face.

"Goodbye," he said.

Felix put his own hands down on the counter. He looked across at the fat man and he didn't smile. He said, "I got the gun out in the car. I'd like to bring it in here and have you clean it for me."

"Oh, for fuck's sake," the fat man said. "You're under arrest."

He gestured to an older guy in a suit who'd just come in. The older guy was about Felix's height and his skin was cracked and gray. No lips on him, and his eyes were the color of rubber bands. The guys in uniform watched Felix without too much interest. Just another dickhead out to ruin their lunchtime shopping.

The guy in the suit came up close to Felix and looked at him. Felix smelled cigarettes and something else, a musty odor that told him the guy's suit probably made the trip to the dry cleaners less than once a year.

The gray guy said, "Okay, Jerry needs a problem solved. Which of you guys wants an easy collar?"

The uniforms began to mutter complaints. They didn't want the bother of filling out the ticket.

Felix said, "And I need a shoulder holster, whatever design you think is best."

"Hey, Mike," the fat man said to the guy in the suit. "You want to try out the new Sig-Sauer stun on him? See if he dies?"

The guy he'd called Mike leaned against the counter next to Felix. He twined his fingers over his belly. His hands were just as dry and gray as his face.

"What's the angle?" Mike said. His voice was an unpleasant mixture of crackle and slur.

"I need my gun cleaned and loaded. I'm Felix Novak."

"Nah," Mike said. "You got it confused. You're Franklin Novak. But he's older than you by about twenty-five years and I know him. So your scam is shit."

"I'm his son."

The blip of silence that followed was filled by the radio, which had switched from Dion to Sam Cooke, "Mean Old World."

"No kidding," Mike said. His voice had gone real easy. "I guess I know why you're in town. That's your ride out front? I knew I was coming in here for a better reason than to check out the new Kahr superlightweights."

"Yeah," Felix said. "And all I've got is an old pistol that's rusted out. I need some bullets and some other stuff."

The fat man behind the counter had one hand slipped in his belt. He brought the other to his mouth and chewed on his thumb. He looked at Mike. Mike looked at Felix.

Mike said, "If you're Felix Novak, then I met you back when you were two or three. You had a snappy line for all your dad's cop buddies back then. What was it?"

Now the uniform cops had grown interested—they were standing in a loose circle, a few feet away. A stock boy came out of the back. Felix watched the fat man reach under the counter. The radio went off. The front door lock clicked.

Felix leaned right up near Mike's ear. He felt the stillness, how everybody in the place had their hand on a gun. The smell of old dust was strong on Mike, but Felix ignored it. He cupped his hand over his mouth and whispered in a high-pitched kid's voice, "Don't do me any fucking favors."

"Holy shit," Mike said. He hugged Felix hard across the chest. "My sincere regrets about your sister. Jerry, hook him up. Give him the DeSantis New York rig and the, uh . . . oh, give him a whole setup. Let him bring his piece in. Put it all on Special Ops's tab."

Jerry unlocked the front door and Felix went out to get the gun from his trunk. He figured he had maybe half a dozen hours before his father knew he was in town—not longer. When he got back to the store the detective they'd called Mike was gone. But Jerry was patiently filling out a gun license with a ballpoint pen, his tongue peeping out from between his lips.

"We keep these around for special customers," Jerry said. "Sharpman okayed it. You want to check out the Glocks while you're here? How do you spell your first name?"

"Mike Sharpman?" Felix frowned. That name was on Penelope's police report.

"Your name, not his."

Felix wrote out his name. He felt cold beads of sweat on the interstices of his fingers.

"There's nobody like Mike Sharpman," Jerry said as he took the Thompson. "There's a cop out of the old school who could give a shit for rules."

"Gotta love cops like that," Felix said.

8

"Well, hey, baby!" Gus said. "I thought I said I'd see you later at Eden-Roc."

"But I wanted to see you now, baby," Soraya said. She let the door to Sanction, the lounge at the Official, shut behind her. Gus was at the far end of the bar, where he'd been talking to Kashmira. She was behind the bar in a body-hugging black cat suit. They were both finishing tall glasses of what looked like orange juice. They looked a little dour, as if they'd just been disagreeing about something.

"Hi, Kashmira," Soraya said. "Honey, can you give us a minute?"

The bartender nodded and went to the other end of the bar.

Gus said, "It's good to see you. You want to get something to eat? We got appetizers in back for this *Paper* magazine party that's happening later—"

"Have you been straight with me?" Soraya asked.

Gus glanced around them. He slipped his arm around her waist and urged her onto a bar stool. She was maybe an inch taller than him. His hands slipped around and tightened on her. She felt herself drawing closer, that weird thoughtless part of her taking hold. She didn't know why—something in his eyes, maybe. Grifter eyes—just exactly the kind of eyes her mother hated.

"I missed you so much these last couple of days," he said.

"Bullshit. What haven't you been telling me?" But she felt her voice grow softer. He didn't let her go.

"There's nothing I wouldn't tell you, Soraya. Baby, you know I'm only about you. And I think it's great what you're doing for Felix Novak. He seems like a confused kid and I'm sure you can help him out, get him through mourning for his sister."

"That's not—there were people with her when she died and he wants to talk to them, and I'm going to help him. And Lord help you if I find out it was somebody she met while she was snorting junk in the basement at Eden-Roc."

Gus stood up. He slid the empty glass away and put both arms around Soraya. She slid off the bar stool and faced him.

"Let's pray you're wrong," Gus said, and his voice was low and thick, hot wax blanketing their fight. "I don't like anybody using in my places, you know that. Want to take a nap upstairs?"

She felt herself going quiet. She wanted to say no. But he didn't let go of her hands and she didn't pull them away. She heard the door open behind her, people coming in for a quick meeting over an afternoon drink.

"You want to nap with me?" she asked.

"Baby, I am dying to nap with you."

She heard Kashmira say, "Hello, what can I get you?"

Soraya liked Kashmira, but she thought her voice belonged on a phone-sex line. And then Soraya was following Gus. They stepped into an elevator lined in pale red suede.

"I missed you so much," he said. He was opening the buttons on her shirt, his head down, kissing a line between her breasts. She had her eyes closed and they went to his door. They were in the fifth-floor room where he'd been living since he'd met her. The bed wasn't made. She lay down then and closed her eyes. She felt herself exhale, all the pressure of school disappearing, replaced by the good pressure of Gus as he moved on top of her.

She said, "I missed you, too. I've been so worried about Felix."

"Forget him," Gus said.

"And that bitch Lanie's around again . . ."

"Come on, Soraya. You know I don't want to talk about anybody else when I'm alone with you."

"I was going to ask you about that room downstairs where they found Penelope; it says it's a house room. What does that mean?"

"It means somebody was comped. I'll check on who, but listen, remind me about that 'cause I can't think about anything else but you right now."

* * *

Felix walked down Hudson Street, got some black coffee and a piece of rhubarb pie in a takeout shop called Delia's. He still had some of the afternoon to kill before meeting Soraya. He stood alone at the counter by the window and ate and drank. The Thompson itched him and he silently agreed with his new friend, Fat Jerry—lucky he was built big across the chest and shoulders because otherwise the gun sure wouldn't be easy to conceal. He looked around the little shop and saw the girl behind the counter smiling at him. There were an awful lot of pretty girls in New York, and they all seemed real friendly. He wondered why he'd always been so quick to agree with his mom when she bashed the big city.

"I like your hat," said the girl behind the counter. "We should go dancing sometime. I could wear my hat, too."

She laughed and he saw big white teeth, an easy smile. She had straight black hair parted in the middle and she was easily as tall as him. He thought she was about twenty, maybe younger. Another little sister.

"Actually, I heard about a party tonight," he said. "Do you know about Orange Glow?"

"Whoa, now." She laughed. "There's a party that's a little too rich for my young blood."

"Why's that?" he asked. But she'd already turned to help someone who'd just come in. Idly, he thought about what he'd do to Gus if he found out Gus knew anything, anything at all, about what had happened to his sister. A million sorries from Soraya and then he'd work Gus over till he was pulp. As of right now, he didn't know that Gus was covering anything, had no idea how many people he'd dealt with, how many people Penelope knew when she was here. But he'd learn, just as fast as he'd learned how to navigate the Manhattan grid and the surrounding boroughs.

He finished up his pie. He got into his car and retraced his steps over to Williamsburg. Figured he'd check out Domsey's, buy himself his very first suit. Get something dark and cut loose, cover up the gun.

* * *

"Your face is flushed," Felix said. It was a few hours later and he'd just stepped into Sanction.

"Why shouldn't it be?" Soraya asked. "I just had great sex. Afternoon delight." She pretended to be exhausted, to drop her head down onto the table.

"Nice that you're so bold about it."

"Why shouldn't I be?" Soraya asked. She flashed her eyes at Felix, who looked down and away. They went quiet and Felix looked around the lounge. It was past seven and there were several groups of young people drinking, huddled around the low wooden tables set against the east wall, making their plans for the night.

Felix watched the bartender serve a few drinks, then turn and slip a disc into the stereo. The Rolling Stones, "Angie," and the bartender began to sing along. She was incredible to look at, Felix realized. She was Latin in some way, but not Puerto Rican like Soraya. Cuban, perhaps. Or Mexican. Mayan? No, too tall.

"That's Kashmira—you want some of her action?" Soraya asked. "I hear she's open to suggestions."

Felix looked at Soraya, curled his lip.

"You don't have to put on some blasé show for me," Felix said. "I'm real impressed with you even when you act your age."

"Okay," Soraya said. "It's just that I know you don't like Gus. It makes me want to be brazen."

The pretty bartender came and stood in front of them.

"What can I bring you?" she asked.

"Just give me a Coke," Felix said. "Put a little lemon juice in it."

"Kashmira, this is Felix," Soraya said.

Kashmira looked at Felix. He was in clothes he'd gotten at Domsey's that reminded him of home, a jean jacket and a black button-down shirt with white pearl buttons. He figured he'd save the suit for later. Didn't matter that he'd been born in Brooklyn. Didn't matter that the city gave him a funny thrill. He wasn't ever going to fit back in. He knew that.

"West Coast?" Kashmira asked.

"That's right," Felix said.

"Actually," Soraya said, "Kashmira, you were working the bar at Eden-Roc back in November, weren't you? Before Gus promoted you to over here?"

"Yeah, I was there," Kashmira said. She gave Felix his Coke. "Where on the coast—not LA?"

"Outside Portland."

"Tell me more," Kashmira said.

"Washburn," Felix said, slow. "Just off the Wilson River Highway. At the edge of the Cascade mountain range, along a ridge that leads into the Willamette Valley. From the bedroom in my trailer you can smell the Pacific."

"That sounds beautiful," Kashmira said. She had a piece of green beach glass hanging from a white cord on her neck that nestled low on her chest. She rubbed it while she looked at Felix.

"Huh," Soraya said. "When you worked at Eden-Roc, I was in there one night and I saw that girl Penelope there—you know the one because of what happened to her. Did you ever see her?"

"I heard about her. But I never saw her," Kashmira said. A few after-work guys came in and made some wolf sounds at the end of the bar. Kashmira ignored them. Another bartender came on shift then, a bald guy dressed in Diesel jeans and a black T-shirt.

"Take care of those yahoos," Kashmira said, without taking her eyes off Felix. The bald guy went over to the work guys and they made noises that expressed disappointment.

Soraya said, "You sure you don't remember her? Felix is Felix Novak. Her brother."

"Oh, Lord," Kashmira said. She reached across and pressed her hand down on Felix's. He stared at her.

"Tell me what you heard," Felix said. He put his other hand on top of Kashmira's. She came close then. He smelled a perfume that reminded him, strangely enough, of home. He didn't blink.

"I saw her sometimes. She was always with a rich kid—I don't know his name. He was in a crowd that goes to the Giant's House, that bar built on the roof of that old UPS building at the bottom of Greenwich Street."

"What'd he look like—the rich kid?" Soraya asked.

"I feel so bad for you," Kashmira said to Felix. "Do you want to hang out sometime, talk about it?"

"Kashmira, what'd he look like," Soraya asked. Her voice was flat, and Felix detected in it the same thing he'd heard when she talked about Lanie. She didn't seem to like it much when other women were warm to him. In fact, she looked like she wanted to smack Kashmira's hand away from Felix's. So Felix held Kashmira's hand tighter. He glanced at Soraya's face.

"I didn't like what they were up to," Kashmira said.

Felix said, "Which was . . ."

"Oxy. That stuff's too hot. It's not like straight heroin, where you need a good connection to get it. It's just not here yet, in the city. But that crowd, they let you know they had it. They're into it 'cause it's a white-trash drug and they think that's funny, that and the fact that the high lasts so damn long. When you cut it with cocaine it's like driving all out on the freeway and then it turns into a roller coaster every once in a while. It's wild."

"How do you know?" Soraya asked.

Kashmira shrugged. "I've tried it. Not with them. The guy she hung with, I don't know his name, but he's just a white kid with too much money. A real preppy way about him, the kind of style that's easy to buy, Ralph Lauren cut with Agnes B. and a dash of Thomas Pink. Monochromatic and not friendly at all. I avoid that kind."

"You know anybody over at the Giant's House?"

"There's a guy called Jay Medrano who tends bar there. He might know something. Don't scare him, though. He uses."

"Oxy?" Soraya asked.

Kashmira said, "Last I heard, he was keeping himself strictly to H."

They said goodbye to Kashmira and Felix told her maybe he'd see her again, that he was storing some stuff in a room upstairs. That was where he was sleeping.

"I'll look out for you," Kashmira said. "I'll watch out for that rich kid, too. You'll know him when you find him. He's like . . . he's the opposite of a sweet guy like you."

9

Mike Sharpman sat at his desk in the 5th Precinct, on Elizabeth Street in Chinatown. He was on the second floor, in the detectives' "area," which was little more than a half-dozen desks and chairs arranged near the front windows. They were set off from the rest of the floor by a couple of coat trees and a thin wooden divider that got kicked to the floor by angry sweatshop owners who were rounded up and arrested once every few months.

The area was empty now. The only sound was of the carpenters downstairs, rebuilding the front door to the precinct, which had been ripped apart the night before by a monster on meth who they'd brought in after he'd destroyed a basement mah-jongg parlor. Took the door off its hinges and used it to destroy most of the vestibule. Now the buzz of drills and Sawzalls was ruining Sharpman's lunch, and he resented it, resented that monster on meth and the whole NYPD for not promoting him the hell out of Chinatown.

What few friends he had were across the street, eating lunch at Shanghai Snack Bar. But he'd brought his food back to his desk and now he popped open the styrofoam clamshell. He looked at a mound of waxy rice with some slivers of stringy white chicken and yellowish broccoli sitting on top like an afterthought. He shook his head. Forty-four years old and paying three dollars and fifty cents for his lunch, couldn't even eat in the restaurant off a plate because he wanted to save the tip.

Well, maybe this Novak kid would be worth something. Make a buck, settle an old score—who knew? He played this right and the backdoor politics of the situation could get him transferred right out of the 5th. He knew it'd been a lucky thing when he'd been asked to sign off on Penelope Novak's OD. He wasn't sure how, he just knew. And now it looked like some things might fall right for him for a change. Maybe he'd even get himself transferred over to One Police Plaza, where he could hunker down in style for his final five years. Have a fucking hamburger deluxe for a change. He searched around for a second on the Internet and found a number that he'd always wanted to call, the number of one very rich man who might care quite a bit that Franklin Novak's son, Felix, was in town.

"Let me speak to Starling Furst," he said. "Tell him it's Mike Sharpman, Lieutenant Mike Sharpman of the NYPD. Yeah, I'm sure he *is* in a meeting. I would be, too, if I were him. Put me through. He'll want to talk, believe me. I got information about his grandson. Lady, you can bet your job he'll be happy to hear from me. What the hell? I'm betting mine."

He waited, poked at the mound of rice with his plastic fork. He opened the drawer of his desk, pulled out soy sauce packets, a notepad, and some rubber bands. He felt his dry skin tighten over his face. He picked up a sliver of broccoli root and a rubber band. He made a slingshot, let the thing go, and the broccoli flew across the room and slapped up against a window that looked out on Elizabeth Street. *Thwop.* He shot another, then two more. *Thwop thwop.* Three of them stuck. He looked across the room at a beat cop who was smirking at him.

"Hey, Dandruff," the beat cop said. "You an artist now?"

Sharpman gave him the finger. He shot a last piece of broccoli at the cop and missed him. That was what they all called him, Dandruff. God, he hated this place.

The line came alive.

"What is it?" Starling Furst said.

"Hello, Mr. Furst? Mike Sharpman—yeah, from way back when. Really, you were just thinking of me? Well, likewise. I'll make it quick, sir. You won't believe who I ran into yesterday."

In the Roadrunner on the way over to the Giant's House, Felix and Soraya didn't look at each other.

Soraya said, "So I've been meaning to ask, you have fun with Lanie last night?"

Felix said, "I'm having a good time with everybody in New York who acts nice to me."

"Yes," Soraya said. "I've noticed how well you're handling all the attention. Who'd have thought the sweaty little chocolate-smeared, Power Rangers–tighty-whities–wearing kid you were would turn out be such a big strong man?"

They stopped at a light, at Prince and 6th Avenue. Felix shook his head and looked at the men who walked by, at mean eyes paired up with East Coast prep school clothes. A few of them glanced at the car with what he imagined was snobbish envy. He gunned the engine and the thing growled and hissed like a pissed-off python.

Felix said, "I didn't figure you'd grow up to be so straight-up beautiful and full of wisdom, either. So now, even though I'm older, I'm taking my cues from you."

"Don't be an ass," Soraya said.

Felix slid the car into the intersection. They drove over to Greenwich Street without saying more. Soraya flipped on the radio, found some Roberta Flack that inevitably reminded them both of their mothers. They both hummed and looked elsewhere while Felix eased the Roadrunner into a parking space in front of a low redbrick building.

They went up a flight of concrete stairs and came into the bar. The Giant's House was built around a huge skylight with a tree that shot right up through it. Everything else was set up in relation to that tree. There were low aluminum tables with lounge chairs around them. The bar along the west wall had a twenty-foot-long, two-and-a-half-foot-wide window that looked out over the West Side Highway and the Hudson River, and then over to New Jersey.

"This is very LA," Soraya said. Felix nodded, though he'd never been to LA. Complementing the furniture were six or eight tallish model types, languidly drinking what looked like water, staring at nothing, waiting for the night to begin. Felix looked the scene over. The room was jaw-drop beautiful, he had to admit that, but he was starting to get freaked out by all these folks who seemed so bored by it all. That was why he liked Lanie—at least she seemed excited by life. Clearly, she wasn't the New York City norm.

There were two bartenders at the bar. Both were men. Soraya sat down on a bar stool and smiled at one of them. The other came over. He was overbuilt for his height, with dark, hooded eyes and curly black hair. On his forearm was a complicated tattoo of a weeping tiger, with *Jay* written in one of its wet eyes and *Luz* in the other. Nothing prep school about him, Felix thought.

"I hear you drive up?" Jay asked. He picked up a wineglass and polished it carefully with a white towel.

"That was me," Felix said.

"I'm Jay." The bartender motioned with his head. "You want to show off your whip?"

Felix motioned to Soraya to stay upstairs, to let him ask questions on his own. She nodded a yes, stayed on her bar stool. Jay told the other bartender he'd be gone for a few minutes, and then Felix followed him back out the way they'd come, down the stairs and out into the street.

"Lord above," Jay said. "383 V-8?"

"There was one in there, but I dropped in a Hemi 426."

"A 426? Go on and pop it."

Felix opened the hood and they looked at the engine. It wasn't as shiny as he would've liked, but then, he'd never been obsessive about keeping the car clean. He'd picked the Roadrunner up almost by accident, from a tractor salesman who owed his mother money. He'd gone ahead and pumped it up, but he didn't consider himself crazy for everything Mopar. Still, he suspected he could get this guy Jay going pretty good.

Felix said, "The tranny's a 727 automatic with a 3800 turbo action converter. Carburetor's the Holley 2300 Series Six."

Jay ran his hand over the paint. The original *Roadrunner* was still over the driver's side wheel well. Jay whistled.

"I love this Plum Crazy paint," Jay said. "My Lord. I had a '71 Chevelle painted Go Man Go 'Vitamin C' Competition Orange—me and my brother rebuilt it. We put in a 440 with three two-barrel carburetors and tried to keep it real clean, but then the engine let go one night when we were dragging, blew out at 6600 rpm, and my gearhead days were over."

"Bad accident?"

"I've got metal screws holding both my hips together, so I'm always in a little pain. I figured I'd bring that pain to the city, turn it into an acting career. Turns out I'm not the only guy from out of town who can cry on command."

"You're from where?"

"Idaho, outside Sun Valley."

Felix said, "I'm from outside Portland."

"You drove this thing here and the carburetor held out?"

"I can't believe it either."

"I was friends with a girl from outside Portland. She knew some things about Mopar. We used to say we should get all hopped up hillbilly-style and drag race up and down 10th Avenue. . . ."

Jay Medrano quieted down then. He looked over at Felix, real slow. Then he said, "I guess if I thought about her for a little I'd remember that she mentioned a big brother. I guess that person might be you."

Felix couldn't help his frown. He nodded, slow.

"Penelope Novak," Felix said. "You knew her."

He reached over and closed the hood. A trickle of people were making their way down Greenwich, turning in at the unmarked doorway and moving up the stairs to the bar. Jay checked his watch.

"We used together sometimes when we had money," Jay said. "Me and her, we liked to cut our Oxy with cocaine and do some snorting. But that Oxy—at a dollar-fifty a milligram that stuff does not come cheap. It's like we had the idea to do a cheap drug from the country and then the city ratchets up the price, just like everything. She was one funny girl. But she hung with some rich folks. Off shift, they're not my kind of people."

"What about some preppy guy, dull looking but girls flock to him?"

Jay shrugged. "That's half the guys who come around here. You know where you should go? The Peppermint Lounge. That's where all those kids hang out. Liza Pruitt runs some shit out of there."

"Fair enough," Felix said. "You want to tell me anything else? Considering she was my sister."

Jay looked up and down the street. His eyes danced over the car for a moment, and then he looked up to the windows of the Giant's House. Music was wafting down—old Cassandra Wilson. Then he looked left. More young people were coming toward the bar. He sighed. The muscles in his neck seemed pumped up, even though no voices had been raised. Felix thought this was a user's sign, being all pumped and having no place to go.

"You're on it now," Felix asked.

Jay smiled. His eyes had a yellow cast to them and he seemed like he'd gone into a doze.

"I tried to stick with H, but once you get down with Oxy, it's hard to go back. I crush up an eighty-milligram pill, it gets me through a shift. It hurts, man, standing up all night when you've got screws in your hips. That Oxy, that stuff has a real powerful release, nice and sweet, way better than the H you get on the street."

"Okay," Felix said, real easy. "That's cool."

Jay nodded slow, looked away. He chewed for a moment on nothing and swallowed.

Then he said, "There was one kid in particular from that group who she liked and I didn't. Name of Lem Dawes. Maybe that's who you mean."

"What about Gus Moravia?" Felix said. "Was he . . . connected?"

"Gus?" Jay said, and he smirked. They began to make their way back upstairs.

Jay said, "Connected's not the word for Gus. But you won't hear me say anything against that big boy. He's definitely in control of his shit. Look, about your Roadrunner—you decide to stay here in the city, you don't need a car, you look me up. I'll give you what's left of the damn money I saved for acting lessons that I'm blowing on Oxy and I'll give it to you and drive my ass right back home."

Jay slipped back behind the bar. He nodded a goodbye to Felix and Felix nodded back. And then Soraya was next to him.

She said, "Ready to go?"

They went out. Behind them, the place had begun to heat up. They were playing a new thing, a smashup of Ludacris over Led Zeppelin's "D'yer Mak'er." There were whoops from the bar.

Felix said, "He said we should check out the Peppermint Lounge."

Soraya said, "That place isn't open for business yet." She put her hand on his back, said, "Users will lie like that. They don't even notice it. Listen, could you drive me uptown? I need to study."

"But that woman who opened the door at Udris's place. Didn't she mention the Peppermint Lounge?" Felix asked. He waited a moment. Then he said, "Liza Pruitt?"

Soraya frowned. "Shit, you're right. I don't see how Jay would know Liza. Still . . ."

Felix was watching Soraya carefully. He felt a little weary. He wasn't so surprised that there were things and people who fit together that Soraya didn't want to see. In fact, her not seeing things made a certain sad kind of sense. He said nothing more.

Felix found himself sitting alone at a white Formica table in Wok-n-Roll, the Chinese restaurant on Broadway and 113th, across from Soraya's dorm. He'd dropped off Soraya and found himself famished. He had his cowboy hat tipped back as he paged through the *Spectator.*

He drank a Coke, ate a dish of beef with dried bean curd. He'd pulled all the beef but left most of the bean curd. He'd figured it'd be like potatoes, but it wasn't like potatoes at all. No matter how she'd tried, Ellie couldn't get him to be adventurous with food. He liked beef, mounds of mashed-up vegetables, and potatoes. That was all, really. He liked Coca-Cola and had developed a taste for beer brewed in small batches, which he'd refined at the Smuggler's Notch, back home. But he liked his Budweiser, too. So while he was trying to be adventurous, now that he was here, he was finding it difficult.

He wondered the same thing he'd wondered for years: how Penelope could have been born hungry for drugs and why he didn't feel that way at all. He pushed the plate forward and took a toothpick from the red plastic dispenser on the table.

He'd seen her once, entertaining a crowd of homeless kids in Pioneer Courthouse Square. This was back when she was just fourteen and he was seventeen, the second or third time she'd run away. Ellie had sent him out after her and he'd driven down to Portland to try to figure out what drew her there when he felt so unmoved. She was tall and gangly then and she was in front of a dozen or so kids who were draped over skateboards and each other, sodden in dirty jeans and unlaced combat boots, their dyed hair blowing around in the cool fall evening. She'd spread her arms out wide, and she was telling the story of why she was there.

"So my daddy, he's a cop, and he sees his partner get shot again and again and again by some drug dealer, and he tucks his little Jewish tail under his butt and he runs. My old-school Wasp mom hears that he did this shit? She freaks, sleeping next to a coward and all and she's one dried-out tough bitch, you can bet on that. Next thing I know, I'm out in the goddamned valley, hoeing God's green earth!" She pretended to hoe the bricks in the square.

"I say, 'Mommy, tell me about Daddy?'" She made her voice sound high and childish, which wasn't much of a stretch.

"And her, what's she say?"

Penelope reared up then, cupped her hands to her ears, and leaned forward at her waist. All the kids watching her drew in a big breath and then they yelled out, "Your daddy's a coward!"

The noise was big and plenty of folks looked over. Felix watched from twenty feet away. He guessed the other kids were familiar with this, that their fathers were cowards, too.

"Now who's gonna get me high?" his sister asked. And she was enveloped by the group. He remembered watching her disappear in the haze as the group got up and went to walk and smoke, and he didn't follow.

He went back to the spot on Southwest Yamhill where he'd parked the old Toyota truck he'd borrowed from Ellie, and he just drove on home. When Ellie asked he said he couldn't find her, couldn't imagine where she was.

He paid his check and stepped out onto Broadway, with his hat in his hand. He figured that while he was in town he should probably ask the old man how it felt to be a coward, get right up in his face and scream it at him. Straighten that out, too.

10

Midnight Thursday found Franklin Novak at his favorite table, against the middle of the brick wall on the south side of the back room at Elaine's. The place was wild with noisy old drunks, most of them rich and nearly all of them friendly with one another, so the difference between the room and a high school cafeteria was just about nothing, except for a big dose of age and money. The loud blasts of conversation flowed as fast as the mixed drinks, but Franklin watched without getting into the middle of it. He only occasionally nodded to the men and women who caught his eye.

He sat with Chris Gennardi, his wife, Diane, and their daughter, Lisa, an eleven-year-old kid with honey-colored hair, espresso-bean eyes, and freckles sprayed across her nose and cheeks. Lisa was doing her math homework by candlelight while she drank a tonic water with extra limes. She had headphones on, too, big ones that completely covered the sides of her head.

Diane was tipped back in her chair, one hand on her daughter's shoulder, the other gripping a Sauza margarita. She was talking with a woman at the next table about a resort in Cancún where they'd both just been. They were trying to decide who'd had a worse experience. Both women had bronze-colored skin. They wore chunky gold Elsa Peretti jewelry on their ears and necks.

Gennardi was eating a piece of halibut that was as big as a baseball mitt. He had his mouth down close to the plate and his eyes flitted around, landing evenly on his wife, his daughter, his boss. Franklin, meanwhile, was in family heaven. His hands were clasped over his belly. A plate of Elaine's famous macaroni sat in front of him, but he'd barely touched it. He nipped from his glass of Bushmills, and he glowed.

The cell phone in front of Gennardi lit up.

"Philip's got the car outside," Gennardi said. He pushed the plate of fish away, leaving the ratatouille and the baked potato, and he yawned. He was in a black turtleneck and a black suit. His gray-and-black hair was brushed back.

"Tell him to give us a few more minutes," Franklin said. He reached out and tapped on Lisa's notebook. She'd been about to do a long division problem completely wrong and he traced backward, toward her mistake. She looked up and nodded, curled her lip at him. She gulped her tonic water and slipped off her headphones.

"We need anything?" Gennardi asked.

"Nah," Franklin said. "Let me just soak up some more of this familial warmth before we head down to bang some teenage heads together."

Gennardi shrugged, said, "Only to you would this look warm."

"What the hell is it if not that?" Franklin said.

"Okay, okay. That's what it is," Gennardi said.

Across the room, Jimmy Tzatziki, the metro editor at the *Spectator*, stood up to make a toast and spilled champagne down his blue-and-white–checked shirtfront. He saw what he'd done and threw the rest of the glass at himself. There were cheers.

"What's the numerator there?" Franklin said to Lisa. He tapped his finger on her paper. She looked up, reached out, and shoved her middle finger under his chin. Franklin smiled.

"Let's go," Franklin said. "I can't stand your kid, anyway."

"Yeah, get out of here, you creeps," Lisa said.

"Watch it, Lisa," Gennardi said.

"What the hell are they if not creeps?" Lisa asked her mom.

"You can finish my macaroni," Franklin said. "If you promise to work on your manners and stop imitating me."

"It's too late for her to eat," Diane said. "And she imitates you because you remind her of the little bullies in her class."

Diane kissed her husband goodbye. Lisa slid Franklin's plate over to her side of the table and started to pick at it.

On the way out they saw Elaine at her place at the bar and they both hugged her tight. She pointed out a small dark man with a bulbous forehead. His gray hair was swept up from the edges of his head so that it covered the top like whipped cream on a butterscotch sundae. He had on a black suit and a champagne-colored tie with a knot the size of a tennis ball.

"Little fella's been wanting to meet you," Elaine said. "Name of Leon Edelstein."

While Gennardi waited with Elaine, Franklin ambled over and shook the guy's hand. Franklin listened and Edelstein said something about Jews having to stick together, and Franklin gave a shrug that could have been interpreted as agreement. After a few minutes, Gennardi and Franklin left. A brown van with tinted windows pulled up. The two men got in.

"You make a deal?" Gennardi asked.

"Yeah. There's at least three hundred thousand there for Novak and Associates, assuming the thing is ongoing. That and you two can go over there and do a sweep next week sometime. He's bugged."

"Crazy?"

"No, Edelstein says he's got competitors. I know who those guys are and they're nothing. I can tell them to lay off. So the deal's done."

"We need the money," Gennardi said. "There's so much to be made with all that computer bullshit—people bugging people so they can go to court—why don't we do more of it?"

"'Cause it's ass-dull is why, but we'll do this and keep a finger in. Also I told Edelstein that you and Philip are Jewish like me, okay? So don't contradict that when you go over there."

Philip turned around and smiled. He was Zimbabwean, a former MDC rebel who had tried unsuccessfully to kill President Mugabe. After that, he'd traded himself out of the country for eleven thousand dollars and a Yugoslav-made antiaircraft gun.

"Fair enough," Philip said. "I'll be an African Jew, the world's oldest people. I was thinking about converting, so this will give me some practice."

"Were you?" Gennardi asked.

"No," Philip said.

"Pretend it's true for the purposes of this assignment," Franklin said. "Keep Edelstein happy and we can all go to temple together. Okay, Philip—no problem, right? You know this place we're going?"

"Yeah," Philip said. "I know the place."

"Hey, Gennardi, I'm sorry, man. I forgot to say goodbye to your wife," Franklin said.

"She'll get over it," Gennardi said.

Felix stood behind his car under the Manhattan Bridge and shimmied out of his jeans and sweatshirt. He put on the suit he'd bought, a black number with some strategic dark blue piping. Now that he saw the suit in the streetlight he realized that it was maybe a little more country than was quite right. But he figured nobody else'd care. He had a shirt, too, white and none too clean. Soraya waited in the car. He'd picked her up at Barnard, where she'd been getting in some work. It was Thursday, nearly midnight, time for Orange Glow.

"Looks good," Soraya said when Felix came around to the front of the car. He got in and sat down. She was in a white APC Listen to This Picture T-shirt and jeans, with a pair of dove-colored high-heeled pumps. Felix thought she looked good, but he didn't exactly understand why.

Soraya said, "Maybe I'll ask Gus to install a mechanical bull so you'll feel more at home."

"I'm sure me and Lanie would enjoy that," Felix said, though he hadn't actually seen Lanie again. He watched Soraya's face to see if she'd show anything resembling jealousy.

"You might." Soraya sighed. "But I doubt her skinny ass could handle a big bull. What'd you two talk about, anyway?"

"Not about you." Felix turned the car on and began to drive north.

"Make a right here."

"I know a better way."

"You always were a fast learner," Soraya said.

Felix braked at a light, down in the projects, at Henry and Rutgers. There was no moon and the streetlights felt flat to him, fake. He didn't like that about the city, that the nature of the sky went so forgotten against the hard grain of the street.

Felix asked, "You think Lem Dawes will be there?"

"Probably," Soraya said. "I need to see him from the back to recognize him."

Then she said nothing. Felix looked over at her, but she was looking away, out the side window. She blew on the glass and drew a man's shoulders.

"What's the matter?" Felix asked. They drove by Eden-Roc slowly and Felix kept going. There was a crowd of more than fifty people outside and cabs and black cars lined both sides of the street, making it impossible to park. Felix watched the neighborhood people who were watching the crowd outside the club. The older people pointed at strange characters, at the overserious men from Wall Street and the women with beautiful hair who were chattering in the evening chill.

"What's the matter?" Felix asked again.

Soraya looked over at him. They hadn't spoken about Penelope after Felix had talked with Jay Medrano. They knew they wanted to talk to somebody called Lem Dawes, but Felix had told Soraya nothing else.

Suddenly Soraya erupted, "What's the matter? Fuck you, what's the matter, Felix! You don't trust me and I'm all you've got."

"Why do you think I don't trust you?"

"I know you asked Jay Medrano about Gus. He called Kashmira and told her, and she told me. You really think I'd be with Gus if I suspected him of anything? I love Gus. I really do. He didn't do anything to Penelope. You need to understand who your friends are. Park here."

"I'm sorry," Felix said.

"I am, too. I thought you trusted me."

"I do, it's just—"

"You think there's something wrong with Gus."

Felix nodded. He wanted to say how hard it was for him to trust people, but he just couldn't get it out. And he could see that Soraya was furious at him. But it felt like there was nothing he could do. And no matter what, he did suspect Gus, and he wouldn't be able to do anything but keep on wondering about him until he was proved completely wrong.

Felix slid into a spot and they got out, walked back toward the club. She wouldn't look at him. Traffic sped by on Allen Street. Felix tried to imagine how it would feel to be in love and to have your rational head clouded by how you felt. He was afraid to even imagine it. His mother had trained him hard against that kind of thing.

"I'm sorry I didn't tell you I asked about Gus," Felix said. His voice was low.

Soraya said, "Let's try to concentrate on what we know for real. All we've got now is some wacko stone importer with a connection to Terry Cheng and a rich kid who people don't seem to like, of which there are tons in this city, believe me. If Gus connects I'll be the first person to admit it, but he hasn't yet, and I don't believe he will."

"Okay, okay," Felix said. They came up to the crowd and Soraya raised her arm and waved. Danny spied her and yelled, "Incoming!"

Two bouncers swept out through the group and surrounded Soraya and started to bring her in. Soraya looked over her shoulder and didn't smile.

After a moment she said, "Him too," and Felix was included.

"Too busy for the dog, huh?" Felix said to Danny.

"He's inside somewhere," Danny said. "And believe me, on the inside, he's the only friend you got."

"Everybody's got to start somewhere," Felix said. He took a quick look at the crowd before they went inside. They just looked like a lot of young people, hopeful and harmless. A soot-colored cloud of cigarette smoke hovered above them. Then a brown van pulled up and Felix wondered who would show up at a spot like Eden-Roc in such an ugly ride. The thing idled, but nobody got out. Then he was inside.

By the time Felix's eyes adjusted to the light, Gus already had his arms around Soraya. He was nuzzling her neck. She held him and Felix looked away. He saw Lanie Salisbury sitting with some guys in blazers who looked like computer technicians. One had a camera with a tall flash.

"You let that bitch in again?" Soraya said to Gus. "After what I said?"

"Media is media," Gus said. "And everybody reads the *Spectator* even though nobody admits it. Nice suit, Felix."

"You want to talk to Lanie," Soraya said, "you go ahead."

"Bitter mood," Felix said. "Attitude will get you nowhere."

"Fuck you, big brother," Soraya said. Gus raised an eyebrow and said nothing. For once, Felix thought. Then Gus and Soraya were pulled away through the crowd. Felix stood quietly. The room where he'd drunk with Soraya just two nights before was somewhere beneath them. He was in the main space now.

But nobody was dancing. Instead everyone seemed to be undulating to pulsing music while they talked in large groups, of five and seven and more. It occurred to Felix that he didn't even know what Orange Glow meant. He frowned and looked around for a bar. An Asian man walked by without looking at anyone and people gazed after him. He was short and wiry, not unlike Gus, but he was older, perhaps forty, and he was dressed in a dark jacket that looked to Felix like cheap leather or some synthetic. Felix watched him stride around the bar and through a low door, a door that was not the door to downstairs. He disappeared. Terrence Cheng, Felix guessed. The puppet master.

"Hey, Mr. Hopalong Cassidy, what's happening?" Lanie said. She poked a finger into Felix's chest. He tensed around the gun under his arm and felt his skin go cold and tight. He hadn't been thinking about it.

"Hi, Lanie," Felix said. "Nice night."

"Nice night? Yeah, right now the twenty-four-hour party people are calling this place home." Lanie grinned and looked around the club.

"I bet you'd know a guy I'm looking for," Felix said. "Name of Lem Dawes."

"Over there," Lanie said. Felix followed Lanie's finger and saw a guy in a corner who looked like he'd just gotten off the bus from Andover. He was in a blue blazer and white shirt, striped black-and-white tie. His eyebrows were knit together and slanted and he was kissing a tall girl who was dressed all in black, with white hair. She was much taller than he was. To Felix, they looked like a black-and-white photo of themselves.

"Lem Dawes. Like our dearly departed JFK Jr. but totally lacking the necessary innocent charm. Rich little punk. Now that you mention him, I ought to dump his name off to my editor along with a dozen others. I doubt he'll make the final edition, but you never know. Then my work for the night is done." A flashbulb went off behind her, shot in the direction that Lanie had pointed.

Lanie said, "And after that, why don't the two of us meet up and talk about the old times of a day or so ago when we met and fell so hard for each other?"

But just as she was getting out the words, Felix saw two men come moving hard toward the man she'd called Lem. He saw Lem go up in the air and start moving in a direction that he hadn't chosen. The men weren't letting him use his feet.

Felix felt his jaw tighten and the corners of his mouth turn down. One of the men was Franklin Novak. An old tank in a black suit. Where Felix had a gangle to him, an unfinished quality, Franklin was sawed off at the edges. But that was his father, for sure. He felt the same tug he'd felt when he first saw Soraya, but he kicked the weakness of the feeling away like it was ugly and foreign to him. Franklin was seeing nothing but wherever he was taking Lem Dawes. Felix didn't see Soraya, or Gus, or anybody. He felt how close Lanie was to him, how she was waiting.

But Franklin was gone. A bouncer Felix didn't recognize stepped aside when he saw Franklin Novak coming toward him. They were already moving down the stairs toward the room where Felix had first drunk with Soraya. They had the man called Lem by his shoulders. The new bouncer regained his position just as Felix came up. He looked confused. He said, "Get lost," but he didn't put any confidence behind it.

"I work for Franklin," Felix said, fast, and flashed his holstered gun. The bouncer didn't have time to doubt him because Felix was already downstairs. The lounge was full of people and Felix judged from the ripple through the room that the three men must've headed toward a bathroom at the far end, which he'd used only a few nights before. More than anything he wanted to scream at his father, but he didn't have the words, couldn't put how betrayed he felt into a clear framework—all he knew was that he wanted to get at the man, scare him, make him know how wrong he'd been to just let his family go.

When he got to the bathroom, they were standing just in front of the door. His father and the other man stood on either side of Lem. They both had their arms around him and he was shaking slightly, but otherwise they had him locked down.

"We're next," Gennardi said. Felix shook his head, then he ripped the gun out of the holster and got a good grip on it, threw his shoulders back. He heard music surround them. It was something slow, a revamp of the Wailers. His back was to the room, but his face was turned away from his father. Then he looked up fast and shoved the gun in his father's gut. There was no feel of flesh there. Instead there was protection, Kevlar, maybe, and he dragged the muzzle up, pushed the barrel into his father's neck.

He whispered, "You fucking bastard, you let her—"

And he was down on his ass before he could say "die," the gun no longer in his hands. The other man, the one who wasn't his father, had thrown him on the floor. He felt a foot go into his ribs, like he was the dog now, even as his father pulled him back up to his feet.

"Felix?" Franklin asked.

"Die," Felix said. But now that he was looking into his father's eyes, he couldn't raise his hand.

"My kid," Franklin said to Gennardi.

"No?" Gennardi said. "Jesus, I'm sorry, Franklin."

"Nah—how were you gonna remember?" Franklin asked. "I wouldn't have known either except he's my blood."

Franklin ran a hand over his skull. Felix was only a foot from him and he felt his father stare, take in his face. For a moment, Felix couldn't think of a thing to say. And his father squinted at him, kept staring.

"Gimme back my gun," Felix said. He pushed his father's hand off him and staggered back. Another hand caught him and he steadied, gripped a woman's waist. He smelled her first. Soraya.

"Your gun?" Franklin said. He held the big Thompson loosely in his hand. He checked the safety, popped the full magazine, slipped it back in place, and stuck the heavy gun in his waistband. He cocked his eyebrow and frowned hard. Felix was briefly amazed that his father needed only that much time to recompose himself. Incredible. Bastard hasn't seen me in twelve years, he thought. Nice to know he cares so much.

Franklin said, "It's my gun. Carrying it doesn't make it yours."

"Fuck you," Felix said. He glanced once at the boy called Lem. Gennardi hadn't let him go, even while he'd put Felix on the floor. Felix thought the kid looked like he was going to cry—and not over Felix getting knocked down, either.

"Your boy looks good," Gennardi said to Franklin.

"Yeah," Franklin said. "You filled out good, Felix. Now, about your sister. Don't let's start it here. We're checking with this twinkie, he may know something. Or so your uncle Gennardi says."

"You remember me?" Gennardi asked.

"Maybe," Felix said. "You're Chris Gennardi."

"Meanwhile, we're on line for the bathroom," Franklin said. He looked at Soraya, who still had a hand on Felix. "And you, Soraya Navarro—I want to talk to you, too."

"You should've shot him," Soraya said to Felix. "You missed your chance."

"Look," Lem Dawes said. "You all sound way too busy to bother with me right now, and I've got friends waiting for me upstairs, so why don't we meet later at the bar and—"

The four of them looked at Lem Dawes, who had stopped talking when Gennardi glared at him. Now he was hanging by his jacket, which Gennardi held in his fist.

"This is fun—it's been a while since I was the tough," Gennardi said. "Now shut up, fancy boy." He pulled Lem off the wall and banged on the bathroom door. He said, "Out. Now."

The door opened fast and a tall guy in a suit came out. He wrung his wet hands and looked red around the eyes, like he had something to say. Gennardi bugged his own eyes at him and the red drained from the guy's face. He slipped away, quick.

The five of them stepped into the big bathroom and arranged themselves as far apart from each other as they could get. Inside, the walls were pale blue and candles were set on thin glass shelves. The room smelled of incense, patchouli, and marijuana. If the room was dirty, the light didn't reveal it.

"Sit," Franklin said. Lem slumped down on the midnight blue tile.

"Penelope knew this guy," Gennardi said to the room.

"I saw you that night," Soraya said. "You're that little rich—you're Lem Dawes."

Franklin leaned against the sink. He took the Thompson out and examined it, shook his head.

"I always wondered if your mother took this old thing with her." He slipped it away. "You, Lem. Talk to us."

"About what?" Lem said. His voice was shaking. Casually, as if he were going to straighten the knot, Gennardi reached down and pulled on Lem's tie with his thumb and pointer finger. He cinched the knot, and Lem came off the floor like a marionette. Gennardi flipped the tie around.

"Purple label." Gennardi nodded.

"Penelope," Lem said, fast. "Yeah, I knew her. We didn't have anything between us, though."

Franklin said, "Gennardi, stand back. Let's ask another question. Did you do drugs with my daughter?"

"No," Lem said.

"Bullshit," Soraya said.

"Try again," Franklin said. The only noise was the dense wall of the club's sound coming in under the door.

"Maybe a few times, yeah. We shared some stuff," Lem said.

"Where'd you get it?" Franklin asked.

"From around," Lem said.

"Around?" Franklin asked. He stepped in front of Lem Dawes and said, "Look, you want to be a little more helpful here? Do you deal?"

Lem wet his lips and pursed them, looked away, like he was thinking hard but he couldn't understand what "deal" might mean. He said, "Deal? I don't have the guts for that game. It's too dangerous. Guy like me, I'm a buyer, not a seller."

Franklin said, "Let's leave the bullshit aside. What about Penelope?"

"Look, I don't know anything about her," Lem said as Franklin gazed silently at him. His voice slipped up the register, squeaked. "At least no more than I know about anybody who I meet in these places."

Felix watched and realized suddenly that all he was doing was watching. He felt like he was ten, watching his father, fascinated with the intensity of the man's presence. And he couldn't explain it, how he could be furious with him and fascinated at the same time.

Franklin said, "Lem, you know something you need to tell us? Huh, kid? This is a crowded bathroom right now, but everybody else can wait outside and I'll rip some fucking proper names out of your throat, do you understand me?"

Lem frowned with his whole face. Franklin squatted down. He pulled out the Thompson and tapped the butt of it against Lem's cheek, real light. Then he left the gun there. Still, Lem didn't say anything. Felix thought it looked like he was weighing his options. Or maybe he knew nothing. Maybe he was high and stupid and scared. Simple as that.

Franklin said, "She was my daughter, Lem, you know that?"

Lem suddenly scrunched up his legs, rolled himself into a ball, and closed his eyes.

"Did I say you could do that?" Franklin asked. "Stand up. What else do you have to tell me?"

Lem Dawes stood up, slow. He loosened his tie.

"Ah—it was only 'cause we went to the same doctor that we knew each other, that was all. Maybe we were on the same prescription, so we shared once when we ran into each other. But that was it, I swear."

"Prescription for what?"

"Painkillers. Oxy."

"Maybe you did some sharing, huh? What doctor?"

"I don't think he'd be very happy if I told you his name," Lem said. "He's a very private man."

"Are you kidding?" Franklin asked. "You think I'm worried about who might be unhappy?" He sounded genuinely surprised. Gennardi came over then, put a hand on Lem's white neck.

"Doctor who?" Gennardi asked.

Felix looked over at Soraya. She seemed entirely calm, as if she were taking notes on interrogation procedure.

"You're going to get me in a whole lot of trouble," Lem said.

"You're in trouble now," Franklin said. He whipped around suddenly, and Felix heard his neck crack. Then Franklin got up very close to Lem and bared his teeth so his lips went thin, like Hannibal Lecter. Felix saw Lem's eyes flicker closed.

"Say the name," Franklin said.

"Marsden Biddle, on East Seventy-second," Lem Dawes said. "That's all I know about Penelope Novak." He sounded relieved.

"Okay, then," Franklin said. "So now there's a doctor who prescribes Oxy to young people. Now that's interesting. I didn't know she was sick, actually." He gestured to Lem. "Tell us some more."

"That's all I know. I barely knew her. I swear."

"He's lying," Felix said.

"I swear I don't know anything else," Lem said. "I'm not hiding anything, but I think in a second I'm going to do some screaming. You can't interrogate me like this."

"Yeah," Franklin said. "Maybe we should just let you go."

"You're gonna let him regain his composure?" Gennardi asked.

"Hey, come on, it's a fucking family reunion here. I don't want to look at this piece of garbage anymore. He makes me feel extremely depressed."

Franklin yanked Lem's chin up and stared in his eyes. Felix watched Lem try to meet his father's gaze and saw that he couldn't do it. Lem squeezed his eyes shut. Franklin put his hand into Lem's inside jacket pocket. He rooted around for a second, came out with a small smoke-brown vial that held purple pills. He held the vial up to the dim light.

"Look what I found, *around*," Franklin said. "How do you take these?"

"Who said I take them?" Lem asked. He looked around the room. Franklin shook his head. He grabbed Lem by the back of the neck and banged his head into the steel ball at the end of the towel holder. For a moment, Lem held the pose, as if he couldn't believe someone had actually hurt him. Then Franklin pulled Lem's head up and banged it again. Lem had no response beyond covering his forehead. He did all he could to back away from Franklin.

"Bye for now," Franklin said. He waved to Felix and Soraya. "You two, come with me."

"Are you kidding?" Soraya asked. Franklin turned to her.

"No, I'm not kidding. We got things to discuss. I'm serious. I don't want to be near this character anymore. He makes me feel unhappy for the world."

They filed out then and left Lem in the bathroom. Felix looked around as they went through the club. Terrence Cheng was nowhere to be seen. Gus had disappeared, too. He saw Soraya lock eyes with the bartender, Kashmira, who was dancing while she made a cocktail, but that was all. There was too little to see and too much, all at once, a thousand people dancing, so many of them absorbed with nothing but themselves. Felix craned his neck around and tried to find Lanie, but if she was there, she wasn't letting him see her.

Outside they pulled in fresh air. Felix felt the empty holster bounce against his ribs. He closed his suit over it. Danny came over to him.

"Leaving so soon?" Danny said. He was right up in Felix's face.

"Step back," Felix said. He felt tired and sad. The scene with Lem had disgusted him. He couldn't think of a sadder way for Penelope to end her life than hanging around with a desperate little user like that.

"What'd you tell me to do?" Danny asked. He started to follow them. It occurred to Felix that Danny was acting like he had orders from somebody to fuck with him. Gus? It would be Gus. Felix glanced at Soraya. She was watching Franklin.

"He told you to step back," Franklin said. They were twenty feet away from the club. Danny reared up at Franklin's voice. "This is between me and him, old man," Danny said. He grabbed Felix's jacket and Felix flicked him off, but then it didn't matter what Felix did because Franklin was all over Danny. He turned him around and seemed to thump him in the chest—the noise was like a bongo—and Danny was bent over, no air coming out of him.

Then Franklin got up close, kneed him up against the steel door to a tenement, crouched down near him, and next thing, Danny went a few feet up in the air before he was sprawled on the ground. Franklin stood up, straightened himself. He let out a satisfied sigh.

"There wasn't any point in that," Soraya said.

"You're absolutely right," Franklin said. "But he was exhibiting behavior that I felt was inconsiderate, so I took an opportunity to let off something I'll call steam. Now let's all get a coffee."

"No," Felix said. Soraya stood with him.

"You knew Penelope was with Lem Dawes?" Soraya asked Franklin.

"We traced a call from the room she was in at the Official to his cell phone. Now I know they were personally known to each other. But more important, we've learned about a doctor who likes to keep his business private," Franklin said.

The brown van pulled up hard at the corner of Eldridge and Allen.

Franklin said, "This is mine. Let's go somewhere, huh? Even people who don't get along so well talk sometimes. Like us and the French. Am

I wrong? Or do you want me to beg, because now that I lost my temper and hit somebody I'm not above begging, either."

Franklin got into the front passenger seat. Soraya and Felix didn't move.

Franklin said, "Neither of you have seen me in twelve years. My daughter is dead. Get in the van."

Felix felt himself get in the back. He kept flicking his wrist, hard, to feel pain, because none of it seemed real, especially not the way he'd behaved with his father. Soraya followed him in. Gennardi got in the jump seat in the way back. Soraya took the middle with Felix.

He felt her reach for his hand. Her skin was cool and he realized that his was, too. He knew she'd meant it before, about shooting Franklin.

"Just let it play," Felix whispered. She nodded.

"Why don't you drop us at the office," Franklin said. Philip shot up Eldridge Street.

"Hi, Diane," Gennardi said into a cell phone. "Yeah, I'll be home soon. It might be a little while later than I originally said—"

In the front, Franklin and Philip started laughing.

"You two get in a scrap and every time right after he's on the phone to his fuckin' wife," Philip said, "and then Franklin, you put in a call to—"

But Felix saw Franklin shoot a look across at Philip and then he gestured back at Felix and Soraya.

"Leave it," Franklin said. "That kid back there is my son. And the other one, she's a very old family friend."

Philip turned and looked back at the two of them.

"I've heard talk of you," Philip said. "But I never dreamed I'd see your faces."

And then they drove, did nothing but listen to Gennardi talk to Diane about how quickly she'd gotten Lisa to bed.

Franklin told Philip and Gennardi to head on home, so Soraya and Felix went up alone with him in the freight elevator. They walked by the door to Ivan Bulgarov's studio.

Franklin gestured to the door. "My only friend save for Gennardi and Philip. Sad, no?"

Felix wondered why his father was using this questioning inflection, working overtime to make the two of them feel safe. They walked behind him and Felix stared at the back of his thick, bald head. The corridor smelled of old dust and dead flowers from the streets below. Felix thought Soraya was watching him and his father pretty carefully. She certainly wasn't saying much. It occurred to him that in her family, there were no men. If it was like she said, after Billy died, there had never been another man around her house.

"I don't live here," Franklin said as he flipped locks on the steel door. "Got a condo on the East Side. Hardly ever see it, though. You need a place to crash, you can stay there."

"You're a regular welcome wagon," Felix said. Franklin ignored that, flipped on lights. Felix looked around the small front room. There were no windows. Two black leather couches were up against opposite walls, and a cheap metal desk stood in front of the far wall. The desk had a phone on it and a computer monitor. That was all.

"Reception room," Franklin said. "Where Gennardi takes his afternoon naps. Want something? Beer? Water?" He strode over to a minifridge, which sat next to one of the couches.

"I don't want anything from you," Felix said. "I wouldn't drink your water."

"Relax," Franklin said. "Water doesn't care who pours it."

Felix looked at his father. Franklin's eyes were the same murk brown that he remembered. The pouches under them were dusty purple in the fluorescent light. He looked older than forty-seven.

"I care," Felix said. And Franklin only shrugged. They went through the reception room into the room in the back. Again, no windows. Franklin threw his suit jacket over the back of his chair, sat behind his desk. Soraya sat in one of the bucket leather chairs across from him and Felix took the other. Franklin slipped the Thompson out of his waistband and put it next to the Raging Bull.

Felix said, "Let's not bullshit each other. You knew she was in trouble and you sat and did nothing and now she's dead four months and you've done diddly-shit. You checked a phone log. Big deal, so did we. I'd like that gun back and any information you have and then Soraya and I will leave you alone."

Franklin smiled. He said, "Soraya?"

Soraya only shook her head. She rolled her neck, looked around the room, stopped for a second glance at the shotgun on the wall.

Franklin said, "Correct me if I go astray. Things went bad with me and your father and he got killed. You moved to Queens with your mother. You worked hard and won a fat scholarship to Barnard, which you took because your mom is lonely and needs you nearby. You probably got in a scrap or three along the way and so this thing you're doing with Felix—it's out of respect for what you kids had, which I ruined when I lost your father. That accurate?"

"Sure," Soraya said. "So what?"

"You're not too impressed," Franklin said to her.

"With you two? No," Soraya said.

Felix stirred. He'd only expected her to show disgust at his father, not him. But then, he'd forgotten about their argument earlier in the evening, when he'd revealed that he had a slight problem with trust.

"Either your sister overdosed or she was killed." Soraya gestured at Felix. "You need your father to find out who was there and what they were doing. Hold off on the past—it's going nowhere. Franklin's up to something now. Is that right, Franklin?"

Franklin reached into his desk. He pulled out a Smith & Wesson nine millimeter with a four-inch barrel. He popped the magazine, shook it, slipped it back in.

"You want a gun, take something decent—this'll do it. Ten-shot magazine." He pushed the little gun across the desk. There was the long crackle of metal on metal.

Felix said, "I want the Thompson."

Franklin said, "That one's mine."

The three of them sat for a moment. Soraya got up and went out. She came back with three bottles of Budweiser from the refrigerator. She handed them around.

"You're twenty," Franklin said. Soraya cocked her head to the left; her right eyebrow went up. She twisted the cap off and flicked it with her thumb onto his desk, drank long.

"Right—drink up," Franklin said. "Gennardi caught a line on that Lem Dawes kid, like I said. The kid is shit, no doubt about that. Now we have a doctor who prescribes the same pills that killed Penelope. It'd be good to know more about the doctor. But what happened is not going away. She overdosed. There's no doubt about that. There was no killing, no foul play. Nothing. Anything was anything, I'd have heard about it."

Felix said, "You don't need to protect us from the truth. We're grown. She was murdered. She called you for help just days before it happened and you did nothing. You find out who did it, maybe you'll sleep again."

Franklin looked at his son. He said, "You got pretty handsome out there in Oregon, didn't you? Some of your voice is mine, you got my big jaw, my shoulders, but the good parts of you are your mother's—the eyes and a head of hair you'll probably get to keep. . . ."

Felix shook his head. He said, "Don't waste our time. Maybe you can live with the bullshit OD story. I can't. Tell us what you know. Tell us what you'll do next and we can speed this thing up, and then I can go home, tell my mother the truth."

Franklin worked his jaw for a second. "I wish it were that easy," he said. "I wish there were somebody I could go after. I wish I'd even known where she was. I wish a lot of things. You get older, you make mistakes, spend a lot of time wishing instead of sleeping, sure. I'm guilty of that."

"She called you."

"Yeah. No number left, no information. Nothing. You think I enjoy this?"

"You wouldn't go asking questions if something wasn't bothering you."

"Maybe I had time to kill and I wanted to hear Dawes's story."

"That's all you've got is time."

"Okay, boys," Soraya said. "You're going to nip at each other's egos, why don't you make a date for it? Meanwhile, let's say I have a pain somewhere. I call Marsden Biddle, make an appointment to see him. I ask about Penelope, maybe he gives up a clue."

They both turned to her. Felix stole a quick glance at his father. They did have the same vein on the left side of their foreheads, running up from their eye socket, pulsing. But Felix didn't think there was more physical resemblance than that, and that wasn't much. One was old and bald and ugly. One wasn't.

"No," Franklin said. Then he put up a finger. "Scratch that thought. I'd rather not have you visit any doctor."

"You think I take directions from you?" Soraya laughed. "You forget what you are to me."

"Evil incarnate, like that?" Franklin asked.

"However your son feels about you, he can still look at you. I can't look at my father anymore and that's your fault."

"Then what are you doing here?"

Soraya blew air between her teeth. She said, "It's about Penelope, remember? There are things you know. I want to hear them. That's what I'm doing here."

Through all of this, Felix said nothing. He took a long pull on his beer and watched Franklin.

Franklin said, "I don't think you get it. We're not some team working on a case together. There's no clues to give up."

"Nobody said we're a team," Soraya said. "I'm just letting you know what I'm going to do."

Felix watched the two of them. He let out a long sigh and sat back, closed his eyes. He wanted his father to explain things for hours and hours, but it was too late to do that now. He saw how smart his father was. The old man had brought them in, learned what they were doing, and admitted nothing.

Franklin said, "You're going to go to that doctor no matter what I say, aren't you?"

"That's right," Soraya said. "There's only one boss of me, and you're looking at her."

Franklin said, "Then you let me know exactly when that's happening. Looks like I'll have to keep an eye on you two. Shit. I can already see it. You two squirrelly little fuckers are going to be the death of me."

11

Soraya stayed up in her dorm room alone that night. She listened to Roberta Flack's "Compared to What" over and over—her mom's favorite song. She'd called her mom, finally, on the way home. Their conversation was brief. Her mother said she hadn't slept in four days for worrying about Soraya and her third graders were concerned about her. They'd made her a card with lots of glitter and string. Soraya said she was okay—she couldn't explain it all—she'd be up for dinner on Sunday night.

She lay on her bed and listened to Roberta hit her high notes. Where she could, she sang along. All around her, music from the other dorm rooms came through her windows and mixed with her own until McBain sounded like nothing but a big chicken coop.

She thought about Felix and then she got abstracted, wondered why she bothered with these white boys. She'd been happy in high school, at Stuyvesant, keeping to herself, screwing her boyfriend Malik Stamp every chance she got and studying like she had her mother's every wish and hope and dream placed firmly on her head the rest of the time. And now, at twenty, here she was, surrounded by Novaks, dead and alive. As if she were a child all over again. And still no explanation for why Franklin Novak had left her father to die on the street in front of a botched pizza parlor drug bust in Spanish Harlem. The dumbest thing in the world. The saddest thing in the world.

She thought, If I were self-destructive, I'd take a pair of scissors to my neck right now. Go right for the jugular. But she wasn't. Instead she got on the Internet, began reading about Marsden Biddle. Somebody was hiding and soon enough, they'd come out and show themselves. Greed and drugs were straightforward that way. What had gone wrong for her own father—when that answer finally came, it would come hard. She could feel how close she was to some revelation—she'd been in the room with the last man to see him alive.

She could give her mother the answer, and then she would be free. Though, she knew, her mother had never asked her for this favor. She had never said that not knowing the truth was what had kept her from ever allowing herself to move beyond Billy Navarro.

Soraya closed her eyes and sat back, listened to Roberta sing "Angelitos Negros." Gus rang her cell, but she let it go. They were always ringing and beeping, just to let each other know that they were okay, they were thinking of each other.

And then she was just tired and didn't want to think for another second, so she opened last week's *W* magazine. There were some people she knew—uptown types who came down to Eden-Roc and Bungalow 8 and Suite 16 for late night fun. She looked at a page of photographs from a party for the opening of a new perfume store on 57th Street—Distraction. There were the usual suspects, those ridiculously whorish Hilton sisters, Renee Rockefeller, Julia Stiles, Kate Moss, an MTV personality or two—Gideon Yago and Serena Altschul's cuter little sister, Veruka. On the next page there was a photo of her friend Edwige, smiling wide, on the arm of some older guy who was bald and not much bigger than she was. His face seemed severe and he looked rich—like somebody's nutty British uncle. Soraya shook her head. Crazy Edwige—star in two or three teen movies, transfer to Columbia, and suddenly the whole world mistakes flightiness and instability for the next big thing. But she was beautiful. Soraya had to give her that. And it didn't hurt that her father was Sidney Jamison, the director. She and Soraya had been friends since freshman year and no matter what anybody said, the girl really did glow. She read the photo's caption: *Edwige Jamison in Anton Hors at a benefit for New York Hospital, gossiping with family friend Dr. Marsden Biddle.*

Oh, shit.

She smiled. What better way to get to a society doctor than through his society connections? She was always annoyed at how little she used Columbia's network to make connections of her own. There was so much money and influence flowing through the kids she met at school, and she too often made the mistake of ignoring it all in favor of people who had come up a little rougher, like Felix. But she could pretend like she was society, too. And getting to the doctor through Edwige was brilliant. She'd gossip about Edwige and then maybe Biddle could tell her something about Lem and Penelope. And why he was so quick to prescribe Oxy. She needed to learn more about Oxy.

She found her keys, went out to the corridor. It was a Thursday, she realized, nearly 4 A.M. There was as good a chance as any that Edwige would be in. She walked through the corridors of McBain and found Edwige's room. The door was open when she got down there, so she stood in the doorway and peered in. Edwige was sitting at her desk, with her back to the door, typing away on a customized gold-tone G4. Some old Donovan played in the background.

"Hi, baby," Soraya said. Edwige looked up.

"Oh, hi—I'm just working on this paper on Matthew Barney for my American insurgents art class. But come on in, baby."

So Soraya came in and sat on the windowsill. She thought about how it all would have looked so normal, a typical college sophomore pulling an all-nighter for her art history class, except for the two boys asleep on the bed. They were tousle-haired, with sallow faces and newly shaven cheeks, and they were both in what would soon be very rumpled black suits. They slept with their arms intertwined, snoring prettily into each other's faces.

"Who are they?" Soraya asked.

"Oh, that's Sam London and his boyfriend Olly Durell—in from LA to do a photo shoot. They came up to visit and totally crashed. They're cute, though, huh? If only they'd snore a little less. Though at least this way I know they're not OD'ing."

Edwige hit the remote control and turned up "Mellow Yellow." She smiled at Soraya.

"Later I'm going to undress them, stick on some prosthetics, take photos of their manipulated bodies, and include them with my paper. What's up?"

"Oh," Soraya said. "I was just wondering. I've been so tense and I know health services won't prescribe a thing lately 'cause of all the lawsuits, so I was wondering—"

"You want to go to a doctor?"

"That's what I was thinking, that if you knew anybody—"

"Not another word, baby," Edwige said, and raised a finger. She smiled and Soraya noticed the hands-free phone extension hanging from her ear.

"Dr. Booby," Edwige said. The line clicked on.

Soraya raised an eyebrow. She went and stood over the two handsome young men on the bed. The one nearer to the wall stuck his tongue out in his sleep, frowned at an imaginary adversary.

"Hi, this is Edwige Jamison and when my friend Soraya Navarro calls tomorrow for Dr. Biddle I want her to be given an appointment immediately. Thank you. End call."

Soraya watched her friend. Edwige didn't seem high, exactly. Just extremely relaxed.

Edwige typed for a moment, then looked up. She said, "I e-mailed you his contact info. You should've come to me earlier if you were having a problem."

Soraya said, "I didn't know I was in trouble until now."

"You're in pain?"

"Yeah . . . ," Soraya said. "I guess I am."

"Well, Biddle's all about pain management. You've no idea what he's been able to do for me. Look, do you need something to get you through tonight?"

"Sure," Soraya said. "I was hoping you'd offer."

Edwige slid open her desk drawer and pulled out a smoke-brown vial. She popped off the white plastic cap and removed a tiny purple pill. She handed it over.

"This is OxyContin. Some very pure shit, believe me. Mash it up and snort a quarter of it, like you'd snort coke. Or chop it in eighths to start and swallow it with a little red wine; shiraz is best. You'll be okay. These little bitches wear the pain right off and it's so cool—nobody in the city is using them yet. They're all still into crystal meth and all that other party garbage. But of course you know that."

Soraya came over and kissed her. She said, "I knew I could count on you, Edwige."

"The other way you can go is slow release. That's what I do. I'm up to three a day, sixty milligrams a pop, but I'd like to get down to ten milligrams before too long. I know I'm getting thin. You don't have to tell me. Anyway, anyway . . ." Edwige drifted off. Her head jagged to one side.

"I'm going to get back to my room," Soraya said. "Maybe you should get some sleep."

"No, no. No sleep for the . . . is it wicked? Wasted? You want to fondle a pretty boy before you go?" Edwige asked, and laughed.

In the morning, after explaining to a chilly receptionist with a French accent that she was a good friend of Edwige and that she needed to see Dr. Biddle as quickly as possible, Soraya got an appointment for Monday, 7:30 A.M.

"But I can promise only eight to ten minutes with Dr. Biddle," the receptionist said. "And you understand of course that we do not accept insurance."

"Edwige said she'd cover it," Soraya said. She hung up and called the Official, but if Felix was there, he didn't pick up the phone in his room. She looked at the Oxy pill on her desk. It was tiny. She felt the slightest temptation to chop off a corner and snort it up. What with it being too long since she'd been to bed with Gus and Felix taking up so much of her time, she felt nervous, and she thought she could use a little release.

She opened the window in front of her desk and looked out at the traffic on 113th Street. Only a few students were up, walking to breakfast or an early morning class. The light was really nice. She looked at oak trees on the other side of the street and saw how the sun was making the early spring leaves glow an opalescent green. She shook her head, closed her eyes against the small breeze. She took a bottle of Chanel No. 5 perfume that Gus had given her and used it to crush the

Oxy pill against her desk. She felt the thing crunch down to dust. Then she brought her chin down lightly on the desk, squinted, and blew the purple dust out into the spring wind.

Felix got out of a warm bed and looked around at what appeared to be a studio apartment. The place was wrecked. It felt like a team of burglars had come through and shaken the whole room down. Since he'd gotten into town he hadn't really expected to know where he was when he woke up, but still—this was weird.

Then he saw Lanie, her brown curls covering her face, one arm pushed up against the headboard. Felix felt cold air blow across him and goose bumps grew. He was naked. His clothes had been thrown against the far wall of Lanie's apartment like paint splatter. That must've been at about five in the morning, only a couple of hours after he'd left his father and Soraya. He'd called Lanie and come downtown to what he now realized was her tiny studio apartment on Downing Street.

They were on the sixth floor of a walk-up building. He looked out at the sun rising over the buildings to the east. Then he looked around the room. The place couldn't have been more than twice the size of Soraya's dorm room and it held great messy towers of things—books and CDs, magazines and old copies of the *Spectator.* There was a chest of drawers, an open closet with only a few articles of black and gray clothing hung up improperly. Next to the front door there was a kitchenette. The burners on the small white stove were covered with mail. Party invitations, bills, more shiny magazines still in their plastic sheaths, junk mail, and even some letters that had been addressed by hand, as yet unopened. He felt a rustling behind him and he turned. A small black cat peeked out from behind a laundry basket and then disappeared.

He opened the fridge and found batteries, film, a bag of broccoli that looked like it had given up the fight for freshness sometime during the past winter. A bottle of Stolichnaya was in the freezer along with a bag of party ice. There were several packages of frozen White Castle hamburgers, a pint of Häagen-Dazs dulce de leche ice cream, D'Agostino frozen peas, and that was all.

"Happy to see me?" Lanie asked from the bed. He looked over. She was grinning, though her eyes were still nearly closed. She had a big brown-and-pink blanket pulled up to her chin and she was stretching, uncurling her little body. Then she pulled the blanket off and she was nude. She slipped toward the front of the bed and she was sitting up, facing him.

"I don't understand," Felix said.

"I'm happy to see you, too. Now, why don't you bring that big thing over here and we'll see what we can do with it."

"What?" Felix said. He turned red, twisted around in front of her.

"Oh, come on, Felix, kidding, kidding!"

Then Felix felt embarrassed and he grabbed his pants and covered himself. There was something so cute about her—so messy and self-assured. He laughed out loud as he came over to her and, in a rare moment of genuine introspection, realized that maybe he wasn't used to happy girls. The people in and around his family generally weren't disposed toward levity.

She took his hand, said, "When you woke up, did you have the thing happen where you didn't know where you were?"

The radio next to her clicked on. "And in France right-wing protesters attacked the—" She let go of him and reached back, swatted at the radio, knocked it off the wooden nightstand. It fell with a thud onto a crumpled skirt, made no more noise. Then she shivered and got under the covers.

"I did, but I'm clear on it now. I'm happy I called you last night." Felix smiled. When he'd called, he'd just wanted to talk to her, to talk to anybody who didn't know him when he was a child. But then she'd invited him over and they'd ended up having slow, easy sex, as if that were the most natural thing in the world. Felix looked carefully at her. He cocked his head to one side and said, "You know who my father is. Do you know anything else about my family?"

"No." Lanie smiled. "Does it get even better?"

He shook his head. He couldn't figure out whether she'd made the connections that would tell her who his grandfather was, and he wasn't eager to tell her, not yet, anyway. He felt like he'd already revealed quite a bit. The thing about getting played, Felix realized, is that if it's happening, it's not like anybody's going to announce it to you. You've got to figure it out.

"I don't have to be at work for hours and hours," Lanie said.

"That's good. I could use some more sleep," Felix said.

"Sleep? Come here, you," Lanie said.

"The funny thing is," Felix said as he dove back under the covers with her, "I kind of like you."

"Shut up, dickhead. It's love," Lanie said. And he felt her wrap her arms around him.

"If it's even close, I know you wouldn't be using me to get to Gus and Soraya, right? I'm not just research for a story?"

"No, baby, I swear," Lanie said. "I don't mix business with *mmph!* Damn, Felix. Don't stop. Just trust me."

Felix didn't trust her, not yet, but he didn't stop, either. He didn't want to. She wrapped her hands around his shoulders and he saw his broken heart tattoo disappear behind her fingers.

12

Friday morning, 10 A.M., and Jenny Hurly sat across from Franklin in his visitor's chair, sipping an iced coffee. She was a raven-haired thirty-year-old in a black skirt, with a brown cowl neck sweater that gave her jaw some edge. She had round nut-brown eyes and a real Wisconsin smile. She was maybe a little heavy along her curves.

"Why not?" Franklin said.

They'd been discussing why she didn't want to take any more money from Franklin. The room was warm from their talking, but it was quiet. Gennardi and Philip were over at Edelstein's. Ivan Bulgarov wasn't in yet.

"It makes me uncomfortable," she said. Since Franklin had known her, which was over two years, her voice had gotten lower, more confident. "I feel like a whore and I don't like that one bit."

"You're not. But it's not like you don't need the money," Franklin said. He rubbed at his temples with his knuckles, like a little kid trying to figure out a math problem.

"I don't like what it says about us," she said. She finished her iced coffee and popped off the plastic top to the cup, emptied sugar-coated ice into her mouth, and chewed.

"And I want to go out to dinner, too. I want us to double-date with Chris Gennardi and his wife. You sure talk about them enough—now I'd like to be friends with them. No more meeting at your apartment at midnight when you're done working."

"No more weekends holed up at the Gershwin Hotel with pizza and TV in bed Sundays?" Franklin asked.

"Nope. The only thing I want you paying for is brunch at the Lenox Room when my parents come to town."

Franklin stared at her. He had to fight to get his fists off the sides of his head. The *Spectator*'s main line showed up on his caller ID and Franklin's jaw muscle twitched, his mouth pulled hard to the right. Probably Starling Furst. Fucking guy. He'd spoken to him more in the last month than in the last ten years. He knew well enough that if Furst wanted to truly shut him down, he could, but family was family. Further, Starling wasn't stupid. If he was calling, he had a reason. He checked the *Spectator*'s front page on the corner of his desk: MAYOR BUYS NY1TV. CONFLICT? TUNE IN TO FIND OUT!

"I should take this," Franklin said.

"Think about it," Jenny said. She stood up and came over to the desk, kissed the top of his head. "It was cute at first, all those hundred-dollar bills and no commitments, but not anymore. And lock up that gun, would you? That thing's obscene."

He watched her go out through the office door. Lord, was she soft looking. Man, was she determined to change their relationship. He shook his head, looked back at the headline. Like fucking Gotham City, Franklin thought. If the mayor doesn't like something, he buys it and beats it till it behaves. Franklin scratched at his unshaven jaw with the butt of the Raging Bull. He got himself ready for another nasty talking-to from an old rich guy who would never get enough people around him to soak up all his anger. He picked up on the sixth ring.

"Yeah," Franklin said.

"Jack Dawes calls me up, says some sleazy investigator roughed up his son last night in a nightclub. Called me up to complain about it. Leave the kid alone. He's got nothing to do with my granddaughter."

"Other species eat the weakest of their young," Franklin said.

"Sure. If a kid like Lem Dawes were one of mine I'd have him taken out, no doubt about that. Jack's doing his best. He cut the kid's cash supply to nothing and told him to get a job, stay out of the nightclubs. He even sent him to Marsden Biddle to try to cure his habit."

Franklin's voice went to ice. He said, "You know about the doctor? What's the connection? You knew who my daughter didn't know, then maybe you can tell me who she did know?"

Franklin realized, as he placed the Bull flat on the desk, that he'd never hated Starling Furst before, no matter how much dirt and aggravation the old man threw his way. He'd always respected him, for his daughter and for all the behind-the-scenes deals he'd done to help the city during the many and varied economic crises of the last thirty years. No, he'd never hated him until now.

Starling exhaled, long. He said, "Marsden Biddle's a good guy. I couldn't tell you who Penelope knew. I wish I could. I truly do."

"I'm sending Felix over to talk to you," Franklin said. And he hadn't thought of this before, either.

"He got in touch with you before me? Interesting. In any case, I'd love to see him. Turn him against you all over again."

"We took care of that between us already. You better make up some new fun. He'll be by," Franklin said.

Franklin ended the call before Starling could think of anything else to bother him about. Then he dialed the number Soraya had given him, her cell.

"Where's my son?"

He heard her breath drop. That said to him that if he didn't know and she didn't—that bothered her. Bothered them both.

"Him? He should be calling me soon. I can tell him you asked after him if you want. Oh—I'm going in to see our doctor Monday morning, seven-thirty."

"How'd you—don't take a damn thing he gives you and—no. I'll pick you up afterward. We'll discuss what you learned."

"Can't. I've got a class."

"I'll pick you up, like I just said," Franklin said. "I'll wait for you out on Park Avenue and 72nd in my van. And yeah, find Felix and have him call me now."

Felix did put a call in to his father several hours later, from a pay phone. They made plans to meet for dinner at Zitto's, on Lexington and 33rd.

13

Zitto's was famous for its horrible wallpaper: a dense and overwrought pattern of giant sunflowers and gleaming white swords, which regulars called the Zitto crest. Franklin came in through the etched glass doors and said hello to Mickey Pomodoro, the host, who had been working there for thirty years and seating Franklin at the same table in the back for ten, starting right after Franklin had finished his stint down in Florida with Wackenhut.

They'd become friends after he'd found Mickey's sixteen-year-old daughter, Theresa, shacked up with a goalie from the New York Rangers. Franklin told the goalie about statutory rape—suggested that maybe laws were different in Canada. The goalie pointed out that the girl's name was Tomato, after all, and why shouldn't he have her? Because she ain't ripe and she ain't yours, Franklin had said, and he'd broken a stick over the goalie's head. So now Franklin got the back corner table at Zitto's when he needed it and Mickey's daughter had gone safely off to Cornell, where, before going off to law school and then Washington and a promising career in the State Department, she actually *was* a goalie on the girls' hockey team.

Mickey air-kissed Franklin on both cheeks and brushed imaginary dirt off the lapel of Franklin's black-and-white tweed blazer.

Mickey said, "Kid at the bar says he's here for you. I didn't know him, didn't seat him."

"My kid," Franklin said when he saw Felix, who stood at the bar in his cheap black suit, cowboy hat in his hands. He was talking with the bartender, a sweet woman with auburn hair called Felidia, who wore a big gold crucifix on a chain.

Mickey began to apologize, but Franklin stopped him, hugged him around the shoulders. "Forget it," Franklin said. "I wouldn't have thunk it, either."

He walked up to Felix and they shook hands formally, their chins up and their eyes narrowed. Franklin motioned for Felix to follow him into the dining room.

"Can I leave my hat here with you?" Felix asked Felidia.

"You can leave a whole lot more than that, cowboy," Felidia said.

"Watch it," Franklin said. "That's my kid you're talking to."

"I could happily forget my rotten past with you for a fresh slice of future with him," Felidia said, and laughed. She took out a towel and rubbed at the dark mahogany bar.

"Don't believe her," Franklin said as they walked away.

"Better I should believe you?" Felix asked. Franklin didn't respond, and then Felix saw that there was no need to go on the offensive. So he quieted down and followed Franklin.

Other than the wallpaper, the dining room at Zitto's looked like any other typical Murray Hill Italian joint—white tablecloths, brown carpet, a short candle in the middle of each table, and five old waiters standing near the door to the kitchen. There were booths along one wall and two- and four-top tables in the middle of the room for the tourists. Then there was the back wall, where Franklin and the regulars were seated. The light back there was a little dimmer, and the ceiling was lower and dimpled, so voices were muted.

Felix sat down across from his father. He slid his chair a little to the right so his back wasn't completely to the room and he didn't have to look directly in his father's eyes.

"You look tired," Franklin said.

"Met a lady."

"Since I saw you last night? You don't call them ladies if they put bags under your eyes and a shake in your step."

Felix said nothing. Franklin sighed. Richard the waiter showed up and Franklin nodded at him. Richard nodded back. He was past sixty, thin and sallow, a dour man with a pinched mouth that he rarely bothered to open.

"The same for both of us," Franklin said. "Vitello tonnato—you'll love it. We'll have that and tomatoes and mozzarella to start. It's almost spring."

As Richard walked away, Franklin turned to Felix, said, "Me and

Richard, we had a disagreement a bunch of years back about something neither of us can remember—a political thing back when Alfonse D'Amato was using public office for private gain. Now he serves me lunch, and some days he talks, but most days he doesn't. Looks like today's the silent treatment. Crazy, no?"

"I've given up being surprised at how you handle your life," Felix said.

"Now that's not nice," Franklin said. He dragged his palm over his scalp. "I probably asked you this already, but how's your mom? She okay?"

"Call her up," Felix said. "She's home."

"Jeez," Franklin said, low.

The room began to fill with people, mostly neighborhood types since it was the weekend. But the table next to them remained empty. The air around them was quiet, and hardly anybody bustled past their area. It occurred to Felix that in addition to waiting on them, Richard was guarding their table, that his father was not unknown to the rest of the clientele.

Franklin said, "Ellie never explained anything to you about what went wrong between us?"

"Your leaving Billy Navarro to die in the street saved her the trouble. She always said to me that you were a man of action, so your actions spoke much louder than your words."

Richard showed up and placed speckled brown plates covered with slices of shiny red tomatoes, basil, and thick slabs of mozzarella in front of both of them. He set down oversized goblets and filled them with red wine. Then he went away without saying a word.

"Yeah, you might want to think about how little sense that makes, considering that you don't know what my actions actually were," Franklin said. "But I guess I've got a little time to win you over. Better for now you should eat."

And Felix couldn't help himself. He'd barely eaten a thing in days—certainly nothing resembling a vegetable. So they ate quickly, and they ate the same way, strong-armed, using only their forks to cut. When the plates were taken away, Franklin looked back at Felix.

Felix said, "You're right. Best we forget what I think about you. You want to hear why I think she was killed?"

"Sure I do," Franklin said. He sat back and laid a hand over his belly. Felix got ready to talk and struggled to hide the eagerness in his eyes. He used to love to get his father's attention, to tell him his theories about why the Giants were winning or why Ellie was in a lousy mood, and now, though he knew it made him a fool, the soft feeling welled up in him again and he had to bite his lip to kill it.

Felix gulped wine and got started. "She'd been using for years. If she was going to OD like that, she'd have done it already. She called me and she said she was scared and that she was running with some serious people, people who were dealing real volume. I don't know how she got here or what she was doing, but it was a jump into some kind of big leagues and somebody killed her for it. That's what I *know.*"

Richard put down the vitello tonnato—cold veal in a tuna-and-cream sauce over arugula. Felix stared at it. He pushed the meat with his finger, looked up at his father, and squinted.

"Supposed to look that way. It'll keep. Go on."

"So I come here four, five days ago. Soraya's dating a guy, Gus Moravia—I figure it's a rebel thing, against her mother. You ever speak to her?"

"Nancy Navarro? I tried."

"Gus is some kind of manager, dealer, sleaze—I don't know. He's a user, too, I'd say. He works for a guy, Terrence Cheng. There's another guy, Max Udris. These three, they know each other. Soraya doesn't want to see the connections. But they're there."

Franklin said, "She's a kid and she loves this Gus. Terrence Cheng is one of those guys who everybody suspects but who never gets caught. Whether he's a bad guy or not, I don't know. I'm sorry, but I don't see how these people connect up to Penelope. That Soraya has lousy taste in men is nothing but a coincidence. And more, we don't know that they did anything wrong."

"We don't?" Felix asked. "Soraya saw Max Udris with Penelope at Eden-Roc. Somebody else was there, too, Liza Pruitt. They were all using OxyContin. Lem Dawes was there, too. I'm sure that somebody in there was with her when she died or knows somebody who was. She was scared. She said so. Somebody didn't want her around anymore."

"You're making a lot of connections," Franklin said. His voice was dry. He sipped wine. "Soon you'll have all the answers. What about this: *Why* would they kill her?"

"She wouldn't deal for them," Felix said. He knit his brows, like he was confused at his father's stupidity.

"Who asked her to?"

"They did. Cheng, Udris, whoever. And she didn't like being pushed around."

"What about Lem Dawes and this Dr. Marsden Biddle they both went to?"

"She was always good at finding losers to do drugs with—that's all that is. The outcome of weird parentage."

"I was waiting for genes to fit into your explanation," Franklin said. "Come on, Felix. It doesn't make sense. Now an overdose, that *does* make sense. It makes me sick to say it, believe me, but there it is."

"You don't understand the way these users operate," Felix said. He looked down at his plate, made a face, and ate everything on it. Franklin motioned to Richard, held his fingers two inches apart. A few minutes later, Richard brought out a hanger steak, placed it in front of Felix.

"Thank you," Felix said under his breath and dug in.

"Anybody else implicated in this grand scheme of yours?" Franklin asked.

"Far as I can tell, there's bartenders and waitresses all over this city who are eager to chop up Oxy and start popping it like it's aspirin. I met one who's already into it and he mentioned Liza Pruitt, and she's connected to Udris, and Udris connects to Cheng. I think that's Cheng's angle. Deal to customers, staff, everybody. Udris is a good cover: with his stone business he's in and out of all the high-end hotels and restaurants in the city, so he can move the stuff around. I'd like to start killing some people who were in on this, but I can't be sure of what I'm saying, so I won't. You will."

"Say what?" Franklin smiled. He leaned forward, so the dim lights gleamed on his bald head.

"You've got it in you. You kill whoever killed her and I go back home. Tell Ellie that it's been done."

"That's nice—the way you put it," Franklin said. "I thought I was the hardest guy in town. But I was wrong. You are."

"One other thing. I want my gun back."

"I offered you a gun. You wouldn't take it."

"I want the Thompson. I had it fixed up and sighted for me. I got bullets for it and a holster. I need it."

Richard cleared their plates. A moment passed and then he came back, set down cups of espresso and some biscotti. Felix took one, crunched it.

Franklin said, "When I saw you last night, I was afraid that you'd take it hard if there was nobody to blame for her death. And it looks like I was right."

"But Dad, you were looking, too," Felix said. And then he blew out his cheeks and looked away, stunned and embarrassed by the word he'd just used. He shook it off, didn't look at Franklin.

"That Gus character—that guy needs to go down," Felix said.

"You talk about taking people down with about as much emotion as a token-booth clerk giving bad directions," Franklin said, and laughed. Felix had the feeling his father was helping him along, letting him cover up for the "Dad" he hadn't been ready to use. He nodded. Then Franklin took the Thompson from his waistband and slipped it under the table, tapped Felix's knee with it. Felix took it in one swift motion and slipped it into his shoulder holster. He nodded. Another thank-you.

"About Gus. Soraya's with him—he can't be all bad," Franklin said.

"No. He is. He's got her fooled for no other reason than she's a good girl who likes the bad boys—just like Penelope was."

Franklin said, "So you got your theory and your connections—go prove it. Play connect the dots. It's the wrong way to go about it, but I'd be willing to take the other end—connect the dots and see what the hidden picture is—and we meet where we meet. Tail this Gus character and get back to me. You give me something, I'll give you something. Deal? But watch out for Soraya. I wouldn't want to see her hurt."

"Further than that, I want to trust Soraya," Felix said. "Even though she's in a haze with Gus. She can show me the street connections, bring me to the bars and the clubs."

"She's also got the doctor angle covered. You get the evidence on your killers. You want me to tell you I'll make it right? Consider it done." Franklin sat back.

"So Soraya's in this with me. You see it that way?" Felix asked.

"Sure." Franklin smiled wide and leaned forward. Felix looked away. He folded his napkin, placed it on the table. He adjusted the gun under his jacket and stood up. Then he looked at the wallpaper, not at his father.

"Thanks for dinner," Felix said. "I needed it."

"Oh, one other thing—your grandfather called me. He wants you to go see him. Let him fret a little and maybe he'll throw some cash your way. Here's his number. But the way you feel about me? Don't forget to feel that way about him, too."

Felix took a card with Starling Furst's number on it from his father's outstretched hand. He didn't look down at him, didn't mention that he'd planned to see Starling Furst anyway.

"He's still rich?" Felix asked.

"When you've got money like that, it never goes away. You know, I think of what you could learn from me, it's almost worth clearing up the past so you spend less energy on all the hate."

"So do it," Felix said. And he knew he was giving his father something, admitting his need for him, doing just what Ellie had said he should never do, getting ready to trust his father.

"Nah," Franklin said. "If it was that easy, I would've already. Now, get going. You know how to reach me."

"I'll talk to you soon," Felix said. For a second, he met his father's eyes, nodded, and went to the front of the restaurant. He got his hat from Felidia and went into the street. Richard, the waiter, came back to the table.

Richard said, "If your boy can spend all that time talking to you, I guess I can stand it for half a minute."

"Too sweet," Franklin said. "You see how I'm weeping here. What'd you think of him?"

"He looks young to get into your business, but he was talking like he's ready to kill somebody."

"Yeah. He's smart, but he's a little eager. Needs to work on his self-control. Like, I'm eager to have a tartuffo for dessert, but I'm gonna take the self-control road and not have one. You got tomorrow's *Spectator* around that I could look at?"

14

Gus Moravia stood inside Dean & DeLuca, on the corner of Prince and Broadway, at the stainless steel counter that ran along the fourteen-foot-high wall of windows in the coffee area. He'd bought what looked to Felix like a double shot of espresso in a short paper cup. Methodically, he poured five brown sugar packets into it. He sipped once and added another packet. Felix felt his own lips pucker. The coffee probably tasted as thick as the bottom of a streambed. Didn't heroin addicts crave sugar?

Felix was standing across the street, facing west and the Prada store, waiting for the light to change. He wore a pair of cheap mirrored sunglasses he'd bought back in Pierre, South Dakota. He had on black Puma Clydes, jeans, and his gray sweatshirt. He wore a Yankees hat that he'd bought on Canal Street from an eighty-year-old Chinese lady for three dollars. He knew he looked like nothing but a tourist, a college kid in from nowhere, here to ogle the crippled and ever-resilient city. Based on what he'd seen so far, real city people looked through tourists like they were nothing, the visual equivalent of honking horns. So far he'd been pushed out of the way twice. He highly doubted that Gus would make him.

In fact, Gus had only seen him once at Eden-Roc and on his first night in Soraya's room at the Official, when he was barely wearing any clothes at all. He watched Gus quickly shovel what appeared to be an oversized chocolate doughnut into his mouth. Gus finished off the coffee, upended the cup into his mouth. Then he walked out of Dean & DeLuca and headed south on Broadway. Quite a snack for four o'clock on a Saturday afternoon, Felix thought. Fucking drug-addled night bird. And then he cooled, erased that thought and any emotion at all. He turned left on Spring when Gus did. He had his iPod on, tuned to the high lonesome sound of Roscoe Holcomb. Figured he needed the bluegrass to keep his balance.

He watched Gus's spiky hair disappear into a restaurant on the corner of Spring and Crosby, some kind of fake French place with wood and mirrors all over everything, like a New Orleans saloon gone berserk. He crossed the street and stood in front of a Starbucks, felt a big body move past him fast. Max Udris.

Felix's skin went cold as Max passed. He was with the man Soraya had dubbed Kris Kringle. Both of them were in work clothes, blue jeans and Timberlands, Carhartt jackets with the collars turned up. They were speaking in Russian. Merry Christmas, Felix thought. They disappeared into the restaurant.

Felix counted ten seconds, then followed them through a set of double doors that seemed to seal in the noise. He saw them turning left into the dining room and so he turned right, into the bar area. The bar was packed with people and it occurred to Felix that he looked out of place, but it was too late now. He left his shades on. A bartender in a white button-down shirt with short black bangs and long eyelashes caught his eye. Though she was easily six feet tall, he thought she looked about twelve years old.

"Beer?" he asked.

Bored, she spread one hand over the taps, and with the other she gestured behind her at the dozen bottles arranged in front of the rusted-out mirror.

She said, "Care to get specific?"

He looked at the bottles and then his glance traveled up, to where the mirror curved forward. He could easily see down the long cracked leather banquette, where various well-dressed types were tucked in, facing the people who sat on uncomfortable chairs across from them. Sure enough, Gus sat on a chair across from Max Udris. Both of them had their hands on the little slate table between them.

"Want me to choose for you?" the bartender said. She looked a little annoyed, as if Felix was supposed to be made nervous by her. He didn't see why he should be. So he smiled. She twitched her nose in frustration at him, but then she couldn't help it and she smiled, too.

"Why don't you give me what your boyfriend drinks," Felix said. He looked back up to the mirror at Max and Gus.

"Starapromen," she said. "For you, seven dollars."

Felix shook his head and reached for his money clip. But instead of his pocket, he found a hand. Attached to the hand was an arm, and Felix went stiff and pulled forward, but the crowd around him didn't give. He was right next to Kris Kringle, who'd taken Felix's forearm and was gripping it, tight.

"Out," Kringle said. For such a big old man, Felix thought, he sounded more like an angry cat. And then Felix was being pulled behind him. He caught sight of Max and Gus as Kringle pedaled him through the doors. They were arguing over several sheets of paper spread in front of them. They appeared studiously unaware that he'd been near them.

"Off me," Felix said. He tried to twist free of Kringle's grip, but the man didn't let go. People coming into the bar made way for them, but nobody moved to stop or question what was happening. Two men in sky blue suits eyed Felix and Kringle and laughed.

Then they were moving up Spring and around to Kenmare Street, past Lucy's Natural, past a Thai restaurant, an outdoor café called Loup, and a bicycle repair shop, past scrawny trees and a little fenced-in park that was full of psychotic drunks, and past couples walking home for naps and sex in the failing light of a Saturday afternoon. Felix pulled, but Kringle's grip didn't waver and he wouldn't catch Felix's eye.

"Move," the man said, in that same whiny cat voice. They stepped into a wide square parking lot half-filled with SUVs and foreign sedans, at the foot of Kenmare Street. Kringle flipped Felix against the graffittied side of a building that butted up to the lot. Felix felt his back bang against brick. He pushed off with his ass, knee up, and put his fist into Kringle's jaw, but the man backpedaled and the blow was soft. Kringle grabbed his throat and punched him in the gut. Felix took the hit hard, went up against the bricks, felt Kringle's fist press his kidney right up against his spine.

"We're busy. Not with you," Kringle said. He spun Felix around, put him over his knee, gut-punched him again, and then threw him back against the wall. Felix's breath came out of him like an involuntary word, *no.*

"No following," Kringle said. "You see this nice meeting, maybe you see some not so nice ones, nobody wants that. So no more watching."

Felix knew he was blacking out. He was falling face first into a space between the brick wall and two cars. He was protecting the fire that had exploded just beneath his ribs, was reaching for the gun he'd left in his car. Kris Kringle was already gone when Felix looked up. He knew immediately that he had three kinds of pain, and he didn't want to name any of them. It was the same bunch of hurt that he'd felt the first time he'd been thrown off a bull when he was thirteen. Except now he was in a big city and there were firecrackers exploding inside his head.

The parking lot attendant was standing over him and some concerned hipsters were gathered a few feet from the fender of a white Range Rover that was parked next to where he'd come to rest.

"You want me to call the police?" the attendant asked. He was leaned down near Felix so Felix could smell him, and he wanted the guy away from him. He wanted to hug the ground for another few minutes and not stand up so quick.

"Why?" Felix asked, wheezing.

"'Cause you just got knocked on your ass," the attendant said. Felix held up his arm and nobody took it. Not the attendant or any of the people standing—nobody.

"The only person touching you is an EMT," a serious young woman in blue jeans and Reeboks said. She even seemed to be holding back a guy who looked willing to help.

"Oh, for Pete's sake," Felix said, and pulled himself up on the Rover's fender.

"You will wait for the police and an ambulance!" the woman said. She looked like she was ready to push Felix back down. Everyone was paying attention to her now, and the attendant disappeared into his booth at the other end of the lot, where he shut the door and turned off the light.

"Man," Felix said. "You New York people are the biggest bunch of wusses."

He staggered for a moment. But then the young woman's sanctimonious fury was enough to get him moving. He stood. He started walking down Lafayette Street toward Chinatown. He'd parked fairly nearby and he figured a good lie-down was highly necessary. He'd have his Saturday night in the room Soraya was letting him use at the Official. Then he'd call her and lay down his newly confirmed opinion of her boyfriend.

15

Saturday night and Franklin sat on a brown velvet couch in Chris Gennardi's living room in Forest Hills. They had a Yankees–Red Sox game turned on, but they weren't watching it. It was early in the season, so the Sox were eking out a win. The room had some major window treatment, in shades of beige and champagne, and the carpet was champagne colored, too. In the early evening light, the place felt a little like a honeymoon bedroom on the *QE2.*

"She's a great cook," Franklin said.

Gennardi said, "The sausage and peppers were okay. The eggplant was overdone."

"How can you say that?" Franklin asked.

"Jeez! 'Cause I cooked it, okay? You keep forgetting. Diane only made the salad."

Franklin said, "That was really good, the salad." He rubbed his belly. They were drinking small glasses of amaretto. In the other room, they could hear Diane arguing with Lisa about when was bedtime, ten or eleven o'clock? Midnight? Diane was slowly being cowed into making a deal with Lisa that involved mango sorbet and skipping the weekend's social studies homework.

"Man. I could sleep right now," Franklin said.

"You could, but Diane wouldn't like it," Gennardi said. "Remember last time?" He smiled at his partner.

"Okay. I set up another Edelstein appointment with you for Monday. Says he's real pleased that you didn't find anything the first time around. You're supposed to go in with Philip at 10 A.M. Now, what's this about Lionel McTeague?" Franklin asked. McTeague was one of Franklin's best snitches—a midlevel dealer with connections everywhere.

"Turns out he's on Rikers, was why it took a minute to find him. But he says he'd love to see you," Gennardi said. "He's in maximum security, the Bing, in the OBCC building way at the back of the island. He says you were right about him getting out of the heroin business. And now he's got some stories to tell."

"Sweet Lionel McTeague," Franklin said. "What made him kick?"

"Ah, he got arrested out at a Motel 6 near Kennedy. He was waiting to pick up a mule from Colombia. A stupid thing. The mule got sick, so his cabdriver drove him to a hospital. The mule had the hotel room number on him. So the cops went and picked up Lionel in the room."

"That is stupid," Franklin said.

"The mule was twelve," Gennardi said. "A skinny boy with a fat belly full of condoms of H."

"Fucking McTeague," Franklin said.

"Yeah. The Colombians are pissed at McTeague now for getting caught. So he punched a cop at Rikers and they sent him to the Bing, where he's safer. Which reminds me. When I talked to my guy at Rikers who listens to these losers on the phone, Sunny Richter, he mentioned McTeague and that he heard he was interested in OxyContin because of the prescription angle. You know, the shit is American-made and so these guys, they're telling me—get this—that handling Oxy is patriotic 'cause it keeps the money inside the country. Plus it's safer. Colombians are much more violent than the pharmacists at Purdue Pharma, apparently."

"So Lionel McTeague's got a new strategy, and it could be representative," Franklin said. He took the toothpick that was in his mouth and poked it into his upper gum line, hard. He closed his eyes and nestled deeper into Gennardi's couch. "But on the other hand, I don't want to get upset for no reason here."

"You should go see McTeague. Make him give you a list of people who deal Oxy. Maybe there's a doctor on the list. Who knows? Wait to get upset till something clicks."

Lisa walked into the room in a pair of black-and-white-striped pajamas. She delivered small glass bowls of mango sorbet to both men. Gennardi kissed her on the forehead and she went back out. She stuck her tongue out at Franklin.

"She's been into not talking to boys this week," Gennardi said. "And I guess she figures you fit in that category." He put his bowl of sorbet on the coffee table in front of him.

"I'll take it if you're not hungry," Franklin said.

"It's getting late," Gennardi said, and faked a yawn. "Why don't you call up Jenny Hurly, you want company."

"Don't get on me about her. She wants it to be serious or over."

"Hundred-dollar bills on the dresser aren't going to keep her feelings bottled up if she's ready to fall in love with you."

Franklin said, "That's exactly what I didn't want to hear."

"You old rascal. I'll give you some Peggy Lee to play in the van on the way home."

Franklin ignored the hint, shot out his hand, and took Gennardi's sorbet.

Felix woke up at four in the afternoon on Sunday. He was in bed at the Official. The beige curtains were pulled closed so the room was almost dark.

He called Ellie. She answered on the fourth ring.

"I've been picking butter head lettuce all day," she said. "But I heard the phone and came running."

"I'm getting closer to who killed her. Some people here are suspicious of a doctor she saw, but I know better. And I've had to deal with the old man, which couldn't be helped. But I'm pretty sure about the killers. One of them is close to Soraya Navarro, which could make it rough. It's going to get uglier, though, before it all comes clean."

"I'm coming there," Ellie said.

"No need for that."

"You don't understand. Was she sick? Is that why she went to see a doctor?"

"She was hurting. Look, I'll call you back when I know something."

"Felix, I don't think I can wait much longer."

"It'll just be a few more days."

He hung up the phone and pulled himself into the bathroom. He stood there for a moment, looking at the red-glass-tiled floor, the aluminum bathtub, and the recessed lighting that made it hard to see the beginnings of the lines around his eyes. He didn't flip on the lights around the mirror, which felt way too harsh. In the mirror behind him he could see his naked back and the yellow-and-blue outlines of the bricks he'd slammed against clearly drawn on his skin. He put his hands down flat on the cold marble sink and ran warm water, tried to drink some. Instead he found that he needed to hug his ribs. And then he was over the toilet, where he retched blood.

Gus sat in Sanction, the bar at the Official, on Sunday afternoon and read Lanie Salisbury's piece in the *Spectator* on drug use in nightclubs. He sipped a Bloody Mary he'd made himself, with a half dose of Worcestershire sauce and sugar in place of pepper. The slight spice in the drink wasn't helping to whip the nervous feeling out of his head. He had one eye on the paper and the other on the blank face of his cell phone. The headline read:

MANHATTAN'S NIGHTCRAWLERS EMBRACE HILLBILLY HEROIN

There was a wide-shot photograph of a throng of dancers at the unofficial opening of Terry's new club, the Peppermint Lounge. Gus read the first few paragraphs of the piece again. It started out: "Your intrepid reporter has found herself in a lot of funny places lately, like the dance floors and bathrooms of some of Gotham's hottest clubs—and what has she found? There's a new drug of choice in this town, and it's not coming from Colombia or anywhere south of Texas or Miami. Nope, we're talking about OxyContin, and just the prescription strength packs quite a wallop. Worst of all, this stuff is made in the good old U.S. by Purdue Pharma. The nifty way to abuse it comes from the same folks who gave us moonshine, the Dukes of Hazzard, and Loretta Lynn."

It went on that way, in typical glammed-up *Spectator* style. Eden-Roc was mentioned once, in a paragraph with several other clubs: Sleepy Hollow, Sylvester's, and Bump Town. Lanie promised to keep *Spectator* readers informed on what she discovered. "This is looking like an epidemic," she said, "and it's making our candy-apple city just a little more rotten at the core."

Gus's phone lit up. Terry. Gus sucked air and answered.

"The *Spectator* girl is eighty-sixed," Terry said.

"Of course," Gus said.

The phone went blank. Gus shook his head and pushed the paper aside. Kashmira came over and looked at him. She reached across the bar and rubbed his temples. He pushed his drink toward her and frowned.

"Who's unhappy?" she asked.

Gus said, "Give me an espresso—and see if you can't get some chocolate beignets from the kitchen, okay? Chocolate sauce, too."

"Shitty Sunday?" Kashmira asked.

"Yeah," Gus said. "Shitty Sunday. Here, throw this rag away."

Kashmira turned the espresso machine on behind her. They were listening to slow music, Sade.

Kashmira said, "Does my baby need something stronger than chocolate to get him through?"

"Oh, that's just terrific," Gus said. "Now everybody and their old lady's a dealer."

16

Soraya sat in Dr. Biddle's waiting room at a quarter after seven on Monday morning. She'd forced herself awake an hour earlier and had taken a cab across the park. The waiting room was in a front parlor on the ground floor of a town house that appeared to be occupied entirely by Biddle.

She'd checked in with an assistant called Anne Cruz, who didn't look much older than her and who appeared unfazed by the early hour. Anne Cruz wore a simple gray dress and a rather tight blue sweater. She smiled without opening her mouth.

"I'll bring you in to see the doctor in one or two minutes," Anne Cruz said, and disappeared through a door that looked like another panel in the wall. It was made of the same shimmering blond wood and had no distinguishing mark. Soraya thought she heard her go up some steps.

The few details the room had were all about serious money—there was a thick brown-and-red Iranian rug. Cream-colored Florence Knoll couches were set across from dark brown Mies chairs. There were bookshelves built into the walls; light shone from inside them. A black marble sculpture of an angel stood on a pedestal inside a glass case. The fireplace at the far corner of the room was all black marble, too.

She'd dressed for the appointment in a black skirt and dark red sweater and she was thankful that she'd made the effort to appear as subtle and rich as anybody else who might visit the good doctor. While she waited, two other women were buzzed in. They went and sat on a gray leather couch at the far end of the room. The older one took out a cell phone and began to speak quietly into it. The younger one sat forward, looking at nothing. She clutched a bottle of Evian. She darted her tongue out and licked at her dry lips. Soraya's Internet research had revealed only that Biddle specialized in pain management. But this girl appeared to have gone beyond simple pain.

The door in the wall opened and Anne Cruz beckoned to Soraya.

She seemed not to see the other two women in the room, though Soraya thought they looked at her with longing.

She followed Anne Cruz down a white corridor that smelled of chemical astringent and coffee and entered a large office with glass patio doors along one side. The room looked out onto a garden that had a slate floor and, save for something that looked like a miniature weeping willow, was devoid of greenery.

"Wait here, please," Anne Cruz said. Soraya sat down in a black leather chair across from a desk that was cluttered with papers. Three doors on her right appeared to lead to examination rooms, but this room seemed to be solely for consultations. She saw no diplomas, no medical supplies of any kind.

She heard a movement behind her and forced herself to turn around without betraying nervousness or surprise. A man strode quickly to the middle of the room and stood in front of her.

"I'm Marsden Biddle," he said. "My assistant says you were referred to me by my young friend Edwige Jamison."

He offered his hand and she took it. It was fleshy and soft, like the rest of him. He wore a blue double-breasted suit that was carefully cut but could not obscure the fact that his body was small and round. His tiny eyes were brown, and they protruded a bit from his head, so that it looked like they might occasionally butt up against his square-framed glasses. *Owlish* would be kind, Soraya thought. The skin on his forehead was mottled and pink.

"Edwige and I go to college together," Soraya said. She smiled at the doctor and felt cold air suddenly surround her. She had the uncertain feeling that she was in the presence of someone she'd seen somewhere before. But perhaps it was just the picture in the magazine. She told herself that was what it must be.

"Edwige has an amazing talent," he said. His voice was wheedling and high. "I adore her almost as much as I adore her father. Now, how can I help you?"

"Well," Soraya said. "I'm in pain."

Biddle said nothing, only looked out at his weeping willow.

"It's two kinds of pain, in fact. I was hurt in a—it was a date that I went on last semester that turned into . . . well, it got violent—I guess you could call it date rape—and I was pretty banged up and upset. And then I've been depressed since. Health Services at Barnard hasn't been helpful. Um, I'm embarrassed to go back to them."

"Oh, I don't believe any of that," the doctor said, and smiled. His front teeth were spread apart like a rabbit's. "Barnard's nurses are among the best in the country. And you don't strike me as the sort of girl who would allow any situation to escalate into date rape."

"Your judgment is sexist," Soraya said, without thinking.

The doctor looked around the room. Soraya realized that the glass doors must be triple paned, that the walls were all reinforced—no sounds were coming in or out. He seemed to smile at the silent world he'd created.

"Sexist? You must know I'm too old to care," he said. "Why are you here?"

"I am in pain," Soraya said.

"Fine. Does this pain stem from that false story or from some other, real one?"

And then she had the oddest sensation. She wanted to tell him about losing her father. She wanted to say how she felt like she had to protect her mother. Her mother, who called her no fewer than three times a day, who slept less than four hours a night, and who had dedicated the last dozen years to her third-grade class, as if there were nothing else to life. She wanted to talk about how much she loved Gus and about Felix and how sorry she was for him, about all of it.

But he wasn't that kind of doctor, and she felt tears begin to form. She saw him glance at his watch—a Cartier tank the size of a Chunky bar. She focused then on the stupidly ostentatious watch, and she threw away all thoughts of self. She drew herself up. Wiped away the tear.

"The truth is I had a friend who died, and I can't get over it. She overdosed on OxyContin. Her name was Penelope Novak."

"And the appointment book says that you are Soraya Navarro."

"Yes."

The doctor nodded to himself. He stared at her.

"Well, then. You've mentioned the name, because you presume I helped Penelope, and you are correct. Though your paths are so different . . . you must be very old friends. But no matter. Penelope Novak came to me soon after she arrived in New York. She'd been in a minor car accident a few weeks earlier in the city of Portland, I believe. She had a concussion that was healing nicely, but not as quickly as one would hope. She visited me several times and it was clear to me that she was in immense physical pain. I prescribed OxyContin. It's a wonderful drug. I gave her a very low dosage. Not enough to make a child sick, much less a healthy girl of nineteen who had come from such enormously impressive lineage—on her mother's side, at least."

"Lineage—that can keep you from getting sick?" Soraya asked. She made her face open, so that she only looked like she had the curiosity of a college student.

"Oh, that's just my old-fashioned side talking again. Sexist, patriarchal, that's me. Please forgive my foolish notions."

"Whether she was strong wouldn't have mattered, anyway. She died of a massive overdose."

"I heard you say that, yes. I realize now that she lied to me. She was using other drugs, too. She came to me as someone who suffered from a specific pain and she masked her drug abuse. Her misrepresentation of her condition indemnifies me. But it does not make me any less sorry that she has since died."

The doctor went silent. His eyes looked glassy and wet behind his glasses.

Soraya asked, "How did she come to you?"

"I didn't know Barnard had a class in private investigation."

"She was my friend. That's all."

"She was referred, as you were. Except your arrival here seems predicated on some kind of coincidence. And I don't much believe in coincidence."

Soraya remembered her father saying that only honest people and children believe in coincidence. Now she said nothing. Saying nothing and waiting for something to be revealed was simple—Psych 102.

"Soraya Navarro," he said slowly, and he rolled his *r*'s. He stood up. "You wouldn't want me to speak about you to another patient, would you? I treat many young people for pain. In life there are networks, and I am sought after, within a certain network, for the relief I can give. Perhaps this is why I don't believe in coincidence. I'm afraid that you'd be better served by Barnard's excellent health services. Please give Edwige my fondest regards."

Soraya felt the door behind her open, and Anne Cruz was standing in the doorway. She said nothing as she escorted Soraya out. The outer door buzzed, and Soraya found herself going through it.

She went out to the street. She took a deep breath and looked up at the sky, which was darker than it had been when she'd come across the park. She turned left and walked to Park Avenue and found she couldn't shake the uneasy sense that she'd left something in Dr. Biddle's office. But she carried her bag, and in fact, she hadn't opened it. She was all there, yet she felt like she'd been touched somehow, frisked.

Around her, men and women were stepping into black cars, were on their way to their offices. Nannies pushed baby carriages and the trees rustled in an easy breeze that blew east, rolling down the street from Central Park. Soraya took in the general sense that it was time for the day and, further, the workweek, to begin.

She went and stood on the appointed corner. Franklin pulled up in his brown van. It occurred to her that it was just the sort of forgettable van one might use in an undercover operation. And that because of that, it wasn't a very sensible vehicle for somebody who actually did undercover operations. Franklin reached over, grunted, and pushed the door open.

"Thanks for picking me up," she said. "But I don't know why you bothered."

"I've got an appointment that's out of town. I'll drop you at school. You okay?"

Franklin went up Park Avenue. He was in his usual: a suit of an indeterminate dark color, off-white shirt, no tie. There was stubble all over his bald head. The remains of an egg sandwich sat in tinfoil on the transmission hump. He crumpled the tinfoil and tossed it into the back of the van.

Soraya knew she was shaking a little. She slapped at goose bumps on her forearms. She felt herself licking her lips.

She said, "That guy knew exactly why I was there. He was one spooky dude."

"You ask him about Penelope?"

"He said he treated her for a recurring pain she had, from a car accident that took place back in Portland."

"What about Lem Dawes?"

"Shit. I forgot. Sorry." She squeezed her eyes shut.

"I wonder how she could afford it," Franklin said quietly.

"He said she was referred." Soraya's voice was even smaller, more defensive.

"That's what you learned, that she didn't find him in the fucking phone book?" Franklin's eyes bulged and he didn't look at the girl in the seat next to him.

"You think he plays into this for real, don't you?" Soraya said. "I guess I didn't get very far in there."

"No, you didn't. And yeah," Franklin said. "Something doesn't feel right about a doctor who spooks out a new patient."

"Well, he wouldn't give me a prescription when I asked for one." She looked down at her shaking hands and braced herself for Franklin's anger. It was his daughter who'd been killed. Regardless of whatever he'd done to her father so many years ago, he was still a man who'd lost a child, and she felt disgusted with how badly she'd handled a meeting that could have revealed a lot about what had happened to Penelope.

Franklin exhaled. After a moment he said, "You took on a lot there. It was hard work. Maybe we'll send Felix in next, mess up his hair and dress him up rich so he looks like a client. I'd like to keep up the pressure on this Biddle. Where is Felix, anyway?"

"I don't know," Soraya said. She wrinkled her nose. Franklin's van smelled of old men, day-old newspapers, cigar smoke, and sweat. She wondered again why she was in it, why Franklin was acting like her personal car service. But she kept quiet because she was grateful to him for not coming out and saying she'd screwed up the appointment.

She said, "If he's at the Official, he doesn't answer his phone."

"He should get a cell or a pager," Franklin said. "This unreachable silent-type stuff is bullshit."

They drove through the park in silence. The day had grown full and bright. They went fast along the transverse road and the green trees blew around above them, light dancing on the dirty windshield. When they came out onto Central Park West, Soraya turned to Franklin. He seemed heavy with thought, his lower lip thrust out in a sad pout, his body laid back in the bucket seat.

"You were circling the block, waiting for me to come out?" Soraya asked.

Franklin said nothing. He cracked a window and put a Bully in his mouth.

Soraya asked, "You thought something was going to happen to me in there, didn't you?"

"It was early for an appointment."

"There were two other women waiting with me."

"What makes you think they were patients?"

Franklin cut down 110th and made his way up Broadway.

"Is 116th okay?" Franklin asked. Soraya nodded, then she exhaled low. She began to rap her fist on the cracked rubber dashboard until Franklin looked over at her, eyebrows hooked together, the cheap cigar screwed into the left side of his mouth. Suddenly the fear that had been building in Soraya kicked in. She had a creepy feeling that she'd been little more than bait.

"What?" Soraya asked. "You think Marsden Biddle is dangerous? Come on, you've got to share what you know."

He said, "Guy's name comes up among users and he prescribes what killed my daughter, what the fuck am I supposed to think? Now, take it easy on the sharing. A few days back, you were saying that my son should've killed me when he had the chance."

"So? That's different. If I was in danger, you need to let me know. You want history to repeat itself on my ass?"

"You're the one who wanted to go in there and I asked you not to, right? So yeah, you might have been in some danger, but I was right there."

Soraya said, "Next time, tell me ahead of time."

"Next time, remember to ask some questions that'll turn into leads."

They were at a stoplight, at 113th Street. Soraya got out of the van, fast. She slammed the door, walked in front of the van, stuck out her left fist, and gave Franklin the finger. She wanted to get coffee at Marie's on the next corner, anyway. And fuck him if he wasn't going to play fair.

Franklin rolled the window down farther and called out, "Tell Felix to call me. We all need to powwow again soon."

Soraya didn't answer, didn't even turn around.

17

Franklin went up Broadway, powered up WABC radio, listened to the announcer mutter, "International terrorism," and flipped it back off. He coasted along, turned right on 125th, threaded his way across quiet Harlem streets to the Triboro Bridge, made as if he were going to LaGuardia Airport. He drove with two fingers on the bottom of the wheel and felt each of his forty-seven years weighing down on him like a succession of broken promises. His phone rang. Gennardi.

"Seems that Dr. Marsden Biddle is having some legal trouble," Gennardi said.

"He's getting sued?"

"Nah, it's not medical. He bought a bunch of buildings in the Bronx and he was going to sell them to the city to build a hospital. Problem is, they're condemned."

"Why's that a problem?"

"He's got to pay to have them knocked down and he can't afford the insurance on the demolition, on top of everything else. And he needs to do the demolition soon; otherwise the deal goes south."

"So he needs money," Franklin said.

"That's right. We're on our way to see Edelstein now."

"Good. Remind Philip that he's an African Jew."

"Uh-huh," Gennardi said. "Philip says shalom to you and this year Passover is at his house."

Franklin drove and felt himself fall deep into his own thoughts. He wished he could break free, crawl out from under the weight of his suspicions. But his thoughts were just like his situation with Jenny Hurly—he'd show up and sit around, but he didn't like it when things got too steamed up. Still, to stew in regret was anathema, was exactly what he never liked to do, because he knew that nothing he ever thought up would vanquish the reality of losing a daughter he'd never known.

He still felt fairly sure she'd overdosed. He respected the power of chaos. And nothing could be worse than the fact that her death was meaningless and sad and beyond anyone's control. And in that way, what had happened to her was very much a by-product of the life he'd had with Ellie, the violent love-struck meander that had sent them both off the rails and landed him here. He wished his daughter hadn't come to New York. Hadn't called him begging for help and then left no possible way to find her.

He got off the bridge and picked up Ditmars Boulevard, doing fifty, a shitty brown Econoline van in a sea of shitty cars and trucks, headed all over Queens and the Bronx to do nothing but support work for the great island of Manhattan. He made a sharp left, before Delta's marine air terminal. And suddenly there was nobody to see but cops, DOC officers, and visitors with badges and long frowns, waiting for the bus that would take them across the Francis Buono Bridge to Rikers Island. Besides himself, he couldn't imagine a sorrier bunch of people than those visitors, having to take a precious day off work to come and visit some relative who'd fucked up enough to get the cops involved and who would spend the hour doing little more than whining about the bad food and the unrelenting noise.

He crouched down in the van, pushed aside the gunky brown carpet, and pulled up a flap in the floor. He unscrewed a panel and dropped his Glock into a white-foam–padded compartment, covered it back up. He could hear the gulls along the water screaming about the coming spring. The sun was full and up now, and he breathed in a little air, sucked back his belly, and pulled up his pants. If somebody had killed Penelope, he'd kill that person and whoever protected them. If nobody had, which was almost certainly the case, he didn't know what the hell he was going to do.

He had a good thing going with Gennardi and Philip. A small and simple operation based on an old network of cops and those who drummed up fear in corporate types, who could get them jobs and money for doing little more than hanging around near executives who made ten million a year and thought that others cared. He was more than happy to have this kind of nosy, vaguely helpful relationship with his city. And sure, he fixed things for people from time to time, things that more connected or popular types couldn't fix. But he'd probably end up half crazy and useless if she really had been killed.

He couldn't stop wondering if someone had counted on just that fact. And that bothered him more than anything else—the possibility that somebody he'd crossed in his work might have done this thing to Penelope to get at him. So he prayed for the random and awful stupidity of overdose.

He went into the built-up mobile home where DOC paperwork was processed. He stood in line between a couple of detectives and waited to get his pass from two newbies who were working the desk. They made their phone calls and stared at him, fingered his driver's license and his private investigator identification card, which was something of a rarity in the city.

"Lionel McTeague," the guy said. "He's in OBCC. Wait. He's in the Bing. Is this Bing day?" the newbie asked a supervisor who stood behind him. Franklin gave the supervisor a tired smile. If it *wasn't* Bing day, then why the fuck would he be here? But he said nothing.

They processed a pass and he stuck it on his lapel and got on the bus with the other visitors. There were always a ton of newbies working the front gates at Rikers and he never knew any of them. It always made his entrance slow. The old yellow bus lumbered across, and then there was a wait at the visitors' center on the other side. He boarded another bus to the Otis Bantum Correctional Center. He kept his face down and his eyes half open. No need to have the relatives of fourteen thousand criminals recognize him once they were all back out in the world.

"Are you a lawyer?" a heavyset woman with a Jamaican accent asked him. She wore a black raincoat over a Marriott maid's uniform, and she carried a big purse with a rainbow patch stitched across it.

"No, ma'am," he said. Lawyers avoided Rikers at just about all costs unless their clients were celebrities, and even then they didn't like to come out here. But he knew he looked like one.

"Come on, a Jewish guy like you. Don't tell me you're here to see a relative?"

Franklin laughed. "You'd be surprised—Rikers takes in its share of Jews. Anyway, I'm not a lawyer, but I know a few. What's your situation?"

The bus came to a stop and they disembarked at the entrance to the visitors' room at OBCC. A gray-haired guard ushered them in, took their passes, and patted them down. Through the whole process, the woman told him about her son Ricky, wrongly accused of selling crack cocaine out of the back of a Popeye's on Bruckner Boulevard. Franklin listened. He gave her a card from a pro bono organization he knew—they'd be too busy to help her, probably, but maybe they'd know somebody else. After they went in, the woman was led to a green, mushroom-shaped table with two stools next to it. Getting assigned to a green table in front rather than a blue table meant that the kid had previously been busted for trying to smuggle in contraband.

Franklin was led into the no-contact area, and the woman raised her eyebrows as she saw him go.

"Your relative must've sure done something awful," she said.

He nodded a short yes as the line of inmates in their gray visit jumpsuits filed in. Most were glum-looking men in their midtwenties, though some were younger and still retained expressions of hope. The ones that were older than thirty never seemed to have visitors.

Franklin settled himself in a chair that stood in front of a room that was about the size of a shower stall. There was a chair in there, some graffiti, and between Franklin and the room was a thick Lucite wall with holes drilled in a circular pattern about four feet from the floor. The door on the other side of the little plastic box of a room opened. Franklin focused and everything but the man who shuffled into the room disappeared. He was about Franklin's height, a black man with a newly shaved head and liquid brown eyes that stared around as if they were loose in their sockets.

"Hey, baby," the man said. His cheekbones were high and his smile was wide—what Franklin imagined some people called genuine. His teeth were clean, too, and he looked relaxed, even beatific. There were no scars on his face and Franklin imagined that Lionel McTeague was proud of this, that he had a clean head at the relatively old age of twenty-eight. His legs and hands were locked down, but his jumpsuit was clean and he wore a pair of contraband black-and-white Adidas shell tops. Just a bit north of the fifty-dollar sneaker limit.

"Lionel," Franklin said. His voice was soft, so Lionel had to lean forward to hear him. "First, tell me what can I do for you."

"Nothing, baby. I'm right where I need to be," Lionel said. His voice was smooth and relaxed, though it was a little scratchy in the high registers.

"Trial coming up?" Franklin asked.

"They got it out here in Queens in some months—we're not sure when yet. But then you know I did this stupid thing in here."

"What's that?"

Lionel gave his genuine smile. "I went and busted on a newjack for some bullshit, stole his mackerel dinner or whatever. Broke his front teeth and then this old guard just *lost it,* got so angry at me. So I smacked him in the face to calm him down and they rearrested me, booked me all over again down at the county courthouse, and now I'm in the max, the Bing, for a year bid."

"How's your witness?"

"The cabdriver? Growing older every day, man," Lionel said.

Franklin nodded. Lionel was peacefully hiding out in the Bing till somebody on the outside made the mule's cabdriver unable to testify. This time at Rikers was like limbo—just waiting for the Colombians to get to the cabdriver so Lionel wouldn't finger them and in turn get himself murdered, either inside or out. Then everybody could walk away. It was a good system, Franklin had to admit, if you were smart enough and mean enough to make it work for you. It occurred to Franklin that part of the reason Lionel was willing to see him was that he needed to build up some goodwill on the outside.

"Sunny tells my friend that now you're done with the Colombians and you're into this new shit—this hillbilly hip-hop or whatever," Franklin said.

"Am I finished with H?" Lionel asked. He nodded, mostly to himself, as if he'd been mulling over this issue and was pleased that Franklin had noticed.

Lionel said, "Could be. This mule incident was unpleasant. Plus anything involving air travel is a major ass pain these days. So yeah, this other thing could be right for me."

"Keep it in the good old US of A?"

"That's right, that's right," Lionel said. He leaned forward and Franklin could smell his Listerine breath through the drilled holes. "This is some Purdue Pharma shit I'm talking about. We're going to go high-low with it, you know? I got this doctor friend who I was supplying H to, and just before I came inside he says he wants to reverse the flow—he's got this new shit and he'll supply me. But he says he's not satisfied with having just one distributor to the street, he wants to branch out—"

"A doctor," Franklin said. He felt his own voice grow hoarse. Lionel drew back then. He reached up with his handcuffed hands and stroked his chin.

"I heard you were curious. What do you want him for?" Lionel asked. Franklin balled his fists, pressed them hard up against the sides of his metal chair.

"You know what happened to my daughter?"

"Look at me, my friend," Lionel said. He held his hands up, palms spread, and he didn't shake. "That was a wrong thing that was done to her, but you know how these greedy motherfuckers get. Anyhow, I don't know those culprits. And I was in here when it happened."

And Franklin felt a falling. His ass through the chair, through the vast bowels of the Otis Bantum Correctional Center, through the muck of seventy years of incarceration, down into the East River and then deeper, into the thick sediment and slime that was the base of all New

York and then out farther, swept far away into the ocean, into great depths of hurt. Someone had done something to Penelope and Lionel had heard about it.

There'd been no overdose. Penelope Novak had been murdered.

"This is unfortunate," Franklin said. He stared across at Lionel, who suddenly looked like the smugness had been sucked out of him, like Franklin's gaze was pulling the air out of the little room. Franklin got up very close to the glass. His mud-brown eyes glistened with tears and he showed Lionel that.

Franklin began to speak very quietly. Lionel had no choice but to come up closer to him, till all that separated them was that Lucite, the space between the few dozen drilled holes.

"Talk now," Franklin said. "If you do not, there is someone in there with you who is contracted to die, tonight, tomorrow, in two weeks, who knows? It will not be you. You will be the one who killed him, and you will go to trial, and you will be transferred to Sing Sing or Coxsackie and you will be in for years and years. Once you're inside people will torture you, as a personal favor to me. You know this is nothing for me. It is a matter of two, perhaps three phone calls. Talk."

"I don't know—"

"Do not begin with 'I don't know.'"

Lionel nodded. Franklin knew he was clicking thoughts. The visit that Lionel had hoped would help pave even smoother time had dissolved into a nasty fuckup. Now there was nothing to be done but make trade-offs that would create amends. The best Lionel could hope for was to talk himself into a place no worse than where he'd been before he'd slipped on a gray jumpsuit and come out to see Franklin.

Lionel looked at the floor. He eased off his right sneaker and scratched his foot through an impossibly clean white sock. He took a long breath.

"I was supplying the doctor with H," Lionel said. "He was dealing the shit to these rich kids who kept blowing rehab, and so they were going to him and he was controlling dosage and just about everything else. Keeping these rich junkies alive for their parents and making straight money all the while. This was right up until this thing that happened with the mule. So his supply went short, but it didn't matter because he was already into this new shit, this Oxy. It's legitimate for him and clean and he said goodbye to H, so I wanted into his new shit, you know, bring it the other way, down into the street—"

"How did my daughter get to him?"

Lionel shook his head. Now his lips were moist. A bell rang. A guard walked behind Franklin, said, "Two minutes." Lionel looked up at the guard with real gratitude in his eyes.

"I don't know about your daughter. That doctor has the power to move quantity on his terms. So he—"

Franklin slapped his hand flat on the Lucite. The sound was like a five-pound rump roast hitting the butcher's block.

Lionel spoke faster. "Somebody wanted to build a supply chain with the doctor. They wanted an easy way to buy Oxy so they could deal it, but then they started to crowd him a little. Skim his shit. Your daughter, somehow she got into the middle of their conflict is the way I see it. Her death was a message between them."

"Who is the somebody?" Franklin said.

"A guy who's in with the nightclubs, as I heard it. Again, it wasn't me, and that's a bet."

Franklin stood up.

"I told you everything," Lionel said. "I'm trying to do smart time. Please, Franklin, don't fuck with my bid."

"If it's the truth, you haven't killed anybody. If it's not—"

Franklin shrugged, walked away from the plastic box that held Lionel McTeague.

"Novak! I worked hard to keep this time smooth. Don't fuck with my bid!"

Franklin was already walking past the guards. One of them looked back at Lionel McTeague, who'd knocked his chair over and was now standing, screaming through the holes in the plastic box.

Franklin stood outside in the sun. The Jamaican lady came out, and they waited for the bus doors to open.

"How's your son?" Franklin asked.

"Good, thanks. Sounds like our visit ended a little better than yours did," the lady said. Behind them, they could still hear Lionel McTeague screaming.

"We had a nice talk. He was just sorry to see me go," Franklin said.

18

A sideways glance when he got out of the shower showed Felix a fat and wide bluish bruise on his lower back. It was an ugly thing, and he hoped like mad that his kidney wasn't ruptured. He pressed carefully and it seemed as if the swelling didn't reach too far below the skin's surface. The pain in his ribs was more pronounced. The lower two on his left side were cracked or fractured. He sliced up a bedsheet, wet it, and wound it tight around his midsection till he was wearing a kind of girdle. It hurt when he stood upright, but he no longer felt like he was on fire. It was Monday, just past noon.

He slipped his clothes on. He didn't strap the gun on under his jacket. The thought of it banging against his ribs was too much, and he didn't want to be quick with it, either. A day and a half of sleep had smoothed out his thoughts. Those killers weren't going anywhere. He wouldn't need to try to shoot them down in the street. He'd see to it that Franklin did it. And then he would go on back home.

The phone rang in the hotel room. Felix slowly brought it up to his ear.

Franklin said, "I've been trying to reach you for days. When we meet later, I'm giving you a beeper and a cell. Now listen: Today you go in to see Starling, you ask him about Dr. Marsden Biddle. Say you heard the doctor's in some financial trouble. See what he does. Then ask him if Penelope ever came to see him, you got that?"

"I got it," Felix said. "But the doctor doesn't matter. Where are you, anyway?"

"I'm driving back from a meeting I had in Queens. Maybe the doctor doesn't matter, maybe he does. I don't care what else you do with Starling. Just do me one favor. Ask him about the doctor."

Franklin hung up. Felix sat on the bed. He spun his hat on his finger. Less than three days had passed, but clearly something had snapped into place in his father's bald head. Something beyond an idle connection between his grandfather and the doctor. Felix wondered what it was. He called Starling Furst's office and explained who he was. A secretary assured him that he was welcome at absolutely any time. So Starling already knew he was in town.

He came out of the Official and fell into the lunchtime pedestrian traffic. According to his map, the *Spectator* building was near the piers that ran under the East Side Drive, where the Fulton Fish Market had once been. He drove over, got a permit to park in the lot.

In the elevator he didn't think of the man he was going to see as his grandfather. No, he needed money and he had several questions that needed answers. There was an old man upstairs. He would give Felix these things.

The elevator stopped on a floor that was filled with people sitting at desks, typing away on computers, a massive network of colored wires running in coils along the ceiling over their heads like lines of thought grown physical and wild. Reporters. He rubbed at his face with the whole of his hand, covering it. He wanted to see Lanie later, not now.

He stepped out on the top floor and a receptionist at a desk that was easily forty feet away stood up to greet him. She strode up to him, held out her hand. She was in her sixties, tall, and built solid, like a Greek statue or Kathleen Turner. She wore charcoal slacks and a blue blazer. Felix caught a flowery scent around her, which nearly masked a thick bottom note of alcohol.

She said, "I've known about you for years. Your coming here . . . it really means a lot to him. He cleared an hour for your visit, which is extremely unusual. Come right this way."

Felix shrugged, followed. He hadn't identified himself and she hadn't, either. So Starling Furst was expecting him, and she'd forgotten his name. They passed a conference room on their right that had a massive picture window, so that they could see the great swell of Manhattan rolling north from where they stood. Felix glanced down. Eden-Roc was just a few blocks up from here, buried somewhere in the thick forest of Chinatown's dead trees and five- and six-story tenements.

They arrived at the end of the corridor and the woman opened a door. "I don't think I've actually brought someone back here myself in years," she said, and smiled and shook her pointer finger at him, like, You, you're a naughty one! If Felix hadn't been afraid for his ribs, he would've laughed.

The secretary left him in the doorway and he looked in at Starling Furst, who was looking back at him and smiling, as if he'd taken the same sweetness pill as his secretary. These were not normally nice people, Felix thought, that much was clear. He looked fast around the room, which was a large cube with floor-to-ceiling windows on two sides. The other two walls were filled with photographs of skyscrapers and old newspaper headlines. The furniture wasn't pretentious. It was neither new looking nor particularly expensive. Felix wondered if his grandfather was so powerful that he'd gone beyond worrying about making an impression. Starling Furst got up and came around his desk, which was square, too, and made of oak.

"Glad to see you, Felix," he said.

He took Felix by the elbow and guided him to a tweed sofa set in front of a glass coffee table in one corner of the office. The man smelled of age and something that might be an old-fashioned hair tonic.

"Settle yourself," Starling said. Felix let himself down carefully on the couch. Starling sat across from him in a hard chair that was half a foot higher than the couch.

"Coffee, water?"

"Coffee'd be good," Felix said.

Starling picked up a phone and asked for coffee and chocolate chip cookies. He glanced out the window while he spoke and absently picked at his nose. He wore a black suit and a blue-and-white-striped shirt, with a thin red tie. He was thin as a sharecropper, looked like a man who'd known real hunger, like a figure from the *Grapes of Wrath.* Or perhaps, Felix thought, a little like the famous photograph of Samuel Beckett that Ellie had up on the fridge back home—that same porcupine hair, same gaunt cheeks. Felix realized that maybe that was why she had it there. His eyes were gray, though, and they had the same harsh, unforgiving quality, Felix realized, as his mother's. Starling's wife, Felix's grandmother, was long dead—killed in a plane crash over Martha's Vineyard before Felix was born. He'd remarried a woman called Vivian who Ellie hated almost as much as she hated Starling—but that was all Felix remembered.

Starling said, "Devastated over your sister's death?"

"Yes," Felix said, before he could calculate his response.

"Only appropriate reaction. I'm sick about it, too. Hate death. Always have."

Felix said nothing. He knew he was being watched, that this wretchedly cold old man was appraising him. This was the other thing he suspected was true of all these New York types—if they *were* going to bother to look at you, they'd take their time with their estimation.

"How is your mother?"

"She's well. I'd say that she sent her regards, but she didn't."

"She burns a lot of bridges, that woman."

"She'd say the same of you."

A young man came in with an aluminum tray. He set down coffee cups in front of Felix and Starling and plates that held two of the biggest chocolate chip cookies Felix had ever seen. The cookies looked like minipizzas, studded with marble-sized chunks of chocolate.

"I like things simple," Starling said. "That's why I'm lousy at family. You're going to change all of that. Planning on staying in town, I assume?"

Felix shook his head. He said, "My sister saw a doctor before she died. Dr. Marsden Biddle. I ran into a friend of hers at a nightclub and he mentioned this. Do you know this doctor?"

"You're the sort of young man who goes to nightclubs?"

"Do you even read your own paper?"

"Our familial bond must not mean much to you if you feel free enough to talk to me that way."

Felix shrugged. "Dr. Marsden Biddle. Do you know him?"

Starling Furst grew quiet. Then he said, "I sent Penelope to him. He's been a family friend for years. He's your parents' age, you know. Your mother's year at school, I believe."

"Why did you send her?"

"Your sister came to me in—I suppose it was the second week in November. I've checked that date. She informed me that she'd recently arrived here and she knew no one. She was in a lot of pain owing to some kind of accident and she asked for my help. But she made me promise not to tell her mother where she was."

"You made a deal with a nineteen-year-old runaway?" Felix asked. In order to still himself, he drank some of the black coffee. It was similar to the stuff his mother made back home with beans she bought from the men who came and stayed with them a few times a season to help with the grapes. Pretty damn good. He drank some more of it.

"I suppose so. I gave her some money and sent her to Dr. Biddle. They had two consultations. He informed me that she was perfectly fine, and he prescribed some painkillers. That's what he does. If I'd spoken to your mother even once in the last twelve years, I would have called her. But I haven't."

The room was not exactly quiet. There was some bustle in the hallway that Felix could hear. Starling's computer's fan seemed to be working overtime. But his phone didn't ring.

Felix listened to these noises and wondered about what had happened twelve years ago. Billy Navarro had been killed. His own parents had divorced. His mother had stopped speaking to her family. Felix and Penelope had been whisked out of town in July—picked up in the middle of their day camp's trip to the Bronx Zoo, where they were yanked away from the pandas and the petting stable, respectively. They were dragged home and told to start packing. He knew the man in front of him had been furious about his daughter's rebellious marriage to a mean-spirited Jewish cop from Brooklyn. But he didn't know more about what had happened during those few days when Billy Navarro was murdered and everything fell apart.

And now he was back here, talking to family members who were strangers, trying to understand a place and a people he didn't know, who he'd been trained to hate, who had accepted his sister and then killed her in a matter of weeks.

"I need some money," Felix said. "I didn't come with much, and I'm here until I understand what happened to my sister."

"Your sister died of a drug overdose. I saw the ME's report. In fact, I've got a copy of it here."

"May I see it?"

"Certainly," Starling said. "I'll have an additional copy made for you and sent to—where are you staying?"

"Send it to Franklin Novak's office," Felix said.

He watched carefully, but there was no flicker of anything like anger in Starling's eyes. There was no flicker at all. Felix sat back for a moment, let the tension die out. If the old man knew more, he wasn't going to just hand it over. And then Felix imagined that Starling probably didn't know more. His phone had been quiet for a long hour and he didn't seem anxious about it. To Felix, it looked like this old man might be out of the running.

"All right," Starling said. "I'll have some money sent there, too. This will all be to your attention, of course."

"Thank you," Felix said. "Do you know a reporter named Lanie Salisbury?"

Again, Felix watched, and again, Starling had virtually no reaction. He'd had to gamble her name, to make sure that Lanie wasn't with him on Starling's orders. Now he was fairly sure that she was acting on her own. What she was up to, exactly, was an entirely different matter.

"Well," Starling said slowly, "I'm sure I do know her work. I'm familiar with all the reporters. The real estate transactions my organization is involved in have grown less and less interesting to me over the years. Instead, I keep up with the life of the paper. Why do you ask?"

"She's a good reporter. That's all. She just had a piece in Sunday's paper on drug use in nightclubs and I guess it's part of a series. I admire her work," Felix said. He stood up. He didn't want to reveal the faintness he felt to Starling. He wanted, instead, to leave.

"Thank you for your help," Felix said. "I'm grateful to you and I look forward to seeing you again."

"Of course you'll share what you learn with me."

"Of course," Felix said.

"The only thing more difficult than death, I'd say, is maintaining relations with family."

"I can see how you'd feel that way," Felix said. And he walked out.

Starling Furst stood in his doorway and looked down the long corridor at his grandson's receding figure. He thought, I like him better than his sister, better than his mother, his father, or any of the rest of them. But then, he asked himself, that isn't saying much, is it?

He went back to his desk and picked up the phone.

He said, "Send a message to someone who works downstairs called Lanie Salisbury. Tell her that I've just been reading her work and I'd like to meet her. Today if possible. Then get me everything's she's written for the paper. And come on in here, won't you? I need to assemble some things for a delivery. And have someone refrigerate these cookies. They can be used again."

Felix called Soraya from a pay phone on Front Street, just under the rumbling West Side Highway. He wanted to talk to her about Gus before he saw his father. Give her a last chance before he told Franklin what he knew. It had been less than two days since he'd been beaten up and now he felt like he was in a rush. He wanted this thing over, Penelope avenged, somebody killed. He listened to Soraya's cell phone ring and was forced to leave a message. He decided to say only that they should pool what they had before moving on. He planned to tell her then that Gus was a large part of why Penelope was dead, that he was sorry, but that he was going to go after Gus, and soon. He felt like he couldn't hold the information back much longer.

He said, "Hey, Soraya, I'll be at Franklin's office tomorrow, say, around two or so." He found he could say nothing else, though he'd never felt so impatient in his life. It was exhausting—all this not admitting, not dealing. He'd just seen his grandfather for the first time since he could remember, and he'd treated the old man like a crime suspect, and then he'd asked him for money. He gripped his ribs.

He called the number he had for Lanie Salisbury and she answered on the first ring.

"Lanie here," she said, and she sounded breathless and alive and curious and Felix found her strangely reassuring.

"It's Felix. What are you doing later?"

"Hanging out with you, I hope. I've got to hit some clubs—want to join me?"

"Sure," Felix said. "But I don't think I'm up for dancing."

19

Gus said, "Tell me again why the fuck we're talking about Lem Dawes?"

"So you do know him?" Soraya asked. She felt her body tighten. They were sharing a bottle of red wine, a Médoc that Gus had brought up from the bar. It was just past eight on Monday night and she needed to get uptown, do some work on her Kristeva/Melanie Klein paper and then get some real rest, but she'd wanted to see Gus. And he had to get over to Eden-Roc, check in and make sure his waiters and bartenders and busboys knew their assignments for the night. But they were both exhausted from too much cocktail-hour lovemaking, and Gus's room had grown warm and drowsy. So they'd been lying quiet, their bodies plastered to the heavy beige sheets on his bed.

And then, seemingly out of nowhere, with her eyes half closed and the pale red blanket wrapped around both of them, her wineglass balanced on her breastbone, she found herself asking him about Lem Dawes. She hadn't talked to Felix in a couple of days and left to herself, she'd begun to worry about the connections Felix was making, about how Gus could manage *not* to be involved in all the shit that was going on around him.

Gus said, "Man, this Penelope thing is really throwing you."

"What's she got to do with Lem?" Soraya asked. She felt herself tense up, slip her hand around the wineglass and hold it tight. "Which reminds me. You were going to check on who paid for that suite."

"Yeah, I'll do that. I'll check with the night manager. But look, about all the questions, it's not like how you were . . ." Gus sighed. "You want a bigger answer?"

"Only if you can give me one," she said. And she was momentarily startled at how willing she was to give him the out.

Gus put his wineglass on the night table and turned toward her, stroked her hair and kissed her.

He said, "The truth is, before I met you, I had a little problem with cocaine. Maybe I told you about it? No? Well, it was right when I started managing for Terry and there was this club called Twylo, and—you know how it goes, I was working the door and people were slipping me mad packets and I was taking little hits, the whole bit. Next thing I knew, I was a pure addict, and what was worse, I *knew I was* because of having to watch my mom give in to H, like I told you. So there I am, snorting a line with my morning grapefruit in the middle of the afternoon. Then Terry comes to me one day, and I'm just shaking. So he grabs me, throws me up against the wall, and tells me that I need to kick or he'll fire me. Terry's like a dad to me, so when he said this, I listened. I get the name of a doctor, this Upper East Side guy, Marsden Biddle, and so I go up there—"

She was listening, and when the goose bumps on her chest and arms erupted, she covered by turning on her side, nestling under the blanket so she was closer, facing him. He wore a platinum coin on a gold chain he'd gotten from Jacob the Jeweler—a present from Aaliyah before she'd passed—and Soraya played with it, bounced it against his chest, all to cover what happened to her when she heard that name.

"And he's this amazing guy. He really helped free me of that shit. A few painkillers, a couple of sessions with him, and then some phone calls after that. He even set me up with a counselor who I still talk to once in a while, when I'm feeling like I need something. I never told you this before 'cause I don't like to admit I'm weak like that, but I guess I am. Maybe I never had it that bad, but I was scared. I admit that. And then about Lem Dawes, that's all I know about him, that he goes to Biddle. We talked about it one night because he was saying he was sick on this country crap, the Oxy, so I mentioned Biddle and he said that he already knew him. That he was weaning him off slow, whatever that means. But I was still like, good for you, man. You'll be off that garbage in no time, you know?"

She was warmer now, listening to him. She ran circles over his biceps with the coin. She said, "I'm glad you told me."

"Dawes, though, he's a party hound. We're going to run a little event on a tugboat in the harbor 'cause he can get some of the permits through his family and I've got the connects. It's less than totally legal, but he's up to the challenge. We just need to clear some shit up first. I know you all came at him the other night, but he doesn't know anything. He's just trying to kick, that's all. And it's hard for him to kick just now 'cause he grew up rich, but his dad just cut him off."

"It's hard for anybody to kick," Soraya whispered.

"You don't mind that I told you that, how I used to be sick for Snow White? I mean, that's embarrassing for me, but I figure with you and me close how we are and you asking about little Lem—"

"I'm happy you had the courage to quit," Soraya said. She dropped his necklace and cocooned into him, closed her eyes and felt her body warm up against his.

She said, "I love you."

Franklin was nearly to the right address in Kew Gardens when his cell rang. Gennardi, so he took it.

"Heard you freaked on our friend McTeague," Gennardi said.

"It's different now. He gave up that she was killed."

"You want to hear the rest of it?"

"Tomorrow. In the office," Franklin said. He hung up the phone and turned off Metropolitan Avenue, went left onto Cleveland Place, and drove slowly on a street lined with white brick two-story semidetached houses. A few had police cruisers parked in front—officers home for evening meals or a quick nap in the middle of their shift. He came to 1687 and stopped, pulled into the driveway behind an old blue Saab with rust marks on the fender and wheel wells. He stared forward, unblinking, into the late afternoon sun. Then he slowly got out of the van. There were a few children playing with a tricycle across the street, dutifully watched by a young mother. That mother looked across at the van and the middle-aged bald man in the suit who got out of it. He headed toward Nancy Navarro's redbrick house.

Mrs. Navarro had few visitors, and anyone watching would have thought that the middle-aged man was some sort of salesman, the least welcome kind, dressed as he was, getting out of an unmarked brown van. A salesman or someone from the policeman's benevolent association, there to spend ten or twenty minutes with Nancy to make sure there were no problems with the secured monthly payments on Billy's pension. The young mother would not have guessed that the bald man would be here to shake the dust off old secrets, to begin to navigate a path backward, toward pacts made long ago, between people who looked away from each other when they spoke.

Franklin approached the door and pressed the buzzer, which sounded a low-pitched *bong* that seemed unwelcome in the old house. Nancy Navarro came quickly to the door. She was in beige pants and a white blouse, a purple sweater drawn over her shoulders. She looked through the glass panes and then opened the front door and stood with the screen between her and Franklin. The years-old frown on her face had drawn her lower lip and her cheeks down. This sad bent fought against the beauty she'd enjoyed in her youth—as if the years of evenings spent alone in the house had found no use for her charm. Her brown hair was swept up in a bun and Franklin could see the lines in her forehead, the pulsing there, which he read as fear.

She asked, "Is this about my daughter?" And if she recognized him, she gave no indication.

He said, "She's okay. I saw her this morning. I'm doing my best to protect her."

"Then what is it?" she asked. Still, she didn't suggest that he pull open the screen door and come in. They waited, looking at each other. Franklin had his hands at his sides. Though he felt that he knew her well, they'd never been friends. He remembered her through Billy's stories, and those stories had all been twisted inside out and destroyed during Franklin's years of rebuilding, years of retrospective thought. And then he saw that she was willing to acknowledge that it was him.

"Are you here because you want to change our agreement?" she said.

"I'm not sure yet," Franklin said. She pushed the screen door open, toward him, and he stepped around it and came inside.

They sat down across from each other in her dining room, which she'd made into a kind of large office. She went into the kitchen and came back with a glass and a bottle of Heineken. She placed the drink in front of him, though she had brought out nothing for herself.

He began. "Everyone still believes there was a disagreement between Billy and that dealer, Kenny Price, and that Kenny never knew we were undercover. Then I got scared because of all the shooting and I ran. I left Billy to die in the street."

She said, "That's correct."

"Twelve years have passed. My daughter is dead. My son is here with me now, and there's a chance of making things right with him. Your daughter is near me, too, as I said. They both want to know what happened to Penelope. But they hate me. I swore to Ellie that I wouldn't become the kind of cop I became, where I couldn't speak to her except to yell, and I did—I turned into the kind of cop who comes home and stays a cop. I admit to that, and if that's part of why she went to Billy, I accept my responsibility. But I let it go too far. If my daughter hadn't hated me so much, she might have called me sooner, and she would not be dead now. The other person who ensured that hatred is you."

"You acknowledged that our agreement was the only solution."

"For me to take all of the blame," he said. And his voice was fast, as if he were saying something he'd been thinking about for years.

Franklin took the cold bottle in his hands and sipped from it. Nancy Navarro's house was tidy, but there were file cabinets jutting out from nearly all the walls. They were filled with assignments, ideas and suggestions and innovations in classroom teaching. There were no pictures of Billy Navarro, only class photographs and snapshots of Soraya, from every year, including the present. The house smelled of fresh flowers and school supplies.

Nancy Navarro didn't seem so different now than when they'd sat down together in this room so long ago, just days after her husband was killed and Ellie left town. It was then that they'd agreed on the story, constructed it out of the threads of truth and fiction that would hide indefinitely the betrayal and infidelity that had destroyed both their marriages.

Nancy said, "If you'd have allowed yourself to see how deeply in love Billy was with Ellie, none of this would have happened. Unfortunately I do believe that Billy might have been driven wild enough to try to kill you, but there is only dishonor for all of us if that's ever revealed."

"Hence the agreement," Franklin said again, as if he'd said it to himself silently thousands of times.

"That's right," Nancy said.

And Franklin looked down at the tabletop, busy with work yet clean, and at his thick hands, which he'd spread flat. He felt his pulse points slow. There was no sound in the room save Nancy Navarro's even breathing.

Nancy said, "I can understand that you'd want to explain the truth to your son. But you can't now. That must not happen until he's much older and you trust him. Of course you understand that. And further, think what the truth would do to Soraya."

"So I can't set it right."

"What's past is past. You said yourself that we'll never know exactly what happened that day. There's nothing to set right. We've all got to go on, bear our equal shares of pain for Billy and Ellie's infidelity."

Franklin said, "My daughter's death changes things."

"It's a great tragedy, and I'm sorry for you and for Ellie. But I don't see how your daughter's overdose changes the way we've agreed to look at our shared past."

"I don't, either. But I can't help wondering," he said.

"Turns out Gus knows Biddle," Soraya said. She was on the phone with Felix, who was in the West Village, at a pay phone around the corner from where he was supposed to meet Lanie.

"No kidding," Felix said.

"Don't get smart. It's not the way you think. He—well, the doctor got Gus off coke some years back."

"You believe that?" Felix asked.

"I do. And you'd better, too, if you want me to keep helping you out here."

"Okay," Felix said. "Okay." He watched people pass him, but as usual, nobody looked his way. There were so many of them. It seemed impossible that in this city, so many people could be connected—but here it was, they *were* all connected. He was beginning to accept that.

"I'm serious, Felix. I've never felt more confident about Gus than I am now. He hates drugs. Really—he's clean."

"That doesn't mean—" But Felix stopped. He said, "What if I told you I saw Gus with Max Udris?"

"That wouldn't mean anything. They do legitimate business together."

So Felix saw that she wouldn't accept what he said, not until he was in front of her, anyway. And he didn't want to say aloud that he'd taken a beating because of what he'd seen.

He said, "So there are no connections."

"I don't know if I trust that doctor, but I don't not trust him, you know? Maybe he really was trying to help Penelope. It's the easiest explanation and that could make it the right one."

"Maybe so," Felix said. He slid his hand over his ribs. But he kept silent.

"I'll see you tomorrow at Franklin's," he said. "I know he knows something, but he won't tell us till we're in front of him. Try to show up in the afternoon."

"I can be there by two," Soraya said. Felix thought she sounded a little urgent, but he didn't mention it. He figured he'd get there first, see what he could get from his father when the two of them were alone.

"See you then," Felix said.

* * *

Felix walked around the corner and met Lanie at a place called the Chocolate Bar on Jane Street. Felix had never seen anything like it—a place set up like a bar, entirely devoted to chocolate. The walls were a soft brown and the place smelled like the first time his mother read him the opening of *Charlie and the Chocolate Factory.* A whole variety of pretty young women were seated around the place. They had their same wan, bored looks, cut with a kind of silent glee in the face of the huge variety of chocolate. There were chocolate clusters, brownies, truffle lollipops, bars, and cookies.

Lanie sat alone at the counter, eating a sundae. She was in a black turtleneck and black pants, her curly hair shooting out in all directions. She kissed him when he came up, put her finger in her sundae, and fed him some chocolate sauce.

"I'm doing a piece about this place for the Living section," she said. "Isn't it incredible? You should have the iced chocolate with crumbled Rocher. I can expense everything, so let's go ahead and make ourselves utterly ill."

He couldn't help smiling. She ordered the iced chocolate for him from the man behind the bar. She wouldn't let go of his hand.

She said, "We can walk after this if you want, but I've got to taste some more things for my piece. What's up?"

He said, "I met your boss."

"Jimmy? That old drunk tell you some tales?"

"Starling Furst."

"Good old Starling Furst," Lanie said. She laughed and looked away. "He's not really my boss—he's the boss of all bosses. But he's an old dear. That's something I wanted to tell you. I met him, too, today. He said he was really happy with my work and I bet I've got you to thank for that."

Felix said, playing dumb, "What do you mean?"

"He read the piece that's coming out tomorrow. The one about Eden-Roc. I guess that's what got his old bones jangling. Speaking of that, there's something you should know."

"What?"

"Well, he said he has such confidence in my work that he was willing to cover me with the legal department, so—I got to take a little extra risk with this article."

"Yeah?" Felix asked. The waiter set down a martini glass filled with iced chocolate. Felix thought, If you know the right people, New York is just one big adult amusement park. He tasted the chocolate. It was sweet and thick and ridiculous, excessive, like nothing he'd ever had before. For the first time that day, he forgot that he was in any pain. He floated for a moment and thought, I don't ever want to leave this town.

She put her hand on his cheek. "Like that?" she asked.

He asked, "What was the risk?"

"Well, I'll show you the piece—it'll be on the stands at midnight and I hope we'll still be together then. But the thing we cleared was that I could make a strong implication that your friend Soraya's boyfriend is running a great big Oxy party out of Eden-Roc and bringing in a ton of money for Terrence Cheng. We don't have proof yet, but an awful lot of kids are coming out of there high on Oxy, and we're all waiting for more ODs. There's no doubt that Gus is at the center of it. You can bet that I won't be too welcome in Cheng's spots once they read this piece."

Lanie stopped and tasted Felix's chocolate.

"That's what okra tastes like in heaven," she said.

"That article sounds right on," Felix said. "I can't give you more details yet, but it's a series, right? I can fill you in when I learn more."

"It's a series for sure—Starling Furst loves it."

"I think we'll be able to really help each other out this week," Felix said. And he kissed her. He slipped his arms around her waist and pulled her between his legs.

"You wondering something?" she asked.

Felix nodded. He felt so proud of himself for not having to come right out and ask what Lanie knew and when she'd known it.

Lanie said, "Did I know that you were Starling Furst's grandson when I met you, and was I immediately drawn to you because I knew that if I played it right, being connected to you would make my career go ballistic?"

Felix only nodded again. He realized that he felt a little dizzy from the chocolate and too many Motrin, from Lanie being so close and everything he'd ever understood about trust being so far away.

"Well, if I didn't tell you then, I'm certainly not going to tell you now. So you'll just have to keep wondering, won't you?"

"So this is how it's done in New York?" Felix asked.

"That's right. Now let's get out of here," Lanie said. "Let's order a whole bunch of stuff and bring it back to my apartment where we can sample each other's grade of purity in private."

20

"Starling's like you in a way," Felix said to his father. "He thinks she died of an overdose, too."

Tuesday, noon, and they were waiting for Starling Furst's package to arrive. Felix watched his father's face—which he found easy to read. Franklin sneered, caught himself, squinted, blew out breath, and rubbed at his bald head.

"Be interesting to see how much money he throws at you. The amount means something. But about her death—you were right. I was wrong. So me and your grandfather are nothing alike."

Felix inclined his head. He tried to let his anger rest somewhere in his spine, let it bubble. But he didn't shift easily in his seat because of his ribs. They could hear the sound of a Spanish language radio station come close, get louder, and then disappear. Felix looked around.

"Freight elevator," Franklin said. "It's behind the wall."

Felix watched his father, but he only looked down, glared at his own hands, which were flat on the table, inactive.

"She was murdered," Felix said. "You acknowledge this now?"

"Yes," Franklin said.

"Tell me how you came to see it this way," Felix said.

"First tell me who hit you," Franklin said.

"Is it that obvious?"

"I've been knocked around enough to know what the wheeze of broken ribs sounds like a day or two later. Are you okay?"

"Yeah," Felix said, short.

Franklin opened a drawer in his desk. The phone on his desk rang and Franklin picked it up while he searched through the drawer.

"Yeah," he said into the phone. "Come on in."

He hung up the phone and found what he was looking for; his bald head popped back up. He tossed a small brown bag to Felix.

"Chinese tea—don't know the proper name. Drink it before bed for the next few nights, and it'll help heal what's broken. You want to see a doctor?"

"I don't think so."

"Let me know. If you're still hurting by the end of the week, I got a guy you can see."

"I don't plan to still be here at the end of the week."

Franklin raised an eyebrow, but all he said was, "Who did it to you?"

"Max Udris sent a guy after me, a Russian who looks like Kris Kringle but angry. I'd been watching Udris meet with Gus, the little fucker who goes out with Soraya and works for Terrence Cheng. Me and Kringle tangled and he knocked me around a parking lot. He knew me from when I visited Udris's marble warehouse with Soraya. The way I see it, Udris murdered Penelope. There's some deal going on with Udris and Cheng, and Gus is the go-between. Penelope got in the middle of it. And that Udris guy didn't like it. He gave her something she couldn't handle."

"You got some things right," Franklin said. "She got in the middle of something, but I'm not sure it was between Udris and Cheng. Aren't you forgetting the doctor?"

Felix said nothing. He felt his jaw set, so he pulled out a toothpick and clamped down on that, fought against his unsteady breath.

"Maybe I am. Let's figure it out," Felix said. "And we better move quick. Ellie's coming to town. I told her to wait, but she won't wait long."

"You're shitting me."

"Nope," Felix said. "What've you got to play on that little box?"

"Country music," Franklin said.

"Johnny Cash?"

"Not the new stuff, the old stuff. *Folsom Prison Blues,* like that." Franklin muttered, "Ellie," under his breath while he slipped in the CD. The intercom on the desk buzzed. Felix turned around and looked at the door like he was ready to jump at whoever came through it.

"Gennardi," Franklin said.

They waited. Gennardi came in holding a white manila envelope. He handed it over to Felix.

"Took it off a messenger in the hall," Gennardi said. "Jenny Hurly stopped me, too. Wants to know if you're seeing her later."

"Who's that?" Felix asked.

"Leave it," Franklin said. "Let's deal with this."

Felix opened the envelope. The ME's report was there along with a check. He looked at the check, let out a low whistle.

"Five?" Franklin asked.

"Ten thousand," Felix said. "And there's a note. 'Evidence of overdose. Looking forward to bringing down these drug-dealing nightclub hoodlums.'"

Gennardi laughed out loud, said, "At least they don't let him write his paper."

Felix stood up slow. He spread the xeroxed pages of the ME's report over Franklin's desk. There were copies of the photographs of her body, too. The room went silent. Felix saw Mike Sharpman's name.

"We just do this," Franklin said. "Like she was anybody."

They went through the material. Penelope Phelps Novak had died of a massive overdose brought on by an intake of somewhere in excess of 320 milligrams of OxyContin, combined with trace content of methamphetamine and a blood alcohol level of .35 percent. There was no evidence of physical harm. Her throat was constricted downward, which suggested she'd tried to breathe before losing consciousness, and she'd choked.

"Looks like she was choking something down," Gennardi said.

"Lot of alcohol there," Franklin said.

"Yeah, but her tolerance was high. She'd been drinking heavily for years," Felix said. He traced his fingers over Sharpman's spindly signature. "Do you know what this guy looks like?"

"Mike Sharpman? Like pizza crust."

"I met him when I was having my gun cleaned."

"Your gun." Franklin shook his head. "That old bastard's still kicking around on the force?"

"He made like you two were friends."

"We were," Franklin said.

Gennardi muttered, "Till the bastard double-crossed Billy and—"

But Franklin looked hard at Gennardi, and he said nothing more. Felix watched the two of them. He figured later he'd give Sharpman a call, learn a little something on his own.

Felix said, "This choking—could somebody force you to choke something down? Make you hold it in?"

"Sure," Gennardi said. "They used to do it in mental hospitals."

"Common dust under her fingernails," Felix said. "Which is odd, 'cause I've been staying at the Official and there isn't a hell of a lot of dust in there, what with the daily vacuuming."

"So maybe she was in a dusty place beforehand," Gennardi said.

"I wonder if marble powder counts as common dust," Felix said. They sat back down. Felix flicked his toothpick into the trash can.

"Who you haven't talked to yet is Terrence Cheng," Franklin said.

"That's right," Felix said. "I've got to get Soraya to hook me up with him."

"And let's not forget our friend Lem Dawes," Franklin said.

Felix nodded, got ready to speak. And then Soraya buzzed in.

"Hello," she said. "I see you've started without me." She sat down and ignored Felix's smile. It was a foregone conclusion that she'd read Lanie's piece in the *Spectator* and was pissed off.

Soraya got up when she saw the ME's report spread over the desk. She looked it over.

"Tell us about your doctor's appointment," Franklin said. She had her bag pressed up to her chest and she didn't let it go as she looked around at the three of them. Gennardi suddenly yawned. He began to step into the outer office.

"Gennardi, call Sharpman," Franklin said. "Tell him we saw his signature and hello from me—tell him we want phone records from

Biddle, Udris, and that hotel room. Not for just that night. For a week on either side of the relevant dates. Get them e-mailed here so we can search them."

"Keep your enemies close," Gennardi said as he began to close the door.

"Yeah," Franklin said. "Though I'm not sure a mess like Sharpman deserves the title."

None of them watched Gennardi go out. The phone rang. Once, twice. Franklin ignored it. After five rings it stopped.

"Who was your friend on the force?" Felix asked Soraya. "Who got you the police report? Was it Sharpman?"

"No," Soraya said. "I told you. It was an ex-boyfriend of mine. Guy I met when I was out dancing one night. Paul Montoya. He's how I met Gus, actually. They went to high school together out in Oyster Bay."

Felix looked at Franklin. Franklin shrugged.

"Never date cops—give you nothing but heartbreak," Franklin said.

"Yeah, my mom complained nonstop till I ended it."

"And you were going to check on who paid for the room?" Felix asked.

Soraya shook her head, as if she'd forgotten something. "Gus is getting me that information."

"Gus," Felix said, and raised his chin to Franklin.

"About the doctor," Franklin said.

"I don't think there's anything there. The doctor might be creepy, but he's okay," Soraya said. "He was suspicious because I grilled him a little, but listen, and don't jump a step forward while I'm talking. Gus told me he'd been to Biddle about three years back and he helped him kick a little coke problem he was having. I believe that Biddle really helped Gus. It wouldn't have been easy for him to get off something, but he did it. So I think Biddle's okay. That's not where the problem lies. The somebody who killed her is on the other side, with Max Udris and those guys, I'd say. And maybe Lem Dawes."

"So we're in agreement," Felix said.

Soraya didn't look at him.

Franklin arched an eyebrow, waited. Then he said, "For one thing, the doctor is not okay. Maybe he helped your friend Gus, but that doesn't make him a good guy. He is involved. Further—" Franklin stopped, said, "You two have an argument about something?"

"Did you see today's *Spectator*?" Soraya asked. Her voice was cool. She could've been asking if anyone had a tissue. She drew her black hair back, pushed it behind her shoulders.

"Yeah," Franklin said. "Somebody called Salisbury said your boyfriend is running drugs through Eden-Roc and the rest of Terry Cheng's ventures. The whole thing is unsubstantiated. Me, I figure that kind of thing is good for business unless it's true."

"His new girlfriend," Soraya said, jerking her head at Felix.

Soraya and Franklin both gazed at Felix. If there'd been a window in the room, he'd have looked out of it. Instead, he stared into space. So far, Lanie had done just what he wanted. As far as he was concerned—and then he realized they should all know this—Lanie was absolutely right on target.

He said, "The piece might have gone farther. I could've given her some facts to play with." He faced Soraya. "You should thank me. I was tempted to lead her straight to Udris and I didn't. I was out the other day and I just happened to see Gus meeting with Max Udris."

Felix shot his father a glance. No reason to tell Soraya that he'd taken a beating.

Felix went on. "That connection would expose the whole operation. The only reason I didn't was that—"

"You don't have any *evidence* on Udris," Soraya said.

"I've got a painful feeling about him, that's for sure. But I don't think we're ready to come down on all of them, not yet, anyway. And I want all the bugs in one place for when I decide to bring down my heel."

"Big talk," Soraya said. "He's here a week, he thinks he understands the way the whole city works."

Felix shrugged, said, "Drugs are drugs. Narco-trafficking is just that. Dealers kill people who get in the way. What's there not to understand?"

"Narco-trafficking?" Soraya said. She laughed low. "I guess I forgot that you can even get CNN back on the farm."

But Felix was watching his father. Something was wrong in his father's eyes. He wasn't laughing at either of them. Instead he was watching carefully and listening. Felix wondered—it was almost as if his father wanted to believe him, wanted to believe it could be that simple.

"Without proof, your girlfriend and the *Spectator* could get sued," Soraya said. "And like I just said, I know Gus is clean."

"I guess Starling Furst has seen the inside of a courtroom before," Felix said. He folded the ten-thousand-dollar check and slipped it into his pocket.

"Enough," Franklin said. But his voice was elsewhere, already moving past what they'd discussed. He went on, "Maybe this whole thing did go down the way Felix says. There's a way for it to have been like that without implicating your Gus. I'm going to do some actual investigating here, figure out how Udris operates, how Cheng's involved, like that. You two get out of here. Go get a drink and hammer out your spat. It's dull to me, watching kids fight over who kissed who last night behind the bleachers."

Felix sighed, nodded like he understood his father completely and wasn't insulted, as if this were all just business.

"You want to buy some of this junk and see where it leads you, you could start with this guy Jay Medrano at a place called the Giant's House. He's ready to give up some names and get out of town. I'll be in tomorrow morning," Felix said. "See if I can't be of some help." He stood up and before he could hide it, he grimaced, cinched his eyes closed, and held hard on the chair.

"What's the matter with you?" Soraya asked. She got up and stood close to him, reached an arm around him. Gennardi walked into the room, surveyed the scene.

"That's my boy, playing the sympathy card," Franklin said. "Look, discuss his pain outside. Me and Gennardi have calls to make. Oh, and one other thing, Felix—would you take a damn phone?"

Franklin thrust an old-fashioned Motorola clamshell cell that was about the size of a baseball into Felix's hand.

"I know it's heavy. But the little ones are for sissies. If somebody's listening to you talk on this you can deck 'em with it. The signal isn't scrambled, though, so don't use it a lot. The number's on there."

Felix slipped the phone into his jacket pocket. The thing weighed about half a pound.

Felix said, "Next thing you're going to give me is brass knuckles."

"You don't have your own?" Franklin asked.

Soraya and Felix left Franklin's office and wandered down Seventh Avenue. They didn't speak for several blocks. Then Soraya suggested that they go to Ciel Rouge, a bar that would be quiet in the early afternoon. The color had come back into Felix's face. He was pretty much done with the pain. It'd been a few days, after all, and all there was left was the time it would take for his ribs to heal.

"So what happened?" Soraya asked. She'd already asked twice, and Felix had said nothing. He wasn't sure why—embarrassment was part of it, a sense that she'd expect more from him.

"I took some hits from that guy you called Kris Kringle, remember? He fucked me up pretty good."

"Why didn't you tell me?" Soraya asked.

The street felt quiet, as if the city were taking in some breath before ending the workday and beginning the night. The cabdrivers were all taking in their cabs for the shift change then, and bike messengers whizzed down the middle of Seventh Avenue, weaving around the few trucks.

"It's like I said, I saw Max Udris with Gus—I guess I got lucky on my very first bit of sleuthing."

"You've got a gift for it," Soraya said. "But seeing them together, it doesn't mean anything."

"They're connected. Soraya, you know that. Things are going to go a lot faster when you stop fighting the reality of what's going on."

"You think so?" Soraya asked. "I knew you were going to tail Gus, no matter what I said. And if you were so smart, why'd you get beat up?"

Felix said, "Because I got close to the truth."

Soraya said, "Stop talking about it like that, like the only answer to be discovered is the one you already figured out. Otherwise I'm not going to listen."

They came up to the front of the bar and stopped there. They pawed the pavement for a moment before going in.

"So many bars," Felix said. "I think I've had more talks in bars and restaurants in the last week than I have in my whole life."

"That's what we do here," Soraya said. "We meet and we talk."

"That's New York?"

"That's right," Soraya said.

"Well, then let's keep at it," Felix said. He opened the door, held it for Soraya. She stepped inside. Ciel Rouge was a dark crimson verging on black. There were red curtains covering the front windows and no light came in from the street. The walls and ceiling were thick with ruby-colored paint, and the bar in back was made of zinc. A man in charcoal slacks and a dark blazer tapped out low chords on the grand piano that was set in the far right corner. Felix sank down into a velvet armchair and Soraya sat in another, facing him. But she was on the edge of her seat. Then she jumped up and went to the bar, ordered whiskey and soda for both of them. She brought the drinks back and set them down.

"Okay, let's have it out," Felix said. "You've been angry about me and Lanie for days. We've got what I'd call a fundamental difference of opinion."

"Where's your car?" Soraya asked.

"I left it in the *Spectator* lot."

Soraya shook her head, like that about summed it up.

"You know something, Felix? You got close to all the wrong people way too fast. After that initial thing with your dad, you curled up with him like a little puppy, didn't you? You care to explain that?"

"I'm only here for one thing," Felix said. "Find out who killed my sister, bring them down, then—"

"Get out of Dodge?"

"That's right."

In the dark of the bar, they glowered at each other. There was no other word for it. The man at the piano began to play Neil Diamond, "Solitary Man." They sipped their drinks.

"Just because you started trusting your father doesn't mean I do."

"I don't trust anybody," Felix said.

"That front—it must be hard to keep up."

Felix shrugged. He realized that no, he hadn't been looking at his father like an enemy, not lately, anyway. But he didn't say the obvious thing—that the man they'd been with today, That's my father. I can't hate him forever, for reasons I don't understand, that Ellie never made clear. Eventually, I've got to trust somebody.

"You ever think about what happened, back when everything went bad for our parents?" Soraya asked.

"Only when I'm awake," Felix said. "Why?"

"There's a lot of unanswered questions. Something came over me in that doctor's office yesterday morning. I wanted to talk about it all of a sudden. I've never talked to anybody about my father dying. My mom won't talk about it. I've checked through the papers from back then, but they all say the same thing."

Felix said, "My father and yours were with some minor-league drug dealer out in Spanish Harlem, trying to do an undercover buy in the back of a pizza parlor. They were made and the thing turned into a shoot-out, Wild West style. Billy got shot and he started shooting back. My father freaked out and ran, left the scene."

"You read the same reports. The dealer and Billy emptied their guns."

"Franklin was the only one who saw the exchange."

Soraya sipped her drink. "Then how do we know he ran?"

"That's the way the papers had it."

"And that broke your mother's heart? Him running?"

"She would've left him, anyway, I suspect. She hated the life and she didn't trust Franklin, thought he took too may risks. And she didn't want to admit that to her father, since she'd crossed him to get married in the first place. It was humiliating."

"She ever tell you that?"

"Not exactly," Felix said. "No. Why?"

"It happened pretty fast, didn't it? And she took money from her father when she went, didn't she?"

"Three days in July—that's all it took. I don't know about the money. My father got kicked off the force. After the official investigation, he went down to Florida, got a job with Wackenhut, the big security company. I only know that because he used to send us mail from there and I saw it before my mom threw it all away. I think, yeah, her father forced some money on her and she had nothing, so she took it."

"And in that same week, my mother scraped out every mention of my father from the house," Soraya said. "It was freaky."

"Nancy never mourned for your father?" Felix asked.

"Didn't seem to, no. Not even when I asked her about him."

"She never said why?"

"I assumed she just wanted to forget," Soraya said.

Felix said nothing. But he wondered at that idea, that Nancy might be angry at her husband, would want to forget him.

The piano player switched over to "Freefallin'." A few more people came in, the after-work crowd. The volume of the place went up and the air grew thick. But Felix and Soraya were deep in it, their heads only a few inches apart.

"I was always furious with my father," Felix said. "Ellie never told me not to be."

Soraya said, "My mother always told me, you want to be angry at somebody, forget the drug dealer, be angry at Franklin Novak."

They sipped their drinks, said nothing for a moment.

"A dozen years of that. Starts to wear on you, huh?" Soraya asked.

"Not as bad as my ribs. But yeah, maybe that's why it hasn't been so hard to talk to him now. I was always instructed to hate him. He wrote and we threw away the letters. It's only now that I'm beginning to not feel like something they need to use against each other."

Soraya reached forward then. She put her hand inside Felix's jacket, felt the bedsheet that Felix had wrapped around his middle. He closed his eyes. For a moment, before they pulled apart, he covered her hand with his own.

"It makes no sense," she said. "Franklin doesn't act guilty, never apologizes. Looks me right in the eye. He wouldn't do that if he'd walked away from my father."

"No man would."

"Nobody would," Soraya said. "Man or woman. I think I should go have dinner with my mom. I blew her off Sunday. We can talk about something else besides her third-grade-class art projects. Who are you going to—forget it. I don't want to know."

They got up and walked out of the bar without looking back. By then the place was crowded, and the noise was high. The piano player had been replaced by the sound system, Spandau Ballet singing "True." Felix looked back for a second, saw nothing, thought it was just the kind of bar where nobody ever got tired of crooners.

After a few minutes, Mike Sharpman slid off his bar stool and walked to the door. He lingered just inside and watched the street. He was older than most everybody, so he was ignored. He went outside and buttoned his cheap houndstooth against the cold wind that was coming down Seventh Avenue. He pulled out a cell phone and called Starling Furst.

"You won't believe who stayed friends even after all these years," he said. Then he listened. "You say the word. I can close the whole thing down right now or just play loose. Yeah, I sent over the phone records, just like you said. Sure. Sure, I can meet with the kid. I'm sure he'd love to have a drink with me. He looks about ready to hear a story."

21

Franklin and Gennardi were slumped down low in the back of the van, headed toward the West Village and the Giant's House. Philip was driving. Franklin scratched at his jaw with the back of his fist. He'd forgotten to shave and he knew the skin under his eyes would show purple and that he probably looked a little sad and a little crazy. He looked over at Gennardi. He had a PalmPilot in his big hand and he was punching at it, probably sending an e-mail to Lisa, who worked on a computer in the family kitchen.

"How much?" Philip asked.

"See what he'll give you for five hundred," Franklin said.

"What should I expect for that?"

"Fuck if I know," Franklin said. "Wait, let's see. . . . Street is around a dollar a milligram and you're above that 'cause you can't pass for a junkie or an idiot, so say twenty-five a pill for sixty-gram pills is twenty pills, plus a few extra that you give back to him to use. In that neighborhood."

Philip said, "Am I a dealer or a user?"

"Oh, hell, Philip," Franklin said. "You decide."

Philip grunted ugly and said, "Don't send me in with a half-assed story, like a bankrupt dictator to your oil companies. Do we know for sure this guy can handle five hundred? I don't want to embarrass him. And how did we get to him?"

Franklin looked over at Gennardi, who shrugged, brought his big mouth down into a frown. Philip parked the van on Hudson, half a block from the bar. He yawned, leaned over to the glove compartment, popped it open, and rooted around through bright orange parking tickets, paper napkins, plastic silverware, a couple of George Jones CDs, a sheathed buck knife, and an old copy of *Sanctuary.* Finally he slipped out a wad of bills held together with a black metal clip.

"I dunno," Franklin said. "Play it how you think he wants it. But remember, you want to come back to him for real quantity next time. If he gets nervous, ask to have his source contact you. Give your cell."

"Gun?" Philip asked.

"Sure," Franklin said. "Impress him. Say you heard about him through somebody at Eden-Roc, you read it in the paper. See what happens."

"I guess I *am* an idiot, then," Philip said. "If I'm trying to buy off reading about a supply in the paper." He slammed the door to the van and walked toward the Giant's House.

Gennardi and Franklin sat for a moment in silence in the back of the van. Franklin massaged his temples. He popped open a warm can of Coke that he'd been holding between his knees and sipped from it.

Gennardi said, "I think it's smart of us to make these legitimate connects. Nice to do a little legwork for a change."

"Of course I'd rather go shoot the Kringle guy in the face," Franklin said. "Work backward from there."

"Better this way," Gennardi said. "We'll learn something, and then we can avoid the bullshit conjecture that we had to go through with the kids this afternoon."

Franklin nodded, though even to Gennardi, he didn't want to admit what he suspected, that there was no logical way that Max Udris had killed Penelope or anybody. Drug dealer, maybe. Businessman, sure. Killer, probably not.

"I do appreciate you helping with this," Franklin said. "It's not a high-income project and I know that, and I know my kid was up to nothing good—"

"Ah, Franklin, don't try to get sweet on me. Your voice goes all high register and you start croaking like Gene Hackman."

"Yeah," Franklin said. "True."

Gennardi started to dial his wife on his cell phone. Franklin saw him doing it, popped open the side door.

"I'm going to go watch. Attach some faces to this bullshit."

Franklin stepped into the street, looked back into the van, where Gennardi was pointing forward and to the left. So Franklin went that way. He found the door to the Giant's House and went up the steps. Philip was walking down as he walked up, followed by a handsome young man in a black T-shirt. Upstairs, Franklin looked around. He told the hostess he was looking for a friend and she gave him a doubtful look, like there wasn't much chance he'd have a friend in such a place.

He checked out the view for a second so it looked like he was doing something, registered New Jersey out there on the other side of the Hudson River and tried to remember when he'd last been there. He stopped for a moment by the hostess stand and grabbed some toothpicks while the memory came clear. It'd been six months earlier, and he'd driven to Upper Saddle River. He'd had to go out and fire a senior executive who worked for his own former employer, Kroll. The man was so crazy and violent that old Jules Kroll was afraid of him. So he'd hired Franklin, who'd made fourteen thousand dollars for the job and filed the payment under private speaking engagements, which it kind of was, after all. He'd delivered a speech and taken some questions and then driven the hell away from the guy's compound before the guy had found the clip for the Tec-9 he'd started babbling about when he figured out he was being fired. The drive back to the city had been pleasant. Franklin had resolved to remember to take more out-of-town work.

Once Franklin had seen enough of the young people and picked his teeth, he headed back downstairs and out to the street.

Paul Montoya sat at a table next to the giant tree with his old friend Gus Moravia. Paul was still on the force, working out of Midtown Central, but he liked to see Gus now and then, remember their old times back in high school when they'd both played on the lacrosse team, stoned out of their minds and hell-bent for violence.

He was a little jealous that Gus was with Soraya now, but it was his own damn fault for taking that risk when he'd introduced them. Soraya was too much for him, anyway. What with her dad being a cop who'd been killed on duty, he suspected her of putting some heavy shit on him, and he didn't want to deal with it. She was too young, too. Though she sure was beautiful—crazy beautiful.

"I wonder what he wanted," Paul said.

"Who?" Gus asked. He'd suggested that they meet at the Giant's House because Terrence Cheng had told him to scout it out, see how the place was doing since it was competition and the design was supposed to be terrific, which it was. But otherwise, Gus was bored. He had to work hard to find things to say to Paul and he was so tired from being up all night dealing with shit at Eden-Roc that he was practically shaking. And the Irish coffee and bread pudding he was eating weren't helping any.

"Franklin Novak. He just came in here, sniffed around, and left."

"Oh, man." Gus sighed. "Did he see me?"

"No, he just looked at the view. Is he looking for you?"

"I don't know. I hope not."

"Man, you attract trouble like pimps to a nymphomaniac convention."

"Huh," Gus said. "That's precinct humor?"

"Yeah," Paul said, and looked at his running sneakers.

"I don't know what Soraya ever saw in you," Gus said.

"Likewise, I'm sure. How's business, anyway?"

"Tense," Gus said. "Everybody wants a piece of the nightlife action, and there's only so much to go around."

Franklin walked back to the van, got in. Gennardi was still on the phone with Diane. He held up a finger, mouthed, One minute.

"I'd rather go to Greece," Gennardi said. "It's hot there and there's plenty of stuff for Lisa to see, like the Kritios boy and the Parthenon and all that shit. The cliché is true. The French are jerks. I don't want to get disrespected by some hotel clerk in front of my only daughter."

Franklin nodded at him, like, Good point.

"Okay, I gotta go, but my vote is for Greece, first Athens, then on to some island hopping. I love you, too."

Gennardi hung up, said, "Summer trip."

"What about Italy?"

"That was last summer. Sicily and Palermo—you remember, we went all around down in the Boot."

Philip got in the van a moment later, didn't look back at them. He turned on the engine and pulled away from the curb. With his right hand, he took the wad of hundreds and slipped them back into the glove compartment.

"Nothing?"

"Said he's not a dealer and he even got a little huffy about it, but I think he's lying. Said to go to Lem Dawes, that he wouldn't be surprised if he'd deal to me. Apparently he has some party on a tugboat. I should go to that. Supposed to be an Oxy bonanza."

"That lying asshole has his own boat?" Franklin asked.

Gennardi nodded, said, "I heard about this. It's a family boat. He wants to rent it for gambling parties is what I hear. They board 'em up off the pier at Fulton Street and then head out and gamble, blow drugs, like that."

Philip said, "Reminds me of the boat we had out on Caborra Bassa, mounted with the antiaircraft gun that got me out of the country. The pirates saw that big toy, they left us the fuck alone, you can bet. Man, that boat was the safest place in the country."

"Philip's lived a real life," Gennardi muttered, with what Franklin heard as envy. But Franklin was still annoyed about Lem Dawes.

"Fucking kid. He's a pretty goddamn good liar, I'll say that for him," Franklin said. "We know anybody in the harbor unit?"

"Leonardo Bolanos. He'd be a lieutenant by now, I'd say."

"So call him up. You deal with that bugging thing?" Franklin asked. And then he swallowed, said, "Hey, Gennardi, I'm sorry. I've been so messed up over this family thing I forgot to ask."

"Right. The Edelstein thing. Turns out he is bugged after all. He wants to see you."

"Where am I going?" Philip asked.

"Ah—out to Williamsburg, let's stake the warehouse, get a look at this Udris character and his employee, the guy who kicked my son's ass."

Philip nodded, turned left on Canal Street, and headed east.

"Okay, we'll do the Edelstein thing tomorrow. Assuage his fears. Where's this warehouse, anyway, what's the address?"

"Renwick Boulevard," Gennardi said.

"Man, we are getting busy here," Franklin said.

"There's another thing," Philip said. "This Jay Medrano, he mentioned a bartender who was all up in Gus's shit. Kashmira, he said. She knows everything. Works at Eden-Roc."

"Gus Moravia came up? How?" Franklin asked.

They stopped at the light at Canal and Broadway. There were vendors selling everything from sweaters from Uruguay, to unlicensed NYPD baseball hats, to sex toys from Thailand masquerading as race cars and fake martial arts weapons. Dealers jostled tourists, and great piles of garbage spilled out into the street. The noise was enormous, of honking, of Somali men playing Whitney Houston while they sold watches out of imitation leather briefcases labeled Carteir instead of Cartier, of suburban kids loading up on art supplies from Pearl Paint and then getting their asses jostled into the never-ending traffic.

"This corner always gets me," Philip said. "Crazy as home. We talked about Gus because Jay mentioned him, said we had to get out of the restaurant 'cause he was there. That he didn't even like to talk about drugs when that guy's around."

"Did you see him?" Gennardi asked.

Franklin shook his head. He said, "Maybe he really is the kingpin. King Oxy, and Soraya goes out with him. Shit. I hope he didn't make me."

22

Soraya sat in front of a half-finished plate of fusilli, eggplant, squash, and kale. In addition to being obsessive about teaching, Nancy Navarro was deeply healthy. She was a vegetarian and she liked to keep her vegetables pure, so she tore them with her fingers rather than use a knife and steamed them only until they were warm. Soraya sipped apple juice that was so pungent her nose wrinkled.

Soraya said, "Can't you tell me anything?"

But Nancy was eating, her head bowed down. Soraya watched her mother chew the crunchy vegetables and al dente pasta. The smell of clean cooking and no oil or fat surrounded them, leaving little mystery in the room beyond the pale scent of loss. In the background, Nancy had on classical radio, WQXR. They listened to a Debussy waltz.

Nancy said, "You want to tell me how you have time for classes when you're so busy asking all these questions?"

"If I don't get answers, I can't think straight in class."

"Always the circle with you," Nancy said.

Soraya folded her arms over her chest.

"Look, Mom, I know it never made sense, how Dad was killed and what happened with the Novaks, but I always let it go because I was concerned about you. It was about respect. Now I'm being honest with you. Penelope is dead, and I'm—damn it, the truth is I'm working with Franklin Novak and Felix to find out why. The least you can do is let me know if I was wrong to hate Franklin all these years."

Her mother seemed to look beyond her then, at the dining room, which she used as her office. The chairs were pulled out in there and Nancy looked at those empty spaces, as if she were remembering something.

She said, "You know, right before the end, they were going to start a private firm. They used to joke about it—Navarro and Novak, LLC. Would've been good at it, too. Safer than being on the force."

Nancy's voice was whisper-soft. Soraya could just hear her over the music, over the vague sense of country that always fought to be heard out in Queens, the rapid movements of the squirrels and the aggressive birds, the first crickets of the late spring. Soraya cooled, concentrated, got ready for her mom to reveal.

"Franklin was here the other day," Nancy said.

"I thought you wouldn't speak to him."

"The way he lost Penelope—I couldn't turn him away."

"So?" Soraya said. And then her mother shuddered, hard, and closed her eyes.

"I'm sorry. He and I have an agreement. I can't explain it to you. I wish I could, but I can't."

"Mom, that's not fair."

"Ask him." Her mother was suddenly loud. "If he wants to talk, he can tell you. Not me."

"At least tell me about Ellie, about why she left Franklin."

"That woman never made sense to me. People just got stuck on her and they couldn't let go. She had people around her from high school, from college. Maybe it made her crazy, how they all loved her. That's all I can say."

"She went to Columbia, right?" Soraya asked.

"Yes?"

"Well, wasn't she friends with somebody there called Sidney Jamison? Remember him? He became a big director."

"Maybe," Nancy said. "So? All those rich people, they know each other."

"I go to school with Sidney Jamison's daughter now."

"That's no surprise," Nancy said. "We all had children around the same time. But those people, they had no time for me and your father—you shouldn't forget that. Working class and Puerto Rican. We were Franklin's friends and they weren't too interested in him, either. In fact, I'd say they were afraid of him, though they always said they weren't interested. The only thing that ever fascinated any of them was Ellie, and sure, she was beautiful, but it didn't hurt that she was rich."

Soraya watched her mom. She was thinking about Sidney Jamison and Ellie, how they'd been old friends. And then there was her friend Edwige and Marsden Biddle, who she'd probably known a long time. Then there was only one person between Ellie and Dr. Biddle and Soraya felt herself grow a little shaky. She tried to smile, and suddenly she wished for something heavy to eat, like steak.

"Please, Mom, tell me the truth about what happened. I need to know it."

"Soraya, I'm sorry. I just can't."

The music ended and a soft-voiced man came on and began to announce the news. The stock market was improving, climbing back up from the endless crashes of the previous summer. They were quiet, watching each other. Nancy had begun to cry. And Soraya felt these other people's worlds pressing down on her but without answers; they only felt hard and heavy. Again she was glad she was with Gus. At least he had nothing to do with the past. His mother was dead, and he'd come up from nothing. She knew that for a fact.

She wondered about something else her mother had said. "What did you mean, people got stuck on Ellie? What people?"

"I'm through with talking," Nancy said.

Soraya said, "That's okay, Mom. What happened with my father, everything that went bad back then—I believe it'll come out when the time is right."

"I'm afraid of that," Nancy said. "I'm increasingly afraid of that."

Felix was back in the Roadrunner, cowboy hat pressed down low, sunglasses perched on his nose. He was parked at the base of the Williamsburg Bridge, pulled over to the curb next to a Burger King on Delancey. He was waiting for Franklin to call so he could pick up the tail on a van they were staking out at Udris's place. Since Udris had made him the other way, as a tourist, he'd decided to dress as himself. And if he was still in any kind of pain, the tension of waiting erased it, replaced with the good cold feel of the gun.

While he waited, he dialed his mother's number because he knew he was making her crazy with his days of silence.

This time she answered on the first ring, said, "What?"

"It's okay, Mom, we're getting closer. We've got a trail now, and we're following it."

"We?"

"I had to get in with Franklin. There was no choice. People here owe him favors. It makes everything easier."

"You are not to trust him! I explained that to you."

"You told me never to trust him—but you never explained why."

"Of course I did. I told you what happened with Billy."

"I've been talking with Soraya," Felix said. "That story—we're not so sure it makes sense." His voice was calm. He wanted to see Udris and the white-haired man again. This time, he'd be ready.

So though he heard Ellie as she said, "I'll be there in two days. It was hell to get somebody who I can stand to trust with the property while I'm gone—before, I always depended on you for that—," he had a call on the other line, and he wanted to take it.

"Mom, I gotta go."

"Wait!" But he clicked over, put the idea of her coming to town out of his head.

"Hello?"

"Felix, this is Mike Sharpman. I just talked to your father. He said it'd be a good idea if we talked. Why don't you come to Chinatown and we can have a conversation."

"I can't right now, Mike, I'm waiting on something."

"No, no—it's cool. Your dad said to come and meet me. We're all more or less on the same team here. It's a place called Garibaldi's on the corner of Mulberry and Mosco, across the street from Mao Park—or that's what cops call it. Anyway, Chinatown, near New York Ironworks. Half an hour?"

"Okay," Felix said. He dropped the phone on the seat next to him and turned on the engine. Then, as he slipped into traffic and headed toward the Bowery, he went ahead and dialed his father. When Franklin didn't answer, he shrugged and kept going. After all, he couldn't figure any other way Sharpman could have gotten the cell's number than through Franklin. And more than that, he wanted to hear what the man had to say.

The brown van was parked in a lot off Renwick Boulevard, across from the back entrance of Udris Stone. The van looked like nothing—it was about as conspicuous as a two-day-old *Spectator* soaking up grease in a gutter. The van's occupants watched as Kris Kringle, Udris, and a boy no older than eighteen loaded a piece of stone into the back of a white delivery van. They slipped the slab into a brace and fitted it to the inside of the truck. Then they threw in some toolboxes and some bags of supplies, and some other small bags that could have contained anything at all.

"Guns and drugs," Philip whispered. "I can tell that from the way they behave—bullshit relaxed." Franklin and Gennardi nodded. Philip knew false cool when he saw it and they trusted him.

Franklin's phone rang. A call from the cell he'd given Felix. He ignored it, kept watching through the van's tinted window. Udris and Kris Kringle gave some orders to the kid, who went back into the shop. Then they got into the van and headed out to the boulevard.

"Let's take them ourselves," Franklin said. Philip started up the van. "We don't need Felix to take over just yet. I want to see where they go." He turned to Gennardi. "These guys, could they know us?"

"Maybe through Lem Dawes, but not faces."

"Okay, who wants to place bets where they go?"

"What's the pot?" Philip asked. "Last time it was what? A cheeseburger? You've got to do better than that."

"Whoever names the right location gets first shot at Kris Kringle."

"No fair," Gennardi said. "We get the opportunity, you'll damn sure forget the bet and take first, second, and third pop."

"True," Franklin said. "Bacon cheeseburger, then."

"Cheap bastard," Philip said. "They'll take us to Peppermint Lounge. Jay Medrano said you can get anything through there."

"I thought that place wasn't open," Gennardi said.

"Opens this week."

"No kidding," Gennardi said.

"Okay," Franklin said. "Lunch on me if you're right and one Kris Kringle pop, no matter what I say in the heat of the moment."

"Yeah, right," Philip said, and punched the gas as they headed up Marcy Avenue.

"Good to see you, kid. Have a beer?" Sharpman held out his hand and Felix took it, shook hard.

"It's early," Felix said. "I'll take a Coke."

Sharpman motioned to a woman in blue jeans and a Jets sweatshirt, with hair the color of dirty pennies and a bosom shaped like the fender on a Ford F-150.

Sharpman said, "You know what I want. For him a Coke."

The woman nodded. She gave Felix a Pepsi from the soda gun and then poured Sharpman a double shot of Gilbey's Gin in a water glass. Felix tasted the Pepsi and pushed it away.

Garibaldi's was a cop bar, on the other side of Mao Park, behind the Tombs. Asian men cooked veal, sausage, and peppers and spaghetti marinara at a hot table in the back. There were dark vinyl booths filled with guys drinking Bud Lite and rum and Cokes. The lights were spots, placed in the ceiling, that shone down and showed nothing but the dust and smoke that the place used to keep a stranglehold on any fresh air. The jukebox played Willie Nelson, though, so that was something. Sharpman was the same as he'd been the week before, gray, musty, and cracked—the walking dead.

"I guess you know that I signed off for the precinct on the—ah, your sister's death. You know that by now?"

"I do," Felix said. He looked away from Sharpman. Through the smoked glass of the bar, he could see old Chinese people in formation in the park across the street, doing what looked like a super-slow-motion version of tai chi.

"Yeah. Well, I know I wasn't quick to tell you when I saw you in the Ironworks, 'cause I don't go yapping for no reason, not till I know all the shit there is to know on a situation. But I will now. I'm not in here to talk about Penelope. That was an OD and I'm sorry for it, but we're all sure that's what it was. No. I'm here to talk to you about something else."

"What's that?" Felix asked. He watched Sharpman look at the dark wood of the bar. Sharpman tapped the wet surface with his fingers, as if he were looking for his drumroll. A cop in plainclothes walked by, angled in between them, and let them soak up some of his cigarette smoke.

"Hey, kid—make sure Dandruff here doesn't stick you for all the rounds."

"Shut up, Mohan, you handsome Irish bastard," Sharpman said, and pretended to laugh. But Felix could see he was tight at the edges, and when Mohan clapped Sharpman on the back and walked away Sharpman didn't look after him with anything resembling warmth.

"Talk to me," Felix said. "I got places to be."

Sharpman looked up quickly, focused on Felix, and frowned.

"Okay, big boy. It's about your father. I don't know what you know or how close you are to him. But he isn't right." Sharpman shook his head. He sipped on his gin and bit his lower lip.

"What's wrong about him?" Felix asked. He knew something was wrong with all this, but he let his curiosity show. Sharpman was looking for him to act naive; he'd give him exactly that.

"It's worse than you think. Ninety-one was a tough year here. The recession hit and there was the Rodney King thing out in LA. We had rivers of crack that summer and nobody in the city liked you if you were a cop—not that these ungrateful bastards ever do. I remember doing a buy-and-bust in the East Village, and we had to fight through rioters in Tompkins Square Park to make our arrests."

"Okay, that's the history part," Felix said. "What about my father?"

"Him and Billy were part of Ray Kelly's antidrug task force and so those bastards, they had citywide passports. They could go anywhere. So they start hanging out up on 118th Street and Third Avenue 'cause they're interested in a dealer called Kenny Price, a white guy out of Florida who's bringing up kilos from Colombia, straight up 95 in the back of a Chevy Nova. So he avoids the profiling issue completely, and he's unloading in the barrio and selling to all kinds of dealers, totally indiscriminate. The task force got it all on tape. They spent eight months building the case. Anyway."

Sharpman stopped. He pointed to his empty glass and the bartender filled. While she did so, she muttered, "Picklehead," without affection. Then, wordlessly, she took away Felix's glass of Pepsi and put a Budweiser in front of him.

"Handsome kid like you has to listen to this broken-down old drunk, you ought to drink, too," she said. "Unless you're A.A.?" Felix shook his head and sipped the beer.

Sharpman said, "Sweet lady. Love her like she was my own great-grandmother, I really do. Okay, so Franklin and Billy go into this pizza place, Ray's Optimistic and Original. And they do this huge buy, twenty-thousand-dollar buy, and they got it all on tape. They're walking out, and Kenny Price, he comes after them—he says, 'You forgot something.' Your father yells, 'Not me, him,' just like that. He screams it and then we hear him trip backward on the curb and fall down. And this is all on tape, we have this: Price and Billy shoot each other to death. Both of them empty their Glocks into each other and all over the street. Was a mess, I'll tell you. And your father, he runs. We took the tape off of Billy's body. Kid, I'm sorry. The fact is, your father paid Kenny Price to kill Billy Navarro, and the thing went wrong. Kenny aimed the gun at him by mistake and so your father had to say that. Then the two guys, they killed each other while he ran."

Felix was looking at his fingers. He saw that if he didn't do some work soon, the calluses on his hands were going to wear off. A week away, he thought, and I get soft in my hands and confused everywhere else. He thought, I am not feeling. I am only hearing.

"So," he said. "How come he never got in trouble for it?"

"We did a cover-up. Because of your grandfather. He quieted the thing, and then your mother left town. Your father left the force and went down to that private security firm in Florida, Wackenhut. Everything got taken care of."

"There's just one thing," Felix said.

"Yeah, I know," Sharpman said. "Why would your father do that to his partner, his best friend of nearly ten years—since right when you were born? Billy was your godfather, even, I think. Why? You sure you want to know?"

"Hit me," Felix said, and his voice was hoarse from the bar's lack of air.

"Billy was in love with your mother. He was going to run away with her. And it was driving your father crazy. So he planned to have him killed."

Felix closed his eyes and wished he didn't know all the other details, the group of so many things that made what he'd just heard entirely possible. Billy and Ellie. No wonder Nancy Navarro didn't mourn. But even if it was all true, it didn't explain why he was hearing this now.

Felix said, "Franklin told you to tell me all this?"

"Well," Sharpman said. "No. I felt like it was my duty to tell you. I mean, if I had a son—"

"You'd want somebody to sit down with him in a bar and turn him against you? Who pays you?" Felix said. And he was a little loud. Some other cops turned around, saw it was Sharpman getting some shit, and looked away.

"Hey, kid—I'm not here for work. This is a moral obligation I've got. You would've found out eventually. This story, it's just the truth. I'm sorry, but there it is." Sharpman's glass was empty.

Quickly, Felix stood up.

"My sister was killed—and all anybody wants to talk about is some bullshit from a dozen years ago. Maybe my father did kill Billy. I don't care about that. I'm done needing a father. What I'm worried about is my sister. You—if I'd known we were here to talk about ancient history, I wouldn't have shown up."

"Nobody likes the messenger," Sharpman said, to himself.

"Try merchant of death," Felix said. "Fuck you, Sharpman. You sanctimonious bastard."

"Big words," Sharpman said. But he said it to Felix's back. Felix was out of the bar, into the street, headed down Baxter to Worth and over to Bowery, where he'd parked his car. A few of the men in the park watched him go. One nodded and made a call on his cell phone.

Sharpman went outside and stood in front of the bar. He breathed long and looked up at the sky. The sun was just down, but there were no stars. He might as well have been staring at a ceiling covered in gray paint. His cell vibrated. He took Starling Furst's call.

Sharpman said, "It got a little messy, but it's done."

"He bought it?"

"It's the truth, isn't it? I'm just the messenger."

"Well, Sharpman, of course it's the truth. There's a Chinese man wearing a Giants baseball hat watching you. See him?"

Sharpman looked across the street. A man was leaning up against the Mao Park fence. His arms were folded over his chest and he chewed on a straw. He nodded once at Sharpman.

"Yeah, I see him."

"He has your cash."

"Terrific," Sharpman said. He looked both ways before quickly crossing the street.

23

They sat in the brown van and watched a white-and-blue sailboat called the *Dancing Bear,* which was docked in an inlet between the Staten Island Ferry and the U.S. Coast Guard station, down at the southernmost tip of Manhattan. The wind was whipping hard and there was no reason to think it was April, since it felt like December. Udris and Kringle had parked their van a few minutes earlier. They'd gotten out, leaving the stone in the back. Kringle carried a crumpled black nylon knapsack in one hand, but that was all. They had no tools. Their clothes were clean.

"It's a sweet little boat," Philip said. "But you couldn't have a party on it."

"How much?" Franklin asked.

"Ninety thousand, minimum."

It was nearly seven. The sun had just set behind the huge Colgate-Palmolive clock far to their right across the Hudson River, in Jersey City. Lem Dawes had greeted Udris and Kringle and ushered them on deck. Philip brought out a pair of Newcon Optic BN-5 night vision binoculars from his tool case. He was able to peer through the boat's tiny windows.

"All I can see is this Lem guy talking nice with Udris. Santa Claus is at a table, smoking a cigarette. I don't get it."

"The question," Gennardi said, "is who is zooming who?"

Philip had killed the engine and now they were all sitting quietly, shivering. To their left, a seemingly unending line of tired commuters made their way into the bowels of the Staten Island Ferry, looking at nothing but the bent back of the person in front of them and their way home.

"Jenny Hurly asked me what was up with you again today," Gennardi said.

"I'm afraid to see her," Franklin said. "But on the other hand, I don't want to let her go."

"Maybe you should decide that you two have a good relationship and go out with her for real. You need me to do a Cyrano thing, tell her how you feel?"

"Say a word to her and I'll kill you," Franklin said. "Don't you know I got a history of dead partners?"

"Marvelous," Gennardi said. "Six hours in the van really brings out your sweet side."

"I don't know why she doesn't like his money," Philip said.

"It lowers her sense of self-worth," Gennardi said. "When you get brought up in Wisconsin, they don't raise you to have thoughts like, Jeez, what I'd really like to do when I'm older is go to New York and get paid to have sex with a morally bereft old man who'd rather pistol-whip coke dealers than talk about love."

"I see," Philip said.

"Hey, Gennardi, when you're thinking something, don't worry about anybody's feelings, just come right out and say it," Franklin said.

"I do," Gennardi said, and smiled. Through the van's front window, they watched Lem come back out. Now the men seemed looser, as if they'd just done business.

"Wait," Philip said. "They're not supplying him. He's supplying them."

And it was true. Kringle carried the knapsack differently now. He cradled it in his arms like a sleeping baby. The men shook hands, clapped each other on the back.

Franklin said, "Supply chain is unclear here."

"Since when does a snot-nosed rich-kid fuck supply a Russian heavy with drugs?" Gennardi asked.

Franklin dialed Felix's cell phone, but he got no response.

Franklin said, "Shit, we could really use Felix right now to pick up this trail. We can follow, but not all the way to their next stop."

"We're going to have to," Gennardi said. They watched Lem disappear into the *Dancing Bear.* Udris and Kringle got back in their van. They turned north, headed toward Church Street and uptown.

"Follow them," Franklin said. "Gennardi's right."

He sat back in the seat. Philip let them get a block ahead and then he started to follow. He peeked out occasionally from behind a dilapidated Time Warner truck.

"God," Franklin said, "I need to piss."

"Shouldn't have drunk that Coke," Gennardi said.

"I needed the caffeine 'cause you put me to sleep."

"This is like the old days," Philip said.

"You weren't here for the old days," Franklin said.

"You're right," Philip said. "If it were my old days I would've slit both your throats and headed downriver, traded your white hides to cannibals for indigenous sculpture."

Gennardi said, "Talk about an upbringing—don't be an ethnic cliché."

"It's okay if I say it. Just like you with your crappy Danny Aiello imitation," Philip said. Then he started to sing "That's Amore" and Gennardi lunged forward for his throat. Franklin caught his hand and settled him back.

"I was gonna tickle him," Gennardi said.

"Okay, both of you shut up and keep them in sight. This delivery is going to clarify some things. It has to. Obviously none of us can stand one more fucking minute in this van. Drop me off wherever they stop and then you two go home. And give me that Glock, would you, Philip? I'm feeling acutely aware of my deep inability to talk about love."

They followed on Sixth Avenue and up to 17th Street, where the white van turned left. They stopped in front of a doorway next to a parking lot. Franklin struggled out of the back of the van.

"Go on and sit up front," Franklin said. "Actually, you two have a beer and talk about the Edelstein thing. Tomorrow you can fill me in on what you figured out."

Franklin slammed the door before either of them could say anything, and Philip drove away so that they didn't get made. Franklin looked up the street and saw Udris's van pull into a parking lot next to

Terrence Cheng's new club, the Peppermint Lounge. He went across to the Peppermint's doorway, pulled out his cell phone, and pretended to speak into it. After a few minutes Udris and Kringle came out and went into the parking lot. Now they were empty-handed and expressionless. The door they closed behind them was painted flat black. It clicked closed when they left. There was no other sound on the street.

Franklin watched them get into the white van and pull out behind a Cadillac SUV. Now Udris was driving. To Franklin, he didn't look too special. Drug dealer, stone importer, what was the difference? He was a cog was what he was. Product distributor. Not too many people in the world would care when Franklin crushed him and his buddy, that was for sure. But he wasn't ready to turn on the personal part, not yet. As he watched the van pull away, he called and left a message with Gennardi to check the van's New York plate and to get whatever other information he could about Udris Stone.

Then he made his way across the street and rang the black plastic buzzer next to the door to the Peppermint Lounge. He'd put what he expected to happen together off of what Felix had told him when they'd had lunch. He was expecting the door to be opened by whoever had dealt with Udris, who would assume that he'd forgotten something. And he figured that if Felix was as smart as he hoped he was, that woman would be Liza Pruitt.

After a minute, a woman in her late twenties opened the door. She was accompanied by a cold breeze. It might have been fifty degrees out in the street. The breeze was much colder. The woman wore jeans and a thick wool sweater with a cowl neck. She had on a black scrunch hat with a pom-pom on top. Platinum-colored hair came out from under the sides. Her teeth were chattering.

Franklin said, "I'm here to see Liza Pruitt." He still hadn't decided whether he was a city investigator, a liquor distributor, or himself.

"You're seeing her," she said.

"It's freezing in there, huh?" Franklin said.

"Management won't turn on the heat till we get our paying customers, and that's not for a couple more hours."

"Terry likes to keep costs down," Franklin said.

"No kidding. What do you want?"

Franklin was too tired to be anything but direct. He said, "Jay Medrano said you were a source."

"He did?"

"Said I could buy in quantity from you."

"Well, I'm flattered. Okay," Liza said. "He didn't call, but that's no surprise. Let's go."

Liza Pruitt walked back into the club. Inside, there was a long hall that felt like a wind tunnel, with framed photos of aged rock stars; Deborah Harry, David Byrne, Joey Ramone, Richard Hell. Then, farther in, the hall opened into a lounge, where a deejay was setting up at a stand that was about ten feet in the air. Two men were behind the bar, filling the steel bins with beer and ice. The sound system played an old Billie Holiday tune, "Violets for Your Furs."

Franklin said, "That's a sweet sound."

"Yeah, I've got a soft spot for anything Billie." Liza folded her arms and stood in front of the bar. She said, "Now tell me, why would my friend Jay give my name to a cop like you?"

Franklin smiled at her. He put a hand on his head and rubbed it, like he didn't know the answer, either. He looked around. The corners of the club were dark and he saw it wasn't a big place, just a room for dancing, with deep blue banquettes along the side wall across from the bar.

He said, "I'm not a cop. I'm a private investigator. And I'm not interested in you or in Jay Medrano—not to bust for distribution, anyway. I could give a shit about that. I'm looking for somebody who can tell me a story about a young lady called Penelope Novak."

Liza didn't bother to hide her recognition. Instead she reared up, her eyelids arching, in a pantomime of nervousness. She said, "Who do you work for?"

"The family. And without going into too much detail, they're not interested in a real investigation because they understand what an overdose is. They just want to know about how she was living. Who might have let her down in those last few days of her life, like that. Did you know her?"

"They're upset."

"Like most rational people would be."

"Well, shit. Let's drink a whiskey," Liza said. She went behind the bar and got a bottle of Maker's Mark from the top shelf and set it on the cold metal bar. She took out glasses and poured a healthy shot for each of them.

"Ice?" she asked.

"Are you kidding?"

Liza laughed. She sipped hers and said, "Penelope. We used together a few times. That was early on, right when she came into town. She was like, heat-seeking when the subject was drugs. She knew who had and who wanted and she put people together. That was her gift, I'd say."

Franklin swished the whiskey in his mouth so he could grumble in his throat first, to kill any sound of emotion. He said, "Then she started slipping."

"She sure did. Fell for some rich kid and started using too much. And he was embarrassed by her, wasn't too nice to her in public, but she wouldn't let him go. He kept saying that they barely knew each other, which might've been true. When you're using that heavily you get confused about who your friends are."

"Where'd she get the money to run with these people?"

"It's funny 'cause I couldn't figure her for rich, but she said her grandfather was supporting her, that he was big."

"Why wouldn't she be rich?"

"For a rich girl, she wore terrible shoes. And she'd reveal sometimes, like she'd talk about feeding chickens and other stuff—made me know she was a farm girl. But she did say that her grandfather was going to send her to a doctor who was going to help her out. This was happening real fast. She was a streak of light, that girl. Within that busy time, November, December, everybody knew her."

The music switched, from Billie Holiday to an old Benny Goodman number, "Somebody Stole My Gal."

"What about Max Udris?"

"What about him? You said you weren't interested in anything but Penelope."

"Did they know each other?"

"I can't imagine why they would, unless—"

"She was carrying for him and then she gave him aggravation, so he put her down?"

Liza Pruitt glared at him. She took off her pom-pom hat and scratched at her wild thatch of hair.

"You presume a lot about people," she said. "It's easy to talk about using, but nobody's talking about who's dealing. And nobody's been implicated. Anyway, the thing you're suggesting isn't Max's style."

"How would you know?"

"Because," Liza said, "I put myself through college working with Max and I've never had a problem. In fact, I feel safer with Max than with Terry Cheng, and Terry's legit."

"Thanks for the drink," Franklin said. He set his glass on the bar and turned toward the hallway.

"Wait, could I get your card? Maybe I'll have something else for you."

"My card? Sure." Franklin took out his card and handed it over. Liza Pruitt looked down at it. The card was blank, save for his name and a number that connected to a voice mail account Gennardi checked every once in a while.

"Oh, shit," Liza said. She looked up at Franklin. "You're her father."

"That's right," Franklin said. He smiled without showing his teeth. Then he said, "I'm going to rain down like hell on these people when I find out who didn't do the right thing, the night she got into too much trouble."

"I can imagine," Liza Pruitt said. "I can imagine."

Franklin didn't say anything else. Liza was professional; she'd already given out everything she'd planned to reveal.

He said, "You ever heard the one about the difference between the Jew and the gentile?"

"What's that?"

"The gentile leaves without saying goodbye; the Jew says goodbye without leaving."

Liza smiled at him.

He said, "This place is for a slightly older crowd than the one Terry's got in Chinatown, huh?"

"That's right."

"Then what are you doing here?"

"I got slightly older," Liza said.

"All right, then. Take care," Franklin said. He went out the way he'd come in.

Behind him, Liza looked at the card and sipped at her whiskey. A minute passed and then Terry Cheng came down the stairs from the deejay booth. He was small and his movements were nimble. He wore black slacks and a black V-necked sweater over a T-shirt, and he looked like anybody's idea of a hip, successful man, the president of a record label or a Hollywood talent manager. He didn't look unhappy, either. He wore gold-framed glasses and he pushed them back on his nose as he strode along the dance floor.

While Liza watched him he went and turned on the big Modine gas heater that hung from the ceiling. Though the music was loud they could still hear the whoosh of the gas jets in the heater as they burned and heated up the steel bars. After another minute the fan at the back of the unit came on and blew hot, dry air down onto the bar area.

Liza watched the heater. "That thing doesn't give any heat that lasts."

"It helps," Terry Cheng said. Neither of them spoke for a minute. Then both of them looked toward the hallway that Franklin had used.

"What are you going to do?" Liza asked.

"Am I connected?" Terry asked. He pushed at the glass Franklin had used.

"Not that I can see," Liza said.

"I'm a businessman," Terry said. "I don't consort with fiends who use heroin and OxyContin and cocaine. I have no reason to be afraid."

"Of course not," Liza said. She went behind the bar, dropped the two glasses in the short sink. She glanced once at the black knapsack that was back there, but she said nothing. When she looked up, Terry was gone. Liza Pruitt put her hand on her forehead, felt the cold sweat there. She poured whiskey into a new glass, drank that, felt her body give off more nervous heat, and she stepped away from the hot air blowing down on her, but the heat didn't go away. She unzipped the knapsack and looked down at several dozen plastic Ziploc bags, each one filled with a hundred purple pills.

"Who's a fiend?" she whispered.

She took out a pill and put it on her finger. She reached under the bar and found a flat-bottomed shot glass. She put the pill on a black plastic coaster and placed the shot glass on top of it, cupped the space the pill made with the *c* of her thumb and pointer finger. Then she pressed the glass down and crushed the pill. Without looking, she slipped a straw from the bar setup on her right.

Felix and Lanie were in the room at the Official. Lanie's apartment had been fumigated for mice and roaches earlier that day and she was unwilling to go back there. She said it smelled too much like Jimmy Tzatziki's office at the *Spectator.* They were naked, postcoital, and they'd been lying there for half an hour. Lanie was dozing. Felix hadn't closed his eyes, not even for a second. But now Lanie was trying to talk to him, though he'd rolled away from her and was lying on his side, facing the window. She was gently touching his bruised ribs, and he put his hands over hers, but that was all.

"You're upset," Lanie said.

"You've got the true beat reporter's gift for insight."

"Don't you dare call me a reporter when we're naked!"

Lanie got out of bed, visibly twitched her little butt, and went and flipped on the television, tuned to CNN.

"I'm sorry," Felix said. He punched his own jaw. "I've got no right to snap at you. It's this mean city."

"Oh, bullshit. Look, Felix, you can tell me anything. They put my stupid nightclubs-and-drugs series on hold till Friday. And anyway, I swore to you that I wouldn't write about you, no matter how juicy your life gets. But don't give me that garbage about this mean city—I never met a guy yet who was more from these streets than you."

"Did you know that my grandfather was your boss or not?" Felix asked.

"Are we still on that?" Lanie frowned. "Look, Felix, I did and I didn't, and that's all I'm going to say about it. The fact is, you can trust me. I won't do anything to harm you because I didn't when it mattered and I don't want to now. We just had some serious sex, for one thing, and I want to keep you."

"Maybe all that's true," Felix said. He swallowed, then he said out loud the single thought that had enveloped him for the last several hours. "I had a drink with somebody called Mike Sharpman this afternoon and he told me more about what happened to my family a dozen years ago. He says the truth is that my father killed Billy Navarro because my mother was having an affair with Billy."

Lanie looked carefully at Felix. The television flickered behind her.

"You must really trust me, to tell me that," Lanie said. "'Cause that's a whole lot bigger than juicy."

"I had to tell somebody."

She came back to the bed and sat down facing the window. She shivered, looked over her shoulder at Felix. He hadn't moved in minutes.

"You want me to dig up background on Sharpman?"

"Why?" Felix asked.

"Stupid—because nobody tells anybody a story like that unless they owe somebody something."

"Oh," Felix said. "Oh, of course."

"Does it hurt?"

"I suspected something, not that—but something. But Sharpman—if he's acting on orders like you say, then that's not the whole story. It can't be."

"It may even be that he told a story that's completely wrong," Lanie said softly.

"Thank you. I wish it didn't fit as well as it does."

Felix pulled her close, slipped his arms around her. He was a lot bigger than she was and he felt like he held her well. And regardless of how upset he was about everything, he was having a difficult time keeping his hands off her. He thought that maybe if he kept his eyes open the ugly visions of his father with a grin that looked like vengeful murder wouldn't crowd in. If he kept his eyes open he wouldn't have to imagine what his parents might have been, and in turn, he wouldn't have to reckon with the fact that if they'd done those things, then inside, he might be capable of them as well.

Lanie said, "I'll check around, see who floats Sharpman's boat."

"Boat?"

"Oh, I know why I'm thinking of boats. You're not going to believe who's hosting tomorrow night's underground party."

"Surprise me," Felix said.

"Gus Moravia and Lem Dawes."

"I'm not surprised," Felix said.

"Lem leased some old tugboat and he's invited five hundred people, but where it'll dock is a secret. He's going to send out a message to everybody's pager at ten."

"Are you going?"

"Of course I'm going," Lanie said. "Even though I'm eighty-sixed from Cheng's clubs, I'm still allowed to go to an outlaw party. Otherwise who would write about it? Richard Johnson? That dog can't dance."

"But you can," Felix said. He sighed, but he found that he was tickling her and then he wouldn't let her go. And then, there in the hotel room, in the dark, among satin sheets and spilled beer, the muted television flickering reports of new skirmishes between India and Pakistan, Iraq and the United States, Felix put his own problems away and focused on the girl in front of him. They pulled each other closer and within a few minutes, nobody was thinking straight.

24

Edwige wasn't in her room when Soraya got there, in the late afternoon on Wednesday. So Soraya walked fast across the street to Columbia's campus. A minute earlier, she'd run into Edwige's friend Maceo on the street, and he'd said that Edwige had been kidnapped by some oaf from the men's water polo team. So Soraya knew what she was looking for.

She came through Columbia's main gate. Edwige was on the Low Library steps with an oversized boy. Soraya remembered that they both had their History of Narcissism class with Tara Barahmpour, one of Edward Said's top acolytes, together in half an hour. A class, Soraya decided ruefully, that she was far too occupied with her own business to attend. Meanwhile, the cell in her hand was ringing. While she walked, she took a call from Felix.

"We need to talk," Felix said. "I'm driving up there now."

"I'm almost ready for you," Soraya said.

Felix said, "What I've got to tell you isn't light."

"Nothing you say ever is. Meet me in front of Italian House—Amsterdam and 118th."

"Done," Felix said. He hung up. Soraya approached Edwige, who was dressed in a brand-new Columbia hooded sweatshirt, a skirt made of yellow and gold thread, and black leather flip-flops. Edwige looked up and smiled. There were purple flowers in her dreadlocks.

Edwige said, "I've been kidnapped by a boy from Iowa. He's on the water polo team. Isn't that exotic?"

Soraya looked at the boy. He was very broad and he had wavy hair that was the color of Edwige's skirt. He smiled up at her and his blue eyes glinted in the sun. He looked more than perfect. It was as if he'd just become animate, as if he'd been sculpted by sand and water and a thousand years.

"I'm Bill," said the boy. Unfortunately his voice had a nasal midwestern twang.

"Bill," Soraya said. "Can I borrow Edwige for just a few minutes?"

Bill turned to Edwige. He put a hand the size of a frying pan around the back of her neck and kissed her. She made cooing noises.

"Promise me that I'll see you again," Bill said.

"I promise," Edwige said. She imitated his accent, dragged out "promise," and laughed. Bill kissed her again. Then he stood up and leaped forward about a dozen steps, took an additional bound, and landed on the grass on the other side of the path.

The girls looked after him.

"Fucking Superman," Soraya said.

"That's about the size of it," Edwige said. "What's up?"

"Look, Edwige, I've got to ask you some stuff that might be uncomfortable for you."

"About Bill? That's impossible," Edwige said. "It's been one of the most comfortable experiences of my young life."

"Not about Bill. Let's walk."

They went into Saint Paul's, the little brick chapel next to Low Library. It was warm in there, and the light was low. They sat down in a pew near the back. In the front pews, several students were praying. Edwige looked up at the altar. An organ lesson was going on, and low notes spewed out at random, long and then short. There were several notes in succession, the introduction of a Bach fugue, and then silence.

"Spooky," Edwige said. "Okay, I'm solemn. What's up?"

"Well, about Dr. Biddle—"

"Booby?"

"Yeah, why do you call him that?"

"He's my godfather. Maybe he looks kind of creepy, but I've known him since I was born. He and my father were at school together. This school, actually."

"Did they know a man named Franklin Novak?"

"I don't know—I never heard of that person," Edwige said. She threw her hood over her head and peeked out of it, made her mouth puckered and small. "Look," she said, "I'm like a nun."

"What about Ellie . . . Furst?"

"Oh yeah, Ellie Furst. She went here, too. Booby had a crush on her. He used to complain to me about it when I was like, eight. He was weird."

"What'd he say?" Soraya asked. She put her fingertips on the wooden pew in front of her, drummed lightly.

"That Ellie married some mean little Jewish cop from Brooklyn."

"Did he ever . . . do anything about it?"

"The crush? No, he was married for a while, but now he dates models. Girls our age. All those rich doctors do that. He told me he slept with Liv Tyler."

"My boyfriend, Gus, says Dr. Biddle was the one who helped him kick cocaine a few years ago."

"Yeah," Edwige said. "He's amazing that way. He's helped so many people."

"But this is the same Dr. Biddle who hooks you up with Oxy."

"Well, it's not quite like that, Soraya," Edwige said. Her voice grew defensive. "I'm very stressed. What are you trying to figure out, anyway?"

"Just—I think I know that cop from Brooklyn, that's all."

"The one Ellie married? My dad always wanted to make a movie of that guy's life, but the cop wouldn't have it. He's not above vigilante justice is what my dad said. But then a long while back, I heard everything went bad for him. He took the blame for something and it never was totally clear if he was guilty. That's what my father said."

"My father's death was the something," Soraya said. "I knew that blaming Franklin was too easy. I just knew it." She dropped her head back and looked at the arched ceiling. She turned and saw Edwige staring at her, confused.

"The cop from Brooklyn. He took the blame for my father's death. They were partners."

"Oh, Soraya—I'm sorry."

"No, it's like, I'm not dealing with that part now. The thing I don't get, though, is about Ellie Furst and Biddle. Did they ever go out?"

"I don't think so—'cause you know Booby's not that hot, even though he's rich now. Back then he was just like—I imagine he was repulsive. Anyway, he wasn't even called Biddle. He was Morton Meyrink."

"He changed his name?"

"Yeah, my dad wanted to make a movie about that, too. Morton Meyrink to Marsden Biddle. But nobody'd fund it. Nobody thought the story was special enough. Biddle's some old writer and Booby liked his book, so he took his name."

"Just like that?"

"I guess. Let's get out of here, Soraya. Really, you're starting to creep me out."

Edwige got up and strode quickly out of the church. She pushed the hood off her head and shook out her locks. Soraya followed her and realized that Felix was probably waiting for her over at Italian House. Edwige headed toward Hamilton Hall.

"You coming to class?" Edwige called.

"No, I've got to work this thing out," Soraya said.

"Hey, is all this why you got me to send you to Booby?"

"Are you angry at me?" Soraya asked.

Edwige frowned. But then she broke into a smile and shook her head. She hugged Soraya.

"Not really," Edwige said. "But damn! You are one sneaky bitch. I get into a bad place, I want you on my side. Find me later—before the party on the tug."

Soraya found Felix idling in the Roadrunner, sunglasses on. He was slumped low in the seat, his hands over his mouth like he was fighting for breath.

"Where do you want to go?" Soraya said when she'd gotten in on the passenger side.

"Out of this town," Felix said. "The fastest way."

"Let's drive up to the suburbs. We'll go up to one of those little towns, Nyack, maybe, walk around in a park."

She turned then and reached for his cowboy hat in the backseat, but he looked over, and she dropped her hand, sat looking forward. She wondered what he knew about his mother's past. She imagined it was very little.

He punched up Johnny Cash on the iPod. *I walk the line.* They drove over to the West Side Highway and Felix opened up the engine till it was roaring. Soraya dropped her head back and closed her eyes, let all the noise wash over her. She tried to think about what Edwige had said. *He took the blame for something and it never was clear that he was guilty.* She played that part through in her head. It fit. And she'd never even thought of it before.

Felix looked over at her. The end of a toothpick showed at the right corner of his mouth. His eyes were tired, with that same wash of purple underneath that his father had. It made him look a little beaten, a little wise, and just a bit too handsome.

"You warm enough?" Felix asked.

She wore jeans and her Adidas yoga shoes and a white button-down shirt—the clothes she'd thoughtlessly thrown on when she'd planned to go to class.

"Grab my jacket," he said. And then she did turn around and slip his white windbreaker over her shoulders. It was the first thing she'd seen him in—she nestled her head in it and thought it felt like what his life on the farm must be like, thick and grassy and muddy.

They drove in silence for a few minutes. There were boats out on the Hudson and the sun was high. Light glinted off the front of the Roadrunner. They had the windows rolled down and the wind blew the air inside the car clear, so it was just the music and the two of them, heavy with what they had to say. But the day was good, Felix thought, and it seemed wrong to disrespect it.

"Let's take this bridge," Felix said. He veered onto the George Washington Bridge and they raced over it, blew away the light midday traffic. Then, on the other side, Felix ran the car around to some high cliffs that overlooked the river and, far down and to their right, the city. The water made everything glint blue. When they parked, they were quiet for a moment, watching. There was nobody else around. They got out and sat on a bench. The drop in front of them was hundreds of feet and they didn't look over it.

Felix said, "A cop told me a story last night, about what happened twelve years ago. It doesn't jibe with what we've been thinking. This cop, he believes Franklin set Billy up to be killed because Billy was having an affair with my mother."

"No," Soraya said. Her voice was low. "I don't want to hear that."

"I don't like it," Felix said. "But if it is that way, then he's a whole lot worse than a coward. And it makes sense that that's why my mother ran and kept us away from him. Maybe my sister found out or something—"

"It doesn't have to tie in to why she died," Soraya said quickly. "These things, they don't have to be connected."

"That's true. But it's because of her dying, that's why I feel like I'm being pushed to discover what happened back then."

And Soraya saw no point in mentioning what she'd heard from Edwige. It didn't matter what Sidney Jamison thought. He was a movie director—a dreamer who wouldn't be concerned with the facts. And this did feel more like the truth. It would be why her mother never spoke about Billy, why she'd tried to erase her husband's memory.

"Lord," Soraya said. "And we've been so close to him."

"To Franklin? Only because we had to. For Penelope."

"You think it's the truth, then, this horrible thing?"

"I don't know," Felix said. He broke the toothpick neatly in half and slipped the pieces into his jeans pocket.

"What's next?" Soraya asked.

"He's been leaving me messages all day. He's been watching Udris and now he thinks that Penelope was helping Udris distribute drugs he's been getting from Lem Dawes, that somewhere in between them, she went down. He thinks Udris and Dawes were the people with her when she died. He's going after them, and he'll find out who was lying."

"But somebody's lying about the past, too, maybe him, maybe somebody else."

"Hard to say," Felix said.

They walked back to the car.

"Do you believe that your mother could have been with my father that way?" Soraya asked. She'd never imagined such a thing before. She couldn't attach the words to pictures, couldn't really envision what they meant.

"I can't imagine it," Felix said. "But then, I thought I'd never talk to my father again, and I did that."

"Wait," Soraya said before they got into the car. "If all of this is true, shouldn't you and I be sworn enemies?"

"Let's pray it isn't true, then," Felix said. "Because I can't lose any more people. We may not get along so easy, but I'd die before I'd be your enemy."

Soraya inclined her head toward him and smiled.

"Did you check out who gave you the information? Because that matters a lot."

"I'm checking on it," Felix said. He thought of Lanie, realized that he needed to call her.

"And we have to see Franklin," Soraya said. "Now."

"Not together. He'll fight and tell us nothing if we do it that way. I want to talk to him alone. I just had to see you first."

"How do you know he'd tell us nothing?"

"I know he'd clam up," Felix said. "Because I would."

Felix paid the toll and they drove back over the bridge. He drove slower and hit random on the iPod, found an old Roger Miller song, "Little Green Apples."

Soraya said, "This car is really starting to charm me. It didn't at first."

"It's the color," Felix said. "Plum Crazy. Just like that fucking Oxy, it sneaks up on you."

Ellie Novak walked through the metal detector at PDX Airport, outside of Portland. Several beeps sounded in succession, and a young security guard with no eyebrows, a crew cut, and a nylon blazer waved her over. She sighed and began to empty her pockets.

In half an hour, she planned to catch a flight to Kennedy. She was in a midnight blue Armani pants suit that she'd worn to the last party she'd been to in New York, back in '91. It wasn't in fashion, but it didn't look ridiculous, either—just old. She'd thrown a brown Woolrich coat over it and she'd brushed her hair back so it was smooth. No makeup, though. She'd tried, looked hard at the lines in her face in the shadowy old mirror she'd propped above the sink in her bathroom back at the house. But it'd been too long—she wasn't even sure where to start, didn't know whether she ought to wear the same burnt umber Estée Lauder lipstick that she wore back then, whether the Kiehl's products she'd buried in the linen closet behind the big white bottles of horse shampoo were even any good anymore.

She had Felix's cell phone number and she had called him several times, but he hadn't answered. Still, she knew it was time to go back. She knew that places never left you, that to stay away from your past forever was an impossible thing.

She dropped her wallet and change into the pink plastic bucket.

"There must be something else that's tripping the alarm," the guard said.

"Oh, maybe this?" she asked. She pulled her keys from the pocket of her coat. She'd used a length of leather cord to attach them to a four-and-a-half-inch folding buck knife.

"You can't take that on the plane," the guard said.

She stared at the guard, fought back the impulse to tell him that she'd chased bigger men than him off her property with no weapon at all, much less her trusty buck.

"We don't allow any sort of sharp object on planes, ma'am, not even nail clippers. It's been that way for more than a year and a half now."

"Well, I'm sorry," Ellie said as she slipped the knife off the cord. "It's been a long time since I was on a plane. Keep it. Give it to your little sister."

The security guard looked down at the big oily knife in his palm.

"Leave us your address," he said. "We'll send it to you."

25

Soraya rode the subway downtown. She switched at Times Square to the One and took it to Franklin Street, to the Official. She chewed on a Cloret and willed the subway to hurry up, which it wouldn't do. She had to meet Gus at Sanction so they could eat dinner together, even though neither of them had time to see each other, much less eat, because Soraya had work to do and Gus had to help Lem prep for the outlaw party later.

Soraya kept picking through what she'd discussed with Felix, trying to make it jibe with things her mother had said over the years, but her mother had been extremely thorough. She'd lived a truly ascetic life since Billy had died, and she'd never talked to her daughter about her father. Once, back in high school when she still went to Saint Valentine's on Sundays with her mother, Soraya had joked that it was as if she wanted Soraya to be a product of immaculate conception. And Nancy Navarro had cocked her head to one side and frowned, eyes opened wide, as if to say, That's a pretty good idea. So now Soraya knew where her mother got some of her mannerisms, but nothing about her father. Still . . . if he'd had that kind of affair and had so deeply betrayed Nancy's trust—that would have been enough to make her erase him. Sure. That was enough.

A man sat across from her, his legs spread wide so that the people on either side of him looked like they were stuck to him, when really, he was pushing himself against them. He was in a Rocafella jean jacket and sweatpants. The man angled forward until his forehead was only a couple of feet from Soraya's knees.

"You fine," he said. He dragged the words out. She bent forward, and he came even with her. He wasn't bad looking, but he smelled of Tommy Hilfiger and she hated scent on a man. Why would a man put another man's smell on him? It was stupid. She never used perfume.

"Thank you," she said. "Now back up off me. I'm thinking."

If Gus ever betrayed her like that, she realized, she'd cut him out like a cancer, just like her mother had with Billy. And then she saw how

Gus was like Billy, how they were both cowboys, living too close to the edgy place where misunderstanding blows up big.

But Gus had never done her wrong yet. And she believed their love was strong.

She sat on the same side of a booth as Gus. They picked through a plate of grilled octopus and marinated vegetables. They drank a bottle of Rioja that Gus had come to favor. He was going on about the night, about how much money they were going to make with five hundred people attending, at fifty bucks to get on the boat and drinks at ten dollars a shot, discounting those people who were stamped for open bar, which basically meant Lem Dawes's fifty best friends.

"But they make up for it in other ways," Gus said. He had one arm draped around Soraya.

"Tell me about Lem," she said.

"Again about Lem? I don't know about Lem—he doesn't tell me what he's up to, but he brings in his friends and their money, even though they don't hardly spend any, and then the people from outside the city come to be near Lem and his people—because Lem's crowd is beautiful and the people who love to watch them bring in the real money. Then—I dunno, there's some magic in there when it works exactly right, when there's just the right mix of those who come to be looked at and those who like to look, and they're all annihilating themselves on my alcohol. I can't explain it any better than that." Gus shrugged. He took a sip of his wine and his left leg jiggled. Soraya put her hand on his thigh until he was still.

"Magic and money," Soraya said.

Gus nodded at her. His eyes were unusually bright and clear, the black irises dilated until they looked like drops of ink. She thought he was impossibly cute, like some crazy-handsome Mickey Mouse. But like him, the problem was that his impish smile made him damn near impossible to read.

"Still no drugs for you?" Soraya asked.

"Soraya, baby, it's the magic trick that gets me now. I don't even drink this wine except for the taste. I told you about my mom, and I admitted that thing to you about kicking. I don't know how much more honest I could be with you," Gus said. "You'd be clean, too, you saw your mom die from that shit. . . . Sorry. I know it wasn't so different with your dad. Look, I need you to trust me 'cause with everybody else I'm all business."

"I don't know how much more honest you could be, either," Soraya said. "And I'm getting so I don't think I should test you anymore."

She sighed. She was looking at his eyes. She was so close to him in the booth, her breasts pressed up against his chest, her forehead against his neck. He pulled her closer, kissed her.

He said, "But don't think the drugs and all that aren't close. They have to be. You know that. I'm not saying it's right, but it's part of the magic."

"Why?" Soraya asked.

"I don't know why," Gus said. "It just is that way."

Then Soraya saw Lem move through the lounge, with his head down. He was moving toward Kashmira, who was working the bar. Gus got free of Soraya then and waved. Lem nodded at him, mouthed, See you on the pier.

"Hey," Soraya said. "Did you check with the night manager about who paid for the room where they found Penelope?"

"I did," Gus said. "He promised he'd get back to me later tonight."

Felix sat down across from his father at Zitto's.

"You look nice," Franklin said.

Richard brought out wine and a plate of stuffed mushrooms. Franklin popped one in his mouth and watched Felix, who only nodded slightly. Felix was being careful with his movements, rationing himself, because there was so much to say. He'd been back to the Official and he'd showered and shaved carefully. He'd washed and brushed his hair and had his black suit cleaned and his white shirt washed. Over the past two days he'd broken in his shoulder holster and now he'd begun to forget that the Thompson was even there, and he knew that was how it should be.

"I thought you preferred Elaine's," Felix said.

"That's for one kind of business, this is for another," Franklin said. He rubbed at his forehead, pushed the thick flesh up and down an inch or two. He wore a blue suit and a blue-and-white-checked shirt. The dark colors did nothing but underline the faint purple under his eyes and the frown lines that were etched right down to his jaw.

"You got a story. You wanted to see me. Let's hear it," Franklin said. Felix could hear his father's short breathing.

"You know Mike Sharpman."

"We put in the call to him about the phone records, yeah. He hasn't called back. So?"

"I had a drink with him yesterday. He said he got my number from you."

"Yeah? He's a liar—what he has is a scanner. You must've been on that phone I gave you and he listened to the call. He's a shit."

"Sorry," Felix said. "I should've suspected."

"You'll learn. Was that when I was trying to get you to tail that fucking Udris character? He's distributing through Lem Dawes, if you can believe that. What's bothering me now is where does Lem get his supply? From the doctor? How hard is it going to be to prove that? And how much of this is mandated by that fucking Terry Cheng character and his boy Gus? And I don't give a shit about any of this except for how it explains the thing with Penelope. And this sickens me, understand that? Which of these four did she annoy?"

"I'm not sure, either," Felix said.

"Usually I can feel an answer pretty easily. Or one of these dickheads will do an unconscious reveal. But because it was her, it's fucking me up. I'll admit that to you."

Franklin sipped his wine. He watched his son and Felix could see that he was looking for him to help—Franklin believed that maybe Felix knew where to look for the reveal.

"There's a party on this boat tonight," Felix said.

"Yeah, that's gonna help. We got a guy on the harbor unit who will let my team ride along. Of course I can't go on the party boat 'cause I might do the wrong thing. But we can pull these guys on the cop boat and then I'll get my answers."

"About Sharpman—" Felix said.

"What about him? A career shit, that's what he is. I wouldn't trust him with a bag of air."

"So," Felix said. He fought for words. He felt the long-ago past fighting for attention, complicating the pain that was Penelope's murder and his ability to look at his father.

"So, come on, what about Sharpman?" Franklin said. He finished the mushrooms and Richard took the plate away.

"Talk," Franklin said.

Richard looked back in surprise. Franklin shook his head at him. "Not you."

Felix leaned in, spoke quickly. "He told me you killed Billy, had him killed, whatever."

"Ah," Franklin said. He rolled his neck and Felix heard the clicks in the older man's spine. Felix's hands were damp right up to his fingertips and he put them down at his sides, stared at his father. He thought, Please, I need you to tell me a better story.

But Felix said, "Sharpman said some drug dealer came out blasting and you said, 'Not me, him.' And then you ran."

Franklin shook his head. "That's the thing about burying an inquiry," he said. "You can't unbury it so easy. So somebody makes up a story, it's easy to believe."

"It didn't happen that way?" Felix asked. He knew how he sounded. Please tell me anything else. Let me believe in you again.

"I said that, yeah. But who did I say it to? I said it to Billy, who was pointing the .38 at me. I don't know if he was going to fire. But then he got shot and he swung on Kenny Price. That's what happened. I was shocked, and then those two, they used up their clips on each other. If I hadn't fallen backward on my ass while I was trying to pull out my gun, I would've taken a bullet from that fucking Kenny Price right in my gut. I was into carrying a magnum back then and it got caught up in my coat. So because I was stupid, I tripped and fell in the gutter. The only time I've ever been lucky."

"That's a different story," Felix said.

"It's my story," Franklin said. "And it's the truth."

Richard came then and put steak in front of both of them. He muttered, "Rare," and walked away. They began to eat in silence. Richard came back with more food, a plate of shiny green broccoli rabe and another of small yellow potatoes, sliced in quarters and sprinkled with fresh oregano. The restaurant had begun to fill, and the noise level went up. Felix watched the muscles in his father's jaw and temples as he chewed. There was no way the man in front of him had killed his partner. He believed that.

"Sharpman say why I'd want to do that to Billy?" Franklin asked, with his mouth full.

"About Mom and Billy Navarro? Yeah."

Franklin didn't pick up his head. He shoveled in a big piece of steak.

"That part's the truth," Franklin said.

"It's terrible," Felix said, and he hoped he only sounded young. He wasn't able to really ask why Billy was killed if Franklin didn't do it. Not yet.

"It's not terrific, that's for sure. Lot of betrayal in there. Years of trust ended up meaning about as much as blood spilled in the gutter. I hope you never get betrayed like that."

"I already did get betrayed like that," Felix said. "A couple of days after it happened. Me and my little sister got played."

Franklin looked up, swallowed. Felix stared at him.

Franklin nodded. "Look, there's no reason to tell Soraya this thing about her father. Better she thinks I'm the coward who ran, you see? Easier that way. This is—I made an agreement with her mother about this, a long time ago. I was never sure that Billy was going to shoot me, and she needed the pension."

"Okay," Felix said. "Except she's more than halfway to knowing the truth. And she already doesn't think you're a coward. There's another thing. Billy tries to shoot at you, and the dealer only shoots at Billy. Why is that? Why doesn't he try to take you both out?"

Franklin looked at his son. Felix nodded, waiting for a response.

So Franklin began to talk. "When they were done fixing the inquiry, I went down to Florida for some years. You know that. I looked around for people who knew Kenny Price and it turned out he was for hire, for gun work, that the drug sales were more or less ancillary to what he considered his profession. But I don't know. I never could figure out who paid him to kill Billy—or if that's even true. There was one way it might've gone down, though, that I figured out. Kenny came out and saw that Billy was going to shoot me. So Kenny waited a beat and figured he'd shoot Billy when he was done with me. Both of us would be dead. But I said what I said and Billy had second thoughts. Both of us were supposed to die, but it got fucked up and the wrong guy came out alive. I swear, every time people plan that kind of shit it never goes right."

"So in the end somebody paid the dealer to kill Billy and you never found out why?"

Richard took their plates then and delivered the bill, which came on a flat silver plate. Franklin didn't look at it. He signed it with a black pen he took from inside his coat, slipped a twenty-dollar bill on top. Then he put the bill on the empty table to their left. He slipped a Bully between his lips and let it dangle there, rubbed his thick neck.

"That's the story that Nancy Navarro and I agreed on. But you're right," Franklin said. "I never did find out the real answer."

"You're okay with that? That you don't know the truth."

"When men are killed, you can never be sure of the why."

"Doesn't that bother you?"

"We'll go to court sometime, watch the lawyers do their tricks. You'll see. Motive is always impossible to prove. That somebody did something, yeah, you can prove that. Why is another thing."

"An impossible thing?"

"Often enough," Franklin said. He breathed heavily. "Didn't think I'd be saying all of that tonight." He stood up then, brushed the crumbs off his jacket front. He nodded at Richard. Felix stood up more slowly. He stared across at his father, who was looking down at his hands. Franklin took a cloth napkin off the table and patted his hands down, ran the thing over his head.

Felix shook his head, said, "'Not me, him.'"

"Imagine saying that and then tripping backward, falling off a curb and then figuring out, in about one second, that anything but running would've destroyed even more lives."

"Quite an agreement."

"I thought your mother'd eventually figure it out."

"I guess she didn't."

"No, and that may have been for the best, too. But you did," Franklin said. "And I've been watching you tonight. Things have changed. Now you can look me in the eye."

And then he stepped forward into the restaurant aisle and hugged Felix hard. Felix was surprised for a second, his hands at his sides, but then he was snuffling, and a big sob came up. He hugged his father back. For a moment the crowd around them looked up and the echo of voices dying down in unison came over the room. Then the people went back to their dinners and Franklin let his son go.

"You want to ride with us later?" Franklin asked.

"Yeah," Felix said. "I do. You know the other thing I don't know is who would want Sharpman to tell me that story."

"Oh," Franklin said. "That could be anybody. I've got a ton of enemies."

Felix stared at his father. Franklin didn't even sound interested in that part. Or, Felix realized, when he saw that his father was suddenly not meeting his gaze, his father knew, and he just didn't want to say. He was intuitively protective, Felix realized. That was what he'd been doing for years—protecting people from too much hurt: Felix and Pen out in Oregon, and Nancy and Soraya here. And he looked away when he felt like he had to protect somebody. His benevolence and suffering were nothing to celebrate. But Felix wondered if it wouldn't be a good thing to learn that kind of behavior from his father, to go back to how he was when he was ten and wanted to be just like him. He smiled to himself. *Not quite.*

"In a couple of hours we'll talk and figure out a place to pick you up," Franklin said. He walked west on 33rd Street, away from his son.

Franklin wriggled out of his suit jacket and threw it over the wooden chair that faced his desk. He dialed Starling Furst's office with the hand that he wasn't using to rub down the ache in his temples. He took a deep breath and smelled something sweet, but he wasn't sure what it was. The phone rang. It was past nine, but Starling was there.

"You told Sharpman to talk to Felix?"

"I thought the boy should know before he went any further with you."

Franklin nodded to himself.

"Tell me about what happened to Penelope," he said. "Tell me or I'll come there and I'll beat it out of you."

There was silence followed by a snort from Starling. Franklin said nothing, waited.

Starling said, "She came to me and said she had a drug habit and she was desperate to get clean. She didn't mention you and neither did I. So I sent her to Marsden Biddle. We discussed this. I assure you, I can vouch for him."

"Do I know this doctor?"

"How should I know?"

Franklin stared straight ahead. And he wondered, What will it be like to deal with the real pain of Penelope's death? So far he'd only indulged in anger, but he knew that compared to the howling pain that would come, this anger meant little. It was a stinging slap, dust blown in the eyes, nothing more.

Starling said, "Biddle only saw her twice. I know because I paid the bill."

"I want to talk to the doctor."

"Call his assistant."

Franklin sniffed deeper. He sensed something sweet and he knew the smell wasn't him. He spun left and looked at the file cabinet. He got up and grabbed a bag of chocolate chip cookies that Gennardi must've brought in, that Lisa and Diane had made at home. Franklin ate one. It was a little burnt, so it was harder than he would've liked. He spoke with his mouth full.

"Why did you do it, Starling? What do you care about how I get along with my son?"

"Isn't that what you did to me, with Ellie?"

"Destroyed your relationship with her? No." Franklin smiled into the phone. "I never said a word about you. You've got a problem with her, why don't you ask her about it?"

"Don't tell me what to do."

"You know what? I'm not going to bother you anymore. When you find out how badly you fucked this up, you'll call me begging for forgiveness and I won't answer your call. Then you're going to beat your own head open and I suggest you have a look in a mirror, 'cause you'll see the evil rot that's taken over your brain."

Franklin hung up and ate a few more of the cookies. They were pretty damn good, once he got through the burned parts. Lisa had drawn a purple cookie monster on the paper bag with an arrow connected to a line that said *Franklin* in black letters. He figured he'd flatten out the bag and put it on the brick wall behind his desk in a carved mahogany frame, right where a diploma might go.

Starling Furst gave himself one minute. He looked at the bright evening lights that were spread out beneath his office window but found, as he always did, that the city offered him no solace. He imagined how good it would feel to go over his present position with a friend, but he had no friends. The next morning's *Spectator* lay on his desk. The headline: HILTON SISTERS GO WILD, KIDNAP PARENTS.

Why do we even have children, he wondered. His answer was a piece of philosophy born of the grizzled bitterness and fury that he'd been holding on to for fifty years: Because we think they'll help us to know ourselves and we're wrong.

He called Marsden Biddle's mobile phone.

"What is it?" Biddle said. In the background, wherever Biddle was, Starling could hear no noise at all.

"Meet me tomorrow morning for breakfast, won't you?" Starling asked.

"The University Club," Biddle said.

"Seven A.M.," Starling said.

"What's this about?"

"I'd like to make sure my retention of what you have and have not done is accurate, that's all. In case of investigation."

Biddle sighed. "See you then," he said.

26

Philip and Franklin went up to Elaine's to pick up Gennardi, who was finishing a meeting with Leon Edelstein. When they pulled up, Franklin looked through the front window and saw Gennardi standing at the bar with Edelstein. Franklin called Gennardi on his mobile.

"He wants to see you," Gennardi said.

"Tell him next week," Franklin said. "Tell him he wouldn't want to be seen with me tonight 'cause we're going to go kill somebody later and he'd end up in court as my alibi and he doesn't want that publicity."

Gennardi chuckled and Franklin heard him say, "You'll love this," to Leon over the bar noise.

Franklin said, "Tell him and then get the hell out here."

Gennardi came out a minute later, with a tray of Bushmills and sodas in go cups. He wore a black leather coat and a black turtleneck. He handed the drinks around and settled himself in the back of the van.

"Elaine sends her love," he said. "Says she'd never make a go cup for anybody but toughs like us. Where's your boy?"

"We're meeting him down at Clarke's parking lot on Houston. We're not looking for proof on the drug thing; we don't care about that. That's on Bolanos—I talked to him and we're going to do a trade. We give him Lem Dawes and the Oxy connection and in return we get to ask a few questions before they take him in."

"That kid's going to be so scared he'll vomit pink rabbits," Gennardi said.

Franklin nodded, said, "He'll vomit black knapsacks."

"The soft white flesh of his victims," Philip said.

"Ick," Gennardi said. And then they drove in silence, cruised along behind a Mayflower moving van, down Second Avenue.

"Leon said he's interested in your diamond scheme," Gennardi said to Philip.

Franklin said, "You pitched him on the Zimbabwean 1459 swindle?"

Philip said, "I told him I could get him diamonds for cheap."

"Can you?"

"Sure," Philip said. "Cheaper than he can get on 47th Street, anyway. But this isn't the Zimbabwean mining swindle, not at all. That'll come later. He's got a mistress called Yolanda who likes expensive things, so I'm going to do the hookup. He's obsessed with her, but he doesn't want to leave his wife. So he's decided to give her all the outsized gifts he can because then the base of their relationship will become material and that'll ensure emotional distance on his part."

"You mean he's scared of love so he wants to treat her like a hooker," Gennardi said.

"Right. It's just like Franklin with—"

"Leave it," Franklin said. He reached down and opened the dig-out in the van's floor. Before he dropped his Glock inside, he eased the magazine out, checked again that it was full. He set the Glock on the pad in the hidden space.

"Either of you carrying?" He looked back at Gennardi, who shook his head. He almost never carried a gun.

"Why?" Philip asked.

"You know how the police get all high-horse when we carry."

Philip put one knee on the steering wheel. He opened his black silk blazer and slipped a Desert Eagle, a .44, from inside the waistband of his white pants. He handed it over to Franklin, who checked the magazine. The chrome finish on the stock shone beneath the streetlights.

"Pretty," Chris said.

"Thanks," Philip said. "Got it from a friend who actually did pull the Zimbabwean 1459."

"How much'd he make?" Chris asked.

"He's dead now," Philip said. "Hence my possession of his firearm."

They nodded quietly, and Franklin buried the gun in the dig-out. They came into Clarke's parking lot on Houston and the sleepy attendant did nothing but nod at the Econoline. They pulled up next to Felix, who was leaning against his Roadrunner. He wore his black suit and his cowboy hat cocked back on his head.

"No guns," Franklin said.

"Course not," Felix said as he locked his car. But when he moved to get into the van, Franklin reached through the open window and patted him down. He pushed at the Thompson under Felix's arm.

"Gimme," Franklin said. "We're going to be around cops."

"Oh," Felix said. "Okay, your plan, your rules."

Franklin reached for the gun.

"But my gun," Felix said, "goes in my car."

He slipped off the gun and went to put it back in the Roadrunner. Afterward, he smiled at his father and slid open the van's side door.

Franklin said, "Where's Soraya?"

"Probably already on the boat," Felix said. Inside the van, he shook hands with Gennardi and Philip.

"When we're in it, I want Gus," Felix said as they drove off. Nobody spoke. Philip tuned from 1010 WINS to 1240, the oldies station. Glen Campbell sang "Southern Nights." Philip sang along and then Gennardi did, too. They pulled up to the pier next to the ferry, parked behind a green dumpster. Gennardi pointed then, before they got out, and the rest of them looked down the block at a white van.

Franklin got out the Newcon binoculars. He watched for a moment.

"I can see them in their side-view mirror. Udris and Kringle. They're just hanging out, looks like they're doing nothing . . . smoking cigarettes, waiting."

"They don't want to be too early to the party," Gennardi said.

"They're a delivery service is what they are," Franklin said. "Where's the camera?"

"I got it," Philip said. He fitted the Newcons onto a digital camera and took several pictures of Udris and Kringle.

"Lay low," Franklin said. They crept out and slipped behind a Dumpster, and then they found themselves standing in a crowd of hundreds of people, all of them swaying quietly. They looked around. But there was no boat, just a big party down at the end of the pier, in between the Coast Guard station and the Staten Island Ferry.

"Just tons and tons of party people," Philip said.

"Guess they overextended the invitation," Gennardi said. The four men walked down toward the water, but instead of a boat, there was only a deejay playing Groove Armada and a bartender standing behind a table, quickly pouring out short glasses of Grey Goose vodka with a dash of orange juice and handing them across the table to grasping young hands. Franklin shouldered past a bouncer and got behind the bartender.

Franklin said, "Where's the host?"

But the bartender didn't have time to do more than shrug. There were dozens and dozens of people pressing up, asking for drinks. So Franklin went over to the deejay. He got his hand on the deejay's shoulder and yelled, "Where's the host?" through the man's headphones. The deejay turned around. He was a bald man with multicolored thunderbolt tattoos on both shoulders. But he had the eyes of an accountant.

The deejay glared for a second and then turned, pointed to a little dot of bouncing light out in the middle of the Hudson.

The deejay said, "They couldn't get the permit for the tugboat at the last minute, so they set us up. We'll do this for another hour or so, just till the police come, so it looks like we made an effort."

"No permit for the pier, either?" Franklin asked. He still had his hand on the deejay.

"I guess not. At least that's the story they told us," he said, frowning, and he put his headphones back on. More people were arriving, in cabs and on foot. A shiny black Denali showed up and several members of the Hollis Crew got out, followed by some bodyguards. Other brightly colored SUVs pulled up, too.

"Looks like there's going to be a party no matter what," Gennardi said. Franklin got on his mobile.

"Bolanos? Yeah, we're at the Whitehall Street terminal, dock A.

They're doing a deal in the water is what it looks like. Smoke screen on the pier so the guys at the First Precinct get confused. Come pick us up."

"Soraya's on that boat," Felix said.

"Take it easy," Franklin said. They stood at the edge of the pier. A dark blue NYPD harbor patrol boat approached from the north. It only had one light on and it nosed over to them. Leonardo Bolanos stood on the foredeck. He wore black jeans and a blue windbreaker.

"Evening, Franklin," he said. They bumped against the pier's black rubber sidewall and Leonardo held out his hand. The deejay turned around then, gave Leonardo a resigned, unhappy stare.

"I'd say you got thirty minutes before the First Precinct boys break it up," Bolanos yelled out. "They know about it, but it's a nice night and they figure you're bringing tourism downtown. So, you know, party on."

"Party on?" the deejay said, and laughed. He turned back to his tables.

"Ignore him. He's a cynical bastard," Franklin said as Bolanos pulled him onto the boat. Bolanos was taller than Franklin, but he had the same shaved head and sleep-deprived eyes. Bolanos was younger, too. Forty or so, and built with great slabs of muscle. Except for his Sperry Topsiders, he looked like any tough cop.

"You guys ready to play pirates?" he asked as Gennardi, Philip, and Felix got on board. Bolanos made a gesture to the cop in the pilot-house, and the patrol boat turned and sped off toward Dawes's boat. They gathered in the back of the boat. Then they could see the city, not a hundred yards away but already remote, the bright outlines of the downtown skyscrapers massed against the blue-paint sky.

"The plan is the same as the deal," Franklin said, and he looked mostly at Felix.

"We have to go on with them 'cause they've got a warrant. They pull off drugs, we get to ask questions of whoever we want. They find nothing, we go away. Understand?"

Felix nodded. Then he said, "There's a girl on board. Soraya Navarro. She's with us."

Gennardi turned to Bolanos, said, "Billy Navarro's daughter."

Bolanos smiled at Franklin. "I knew that sooner or later you'd make good on that nasty rap." Bolanos went up to direct the cop at the controls. Felix followed him. He leaned up against the safety rail and watched the cop at the wheel ease out the clutch and accelerate. They began to head due west. The patrol boat rumbled as they cut through the choppy water.

"Flip off the port light," Bolanos said. And then they were running in near darkness, with nothing but the lights from the console and the flashers on the gunwale.

"This thing runs on diesel, right?" Felix asked.

"Yeah," Bolanos said. "The engine's new, a Kohler 5E0Z. Lot of power for a thirty-footer, but we use most of it."

"Where'd you get it?"

"These guys out in Bayshore called MTS do all our engines. The shop foreman is my cousin, actually."

"Sweet," Felix said. "Listen, there's a guy we're going to pull off of there, a jumpy type with spiky hair called Gus Moravia. I want him for mine."

Bolanos smiled and nodded. He put a foot on the bench seat and cupped a cigarette, lit it. He tossed the match into the wind.

He said, "You're Franklin's son, right?"

"That's right."

"Well, this raid is a payback to Gennardi. I tolerate Franklin 'cause he took a storm of shit way back when, but he's not my man. You drag a guy into the cockpit if we catch him carrying, then yeah, bombs away and I could give a shit, but no special favors. Got it?"

"Even if Gus is the one who killed my sister?"

Bolanos puffed away. They were going at a steady clip and the *Dancing Bear* was only a few hundred feet away.

"That was an OD," Bolanos said carefully. "If it wasn't an OD, you can bet Franklin would've killed the guy by now."

"Okay," Felix said. "Fair enough."

"Looks like your boy's got a Dynasty Marblehead," Bolanos muttered. "Nice boat."

Felix went back down the steps. He twisted slightly and felt the Thompson. Instead of putting it back in his car, he'd slipped it out of the shoulder holster and down into his waistband. Now he fit it back into the holster. They came up alongside the *Dancing Bear.* The boat was quiet and the sails were rolled and covered. There was nobody outside. They came up within feet of the boat and still there was no response. Felix looked into the windows then and saw Lem Dawes sitting alone at a table, calmly counting out purple pills and slipping them into plastic baggies. It looked like he was working hard.

Felix felt the patrol boat's rub rail knock against the port side of the sailboat. Lem looked up and Felix jumped across, caught on a railing, and eased aft.

"Hey," Bolanos yelled. "Me first!"

"Hurry up!" Felix yelled. Felix spider-walked the sheer line and jumped from the foredeck, right at the door leading to the *Dancing Bear*'s cabin. He stepped in and disappeared. Then Philip climbed onto the side deck, grasped the handrail, and leaped onto the boat. Franklin followed him.

"Throw over a rope," Franklin called to Gennardi. But the cop who was driving had the rope. Gennardi hung back. The cop looked at him. "Can't swim," Gennardi said, and shrugged.

Everyone threw themselves through the cabin door and went in. Felix had his hands around Lem's throat. Lem was trying to pull him off.

"Are you alone?" Felix asked. Lem was nodding as much as he could.

On Lem's right there was a wall of dozens of stacked, quart-size containers of Purdue Pharma's OxyContin, in 80- and 160-mg tablets and capsules. The containers were plainly labeled. Lem had been emptying the pills into baggies and stuffing the full baggies into knapsacks.

"Wow," Bolanos said, and his voice was hushed. "I guess I owe you guys for the tip-off. That is one hell of a lot of drugs."

Felix picked up Lem and slammed him down on the table he'd been using, and hundreds of yellow and purple pills spilled off the table and onto the floor.

"Watch it," Bolanos said. "We need to account for all this. I gotta call for a tug. You guys, you get back on my boat. Take this guy with you. Cuff him on the other side, okay? And don't kill him just 'cause I'm busy over here on the radio. Do not kill him."

Felix couldn't seem to take his hands off Lem's throat.

"Seems that you're quite a bit more than a recreational user," Franklin said. "But I suppose I've no right to be surprised."

Franklin grabbed Lem's feet and they dragged him out of the cabin. Gennardi and the cop watched from the other deck. They'd tied the two boats together and now they were holding the sailboat close and waiting.

"Let's throw him over," Franklin said. "Gennardi, don't catch this guy unless we miss."

Dutifully, Gennardi and the cop got out of the way. Franklin and Felix threw Lem across. He landed with a thump and a mewling sound, more like a cat than a man.

"Get used to that noise," Felix said as he leaped across. Franklin clambered after him. When Gennardi caught Franklin, he wouldn't let go.

"Don't kill him," Bolanos yelled from the deck of the *Dancing Bear.* They watched as Lem scuttled across and stood in the corner of the cockpit.

"Let's begin where we left off, when I let you walk away," Franklin said. "Did you kill my daughter?"

"Are you kidding? If I killed her do you think I'd still even be in this country?" Lem asked. Franklin got closer, and Lem slowly slid to the ground.

Felix thought he sounded whiny, and it occurred to him rather suddenly that he didn't like the way he'd talked about his sister, as if there was even a chance that he *had* killed her. So he kicked him in the teeth. Lem's brazen frown turned into a red mess. He gathered up his white shirtfront and pressed his mouth against it. But the blood showed through like blossoming roses. Lem fell on his side and started crying.

Over their shoulder they heard Bolanos say, "We got one guy who needs to go to a hospital. He fell down, yeah. Slipped. We need a tug and we'll need an ambulance when we come in. Take us about fifteen minutes."

Franklin shook his head. "I cannot believe I let you walk."

"I know," Lem said, and he tried to smile through the blood. "I was headed to Cannes tomorrow because I knew when I saw you at Eden-Roc my clock was ticking. I was going to head into the pier and sell as many pills as I could tonight. I was going to live at the Crillon. Just now it's off-season there, so—"

"I don't give a *shit*," Franklin said. His lip was curled almost down to his jaw and his left eyebrow was raised halfway up his forehead. He swung his fist, slow, as if he didn't like the idea of hitting any man who was on the ground. But he connected. Then he raised his fist again so that Lem would understand that now was a good time for honesty.

"So now you got me. You got the stash. What do you want?" Lem asked.

"I asked you a question," Franklin said.

"I don't know anything about Penelope. I told you that last week."

Calmly, Felix slid the Thompson out of his shoulder holster. He brought the gun around, took off the safety, and aimed it at Lem's chest.

"Give me that," Franklin snapped. He took the gun and palmed it, the flat right side of it thick against his hand. He slammed it into the side of Lem's head and Lem made an aggravated noise, a "wauff," as he fell over on his side.

"Next time I let my son shoot you, got that?" Franklin said. He handed the gun back to Felix, who holstered it.

Franklin reached down then and grasped Lem's bloody jaw in his hand as if Lem were a horse and he was going to look at his teeth. Lem made a gurgling sound in his throat.

"Tell me how it went down," Franklin said. Lem's arms crept up and his fingers waved around.

"Make it good or you don't go back to shore," Franklin said.

"I'll tell you everything," Lem said. His voice had a guttural tinge, as if something was caught in his windpipe.

Lem said, "Max Udris killed Penelope. That's the truth. It's all because of Marsden Biddle, I swear. That guy was desperate for money and he had access to tons of Oxy through Purdue Pharma. But he didn't know how to distribute—all he knew on the street level were kids who had come to him over the years to kick heroin. So he figured he'd go through one of them, sell Oxy to some midlevel dealer who could go through to the street, see? So he comes to me, and I figured I'd be both midlevel and the street. I'd sell for him and get rich. But then Penelope shows up in his office and wants to kick—I don't know how she got there. He asks who her last dealer was and she says these stone guys, that when she got to town she was in a lot of pain and she got to them through this guy Jay and his friend Liza Pruitt, who she met at Eden-Roc—I guess they were all from the Northwest or whatever. So she connects Udris and Biddle and I get left out. They want her to carry between them because in New York, nobody's cleaner than she is. Only thing is, she didn't want to carry."

"And you did," Gennardi said. He had one arm firmly on Franklin, who was breathing slowly into his fist.

"That's right," Lem said. "And I've got this boat, which is . . . well, you know what it is. We let the Oxy sit here. But then Biddle, he decides he doesn't want to distribute just to Udris. He's in a rush and he wants to go to other dealers, make more money. Udris didn't think that was fair. And that's when Udris took out Penelope, back at the

Official. Nobody knew she was related to anybody with history in New York. At least I sure didn't."

"Udris killed her as a warning to Biddle," Gennardi said. "To keep the supply chain clean."

"I guess he figured out that she and Biddle were connected somehow and thought it'd matter to the doctor. Thought she was a rich girl and turns out he was right."

"What about Gus Moravia?" Felix asked. Bolanos had his hands on Felix and Felix was still struggling to get at Lem.

Franklin was leaning against the side of the boat. He was squinting at Lem and listening. When Felix asked about Gus, Franklin raised an eyebrow, but that was all.

Lem only looked more pale and confused. He said, "I don't know anything about Gus." He started to shake his head, fast.

"Terrence Cheng?" Gennardi asked.

"Him neither. Those guys run clubs—that's all I know. What they do is none of my business."

"He's more afraid of them than he is of Udris," Felix said.

Gennardi turned to Franklin and said, "Look, Franklin, I know what you're thinking. But I've got to do this so you don't kill them. I'm sorry."

"What're you going to do?" Franklin asked. His voice was level. He only sounded interested.

"You're going to hate me, but it's the only thing." Gennardi turned to Bolanos. "Call Lieutenant Pizzarelli at the First, tell him about a white Chevy van that's sitting at the top of the Whitehall Street pier, plate number EL818. It's got Udris and his buddy in it. They're wanted for murder and if they don't take them in within the next ten minutes, Franklin's going to kill them."

Gennardi looked at Franklin, who was still breathing through his fist.

"I know," Gennardi said, "I know."

Bolanos made the call, and the cop who was driving went up to the console and steadied the patrol boat against the *Dancing Bear.* In the distance, they could see an NYPD tugboat start to chug out toward them. Bolanos let Felix go then, and he walked to the other end of the cockpit, shook himself off.

"You keep whipping out that old piece, but you never get to use it," Franklin said to Felix. "You think these guys were going to let you shoot somebody on a police boat?"

"It's true," Bolanos said. "We would've had to arrest you."

"Thank goodness I kept my head," Felix said.

Franklin cocked his eye at his son. "You pulled that thing out so I'd smack him with it?"

Felix shrugged, smiled. He looked down at the Thompson. "You should've done it back at Eden-Roc. I never shot a gun in my life. You better take it back."

Franklin accepted the gun. He popped the magazine out of the grip and dropped it in the water. Then he tossed the gun over the other side. It disappeared into the black water of the harbor with hardly a sound.

"There's really no need to carry one unless you absolutely plan to kill somebody with it," Franklin said.

"I did," Felix said.

"No, you didn't," Franklin said. "You had a chance, you didn't take it. Just like when you first saw me." But he glanced at his son's face as he spoke. And Felix wasn't smiling. He was looking level at his father.

"You buy Lem's story?" Felix asked. He'd dropped his voice.

"It's a very good story," Franklin said. "It's got everybody in it but Lem. It implicates Udris and the doctor and confirms everything I suspected. But I don't know. You don't sit in a truck and wait to make drug deliveries if you murdered somebody. You might know who did it, but it wouldn't be you. Not that I'm sorry Gennardi put in that call, but I would've liked to see where Udris would lead us next."

Felix looked out at the water. He said, "You think the guys at the First will let us see Udris?"

"We'll see them in a courtroom at best," he said. "And I already explained what happens there. Still, Penelope sitting in a hotel room with those ugly mobsters, accepting pills that would kill her, without a struggle? Does that sit right with you? Let me put it another way: Did she like to get high with that particular brand of loser?"

"I doubt it. And the only time I ever talked to Udris he laughed in my face, like he had nothing to hide."

The tugboat honked at them and they bumped free of the *Dancing Bear.*

"It's not right," Franklin said. "These Russians with their brigades. They grow up quick in a couple of months and then they implode. But them bothering to send a message to a doctor—that I can't quite see. Though Lem sounded pretty sure."

"Fuck that little snake. He lied about Gus Moravia, too."

"You've really got a thing about Gus, don't you?" Franklin asked. "At least he and Soraya weren't on the boat."

"That's true," Felix said. "That's one good thing."

"And now we've got Lem Dawes. He's in custody until we figure out whether his story is right."

They looked back at Lem. He was still sitting on deck, handcuffed. He was staring across at the pier, where he would've made enough money to leave town. He didn't seem eager to come onto the pier and walk through the party looking the way he did, all handcuffed and bloody.

27

Soraya was reading Julia Kristeva in French, her head buried in the crook of her arm, in a carrel at the south end of the East Asian Library in Kent Hall, when she started to cry. It was Wednesday night, just past eleven. She'd remembered where and when she'd first seen Biddle, or Meyrink. It had been at her mother's house, the day after her father was killed. Franklin had spent those days in protective custody, mired in the beginnings of what would be an all too brief internal affairs investigation that had been smeared over the *Spectator*'s front page. Only a few people had been at the Navarros's house. Soraya's grandparents, her mother's sisters, and a few teacher friends from PS 87, Nancy's school. Soraya remembered standing at the front window, watching Ellie Novak drive her battered blue Volvo up the street and park. She came and rang the Navarros's doorbell. Nancy went to greet her, but she didn't invite her in.

"It's awful," Ellie said. She'd been crying. She was a beautiful woman, with long honey-colored hair that was naturally streaked with blond accents. Her nose and mouth were thin and soft. But her green-brown eyes were hard. Soraya remembered how amazed she'd been at Ellie's looks and how envious she'd felt of Penelope for inheriting them. She didn't feel that way anymore.

"I know about you and Billy," Nancy said. There had been reporters in front of the house, newscasters from WPIX and WRTZ, stringers from *Newsday* and the *Times,* and even somebody from UPI. So Nancy had had no choice but to pull Ellie into the house and then out through the back, into the little garden behind the kitchen. Soraya chased the two women through the rooms, but they'd closed the back door. A moment later, Ellie came out with her face set, and she went back through the house the way she'd come. This memory had always been present for Soraya, had always been baffling, until Felix had told her the story he'd heard. Still, it didn't fit. But what she remembered now was new—when Ellie came out to the street, that man, Morton Meyrink, had greeted her.

"You're free now," he'd said. He tried to embrace her, but she pushed him away.

Soraya thought, So there it was, the cold, shuddering feeling that she'd gotten when she was with him in his office.

"You don't know me at all," Ellie had said. "Leave me alone!" And she'd run to her car and disappeared.

Soraya stopped crying. She quickly packed her things and went out of the library. She called Felix's cell as she walked down to 113th Street, but he didn't pick up. And it was then, suddenly, there on the corner of 113th Street and Broadway, that Soraya remembered Felix and Penelope, sitting in the back of that Volvo at the end of Cleveland Place, staring out at her. Felix had been wearing a Yankees hat and he looked scared as he half waved at Soraya, wondering if she could give him answers. And even then, Penelope had looked like she was up to something, her blond hair messily framing her head, her fist balled up in the fabric of her dirty white T-shirt, which she chewed as she suspiciously watched her mother approach their car. Moments later Soraya was gathered up by her mother and carried into the living room and made to sit quietly with her aunts, who cried incessantly, as if they'd spent the last eight years married to Billy, too.

Soraya was desperate to talk to Felix, to go back through what she'd learned with him. There were pieces missing, but they could work together to find them. And she had to tell him about the doctor. She also had to get back to her room at McBain and leave her books, put something good on, and get herself down to the outlaw party on the tug. But she wanted to lie quiet, try to further absorb the way the horrible thing just might fit together.

She arrived in front of the dorm and went through her bag, looking for her ID card. And then she heard a voice behind her.

"Soraya?"

She turned around. It was Gus. He was getting out of the '78 black-on-red Cadillac he sometimes borrowed from Terrence Cheng. He was in khakis and a plaid shirt and New Balance sneakers, his hair tousled. He didn't look like the host of any outlaw party, that was for sure.

"Shouldn't you be down at the dock?" Soraya asked.

"No, Lem couldn't get a permit, or maybe he never had one. I don't know—I was so busy with Eden-Roc that I never really communicated with him. Anyway, the thing is canceled. It'll just be a bunch of people on a dock, waiting for Lem to—are you crying?"

"No," Soraya said. But she was.

"Let's go inside," he said. "There's something I've got to tell you."

They went into the dorm and down the bright, noisy hall and stepped into her room. Soraya dropped her bag and turned on the small light by her desk. She sat on the edge of her bed with her hands curled up in fists and tucked under her thighs.

"I'm ready," she said. "Tell it."

"Well, baby, it's like, this last week you've been so doubtful of me and I've been walking around feeling so weird about us and I just don't want to feel that way anymore. I feel like I should just come clean and hopefully we can still be together."

"Go ahead," she said. And then she already felt like she was walking away. Because once he admitted that he'd been dealing Oxy with Lem, through Udris, and that he'd been in the room with Penelope when she was killed, she knew she'd have to let her love die and tell the Novaks about what he'd done. And they'd kill him. Felix already wanted to. She wouldn't enjoy telling him he was right, but that didn't matter. It was only fair. But then she realized Gus hadn't even started yet and it could be even worse. She looked away. She covered her ears. Gently, Gus took her hands and held them.

"It's important for you to hear this," Gus said. He paused then before going on.

Gus said, "The reason I've been so edgy with you is that I cheated on you during those first weeks we were going out, last fall. I was with Kashmira. Baby, I'm really, really sorry. She feels awful about it, too, 'cause I'm in love with you and it was like, a stupid thing that we did 'cause I was fighting how intense this thing was going to be with you and she's like, nothing but a buddy of mine. Now we're in this mad fight 'cause she's dealing and she simply will not stop and she threatened to tell you about me and her. Fucking blackmail, you believe that? So now, I'm telling you. God, I can't believe I'm saying this."

She imagined that she was feeling something like the strong shock of relief. And then she was crying more and she said, "You never dealt drugs in your life, did you? Not Oxy, not anything?"

Gus stared at her. "No. I mean, me and Terry, we see things, but I've never been involved. But this cheating I did, it's been eating away at me."

"It was only the first few weeks?"

"Twice, actually, in the first month. But we were protected and everything. I can't believe I'm telling you this. I've never been so honest with anybody in my whole life. Why are you smiling?"

"Because you didn't kill anybody."

"So you forgive me?"

"Hell, no, I'm just grateful you didn't kill anybody, that's all."

Then she slapped him, hard. He took the slap, and then he asked her to explain about what she thought he was going to say. And she started to try.

Nancy Navarro opened the screen door and looked at Ellie Furst.

"Thank you for seeing me," Ellie said.

"Of course," Nancy said. She beckoned Ellie in and moved to hug her. Ellie briefly laid her hand on Nancy's back and then moved away from her. It was Wednesday evening, a little past ten. Ellie had taken a cab from the airport.

"I'm so sorry about Penelope," Nancy said. Ellie only flattened her lips over her teeth. She set down her brown canvas bag.

"I've aged," Ellie said. "I'm not who I was when I lived here. And I won't ever get over Pen's death. But it was important for me to see you and I'm grateful."

Nancy didn't speak. Ellie stood in the front foyer and looked at all the framed drawings that Nancy's students had made over the years. The wooden floors she stood on were worn down and no longer shone. Ellie looked around and nodded—her own house was so different, yet in some ways, she saw that as they'd aged, they'd begun to live similar lives.

"I know it's cool out, but let's go and sit in the garden," Nancy said. They walked through the quiet house, past the dining room and the kitchen, where there was a cutting board heaped high with newly washed mesclun and fresh scallions. They went into the garden, where they'd stood nearly a dozen years before. They sat down on iron chairs covered in flaking white paint. Ellie admired the dogwood trees that grew in the garden's back corners.

"I've been cowardly in choosing to never come back. I apologize for that," Ellie said. "And now, arriving at your doorstep when I'm in need. It's wrong."

"I'm the one who should be sorry," Nancy said. "Franklin and I made an agreement a long time ago. It wasn't right, but we did it, anyway. The agreement made me silent, when I might have reached out to you."

"You're in touch with Franklin?" Ellie asked.

"Yes. It was for my pension. If internal affairs found out that my husband tried to kill Franklin in order to be with you, they would have denied that he was killed in the line of duty. That would have left me humiliated and with no legal rights to his pension. When Billy died before he could shoot Franklin, well, Franklin agreed that maybe Billy hesitated, that he didn't have it in his heart to kill him when he had the chance. At least that's what Franklin told me. And Billy did kill that drug dealer after all. That was why Franklin had to shoulder the blame. It was the only honorable thing to do."

"But Nancy," Ellie said. "That's wrong. Franklin tried to kill Billy. He tried to have him assassinated. You know that."

"That's what you thought," Nancy said quietly. "And the police just thought he was a coward because of the tape. But it didn't happen that way. This was our agreement. Franklin didn't know about the affair until I told him. I knew about it nearly from the start, of course."

"And nobody told me any of this," Ellie said.

"You left. You had an affair with my husband and then you ran away. Why should anyone tell you anything?"

The two women were quiet for a moment. They listened to a plane roar overhead, headed east. Nancy shivered, but Ellie didn't move at all.

"But then . . . that drug dealer must have been aiming for Franklin. Why would someone want to kill Franklin? And why did Franklin say what he did?"

"'Not me, him,'" Nancy said. And her voice dropped to a whisper. "Ellie, Franklin said that to Billy. Billy was pointing his own gun at Franklin. Then he turned, saw that man aiming at Franklin, and he shot him. Though he'd meant to kill him, or he was trying to, Billy saved Franklin's life. I've never understood it. But yes, why would the dealer want only to kill Franklin?"

"Good Lord," Ellie said. "All this time I thought my husband had Billy murdered because of what we did."

"Yes," Nancy said. "You never contacted us. Franklin and I—we knew different, but once we saw how you saw it, how the world saw it, we played along. We made our agreement, and we went on with our lives. And you did, too. I never saw Franklin again, until this week."

Ellie dropped her head into her hands. "So I've lost my daughter and I've come to collect my son. He's the only thing that's left. The only one who I didn't destroy. The truth is that I've been angry for a quarter of my life."

Neither woman spoke. Neither said that in addition to being angry for so many years, Ellie had been completely wrong. It was too much, too horrible a thing to accept so quickly.

"In fact," Nancy said after a few minutes, "the only one of us who was ever right was Franklin. The moment I made him promise never to tell the truth, I became wrong, too. All for the price of a policeman's pension. What do you think we should do?"

"I don't even know where to begin," Ellie said. "Where is your daughter? We should tell her first and then Felix."

But Soraya didn't answer her phone, and Felix wasn't reachable, either. Neither woman suggested calling Franklin.

At half-past one in the morning, Lanie Salisbury finished her story. She called it "Urban Outlaws Get Down with Hillbilly Heroin, Go Plum Crazy," and she hoped that'd get through the deputy editor, though she knew it was far too long. It'd probably be reduced to "Club Kids Crushed by Country Smack" or some such thing. The *Spectator* was always hell on titles.

Her story was both dense in detail and entirely clear—she'd been out at the pier for hours and there were numerous dealers there, mostly bartenders from Terry Cheng's clubs, a woman from Peppermint Lounge and another from Sanction. They were taking orders for Oxy at a dollar a milligram, twice that if you looked like a stockbroker or a kid from New Jersey. She had paragraph-long quotes from the deejays, describing the edge that Oxy gave them, a longer high than heroin, cleaner, with fewer bumps. She'd even gotten some photos of people dancing, with just a few fingers over their eyes so they could retain their anonymity. Those club kids would do anything for publicity. But nobody would talk about what it meant when a bloody Lem Dawes had come off a harbor patrol boat in handcuffs and been ushered into a police car. So Lanie had put in some calls and she was waiting to hear back about Lem and what, exactly, he had done. She figured that was another, bigger story. She took a long sip from her cup of Puddle of Mud–brand coffee and pressed send. Then she relaxed.

It was late, but there were dozens of people still in the City room. And the lights were bright. She rubbed her eyes and wondered where Felix was. She'd swiped an undershirt of his when she'd stayed at the room he was using at the Official and she held it to her nose now. It smelled good to her, like honesty and musk and all the sex they'd had. She sank back into her uncomfortable aero chair and closed her eyes. A few minutes later her phone rang, and that woke her from what she realized would've been a very deep, much-needed sleep.

"Lanie here," she said as she blinked.

"It's Jimmy. Look, sorry about your last installment. I'm sure it's excellent, but I'm not going to read it. There's orders from upstairs. The series is killed."

"Killed?" She slapped herself once on the back of the neck to get her blood running.

"Yeah. I just got an e-mail from Starling Furst—says he loves all your shit, but the word is that our readers don't want to hear any more about Oxy. Doesn't help that good old Rudy Giuliani's on Purdue Pharma's payroll. I guess one of his enforcers sent over a note to that effect. So that's it, Lanie. It's over. Congratulations, though—there's some good news—you've been promoted. You're covering city hall."

"You're kidding," Lanie said. She looked at the smelly shirt in her hands and wondered if she was dreaming.

"Nope. No more crime for you."

She thought of the calls she'd put in to see about Lem. She frowned. "What if that's what I want to do?"

"Then do it at another paper. For us, you report on Bloomberg. And you know our position on Bloomberg."

"We love him like he's our daddy except when he raises taxes or messes with the schools. Then we make some graphs and bitch."

"Exactly. All we're asking of him is that he bring us the Olympics and some new stadiums. Other than that we've got nothing but love for our dear mayor. Let's have drinks tomorrow—we'll celebrate and I'll fill you in." Jimmy hung up.

Lanie glanced at her computer and saw that her e-mail icon was pulsing. She clicked it and found a dozen messages. There was a virus warning, party invites, something from a high school friend who was desperate for work. The last message came from P. J. McKenna, in response to an old request about information on Mike Sharpman and her newer question about Lem Dawes's arrest.

It read, *We call him Dandruff. He's a finger man who does double crosses inside the PD for people like your boss. I can't talk about Lem Dawes yet.* And that was it.

She sat for a moment and marveled at the ugliness of it all. Sure, maybe she'd used Felix to do some climbing, but it hadn't played out the way she thought it would, and she liked him in deeper spots than the places where she came up with strategy. Now she felt nothing but bad for him. His family was filled with the biggest creeps. She dialed Felix's cell.

"I've been hoping you'd call," he said.

"You're not going to believe who tells Sharpman what to do."

"I could take a guess," Felix said. He sounded very tired. "But I'd rather play this game in person, in private."

"Like in a bed," Lanie suggested.

"No place I'd rather be," Felix said. "Twenty minutes? Your place."

28

Starling Furst sat with Marsden Biddle in the library in the breakfast room at the University Club. It was seven in the morning. All around them, pairs of men and women muttered to one another over black coffee in chipped white cups and halved pink grapefruits with sides of whole-grain toast. Starling and Marsden looked no different from the others. In here, etiquette demanded that no one approach anyone else. Friends of forty years avoided each other's eyes while they made deals with relative strangers who represented companies and interests that were spread out all over the world. The ceiling was thirty feet above their heads. The hot air that collected up there had begun to rot the paintings of the gates of great universities.

Starling sipped a glass of fresh orange juice. He wore a charcoal double-breasted suit that fit tight over his thin shoulders. His white hair shot out in horizontal lines from the sides of his head, creating the impression that his intensity was a product of some inner static electricity rather than just the poor grooming of someone out of the public eye who answers to no one.

"In a few weeks I should have enough money to put up the bond and demolish all those buildings," Biddle said. "But before I do that piece of business, I imagine I'll short Purdue Pharma's stock. They're in for a PR nightmare with this Oxy. The stuff's a killer, that's for sure."

Starling Furst said, "Let's not be glib. If I find out you were responsible for my granddaughter's death, I'll tell Franklin." His voice was low and cool.

"Responsible? You're mad. Her overdose was just that," Marsden Biddle said. "In the all too human game we play of destroying ourselves, the need for more powerful drugs invariably trumps memories of the nasty experience of what happens when you take them." He sounded bored. He checked his tank watch.

"The user always ups the ante," Starling said.

"Correct," Biddle said. "That's why I'm paid so incredibly well to allocate the chips. But if someone wriggles free of my care, I can't be held responsible for how and when they . . . cash out."

"For your sake, I hope that's true," Starling said.

Biddle sat back in his chair and looked at Starling. Starling avoided the man's beady eyes. Instead, he looked at the scaly red skin on Biddle's hands and wondered how he could have ever trusted him. But he didn't indulge this naiveté for too long. The truth was that Biddle's snobbishness reminded him of his own.

Starling checked the digital Armitron watch that the *Spectator* had sent to its subscribers several years before as a joke gift, which he'd used ever since. The watch said, *Time's a'wastin', better read the* Spectator, on the band in glowing red, which Starling had thought up himself and found amusing. He thought that his use of the freebie watch made him appear eccentric. His employees simply found him charmless and cheap.

Finally Biddle said, "For my sake? Your threats are so antiquated, they're sweet."

"What would Ellie say?" Starling whispered.

"She ought to say, 'Thanks for trying to help my daughter.' But then, you wouldn't know what she'd say. She never spoke to you again, did she?"

"No."

"You hope to fix such a rupture now?"

Starling stared across the table. A small group of muscles began to quiver under his right eye.

"I *had* hoped so. Now, with her daughter dead, I am not so sure."

"Then why did you send her to me?"

"Good God," Starling said. He blew out his cheeks and stared. "You *did* kill her."

"Don't be ridiculous," Biddle said. He smiled, a thin, smirking smile. He said, "I took the Hippocratic oath, just like everyone else."

"But you were involved," Starling said. The muscles in his jaw felt like they were pulling down into his neck.

"Involved? What difference does it make? Your daughter ruined my life. She ruined yours, too. Why do you care what happened to her children?" He leaned forward. "I could've told Penelope to look both ways before running across the street. But it's not my fault she was hit by a car."

A waiter delivered a check and a black pen to the table. Biddle sighed and pulled the check toward him. He signed—the typical indecipherable hieroglyph of a self-important doctor.

Starling said, "She wasn't hit by a car. She overdosed on a drug that you gave her."

Biddle looked up. He slid his chair back half a foot from the table. He said, "I did get in a pinch with these buildings and their need to be knocked down. Legal threats from the community and all that. But money conquers all. And OxyContin really was the magic bullet. Penelope Novak? I wasn't there when she died. I've pumped out so much OxyContin in the last year, who knows whether she took in stuff I sold? Not me, certainly. When I read about what had happened to her, I wondered if you wouldn't be pleased—if you hadn't hoped for that outcome. After my own years-old tiff with your daughter, I can't say I shed tears. And now, with the cash that should be sailing in from my latest shipment, I'll grow very rich—not rich like you, of course, but rich for a man who has to work with his own two hands."

Biddle stood up then and smoothed his double-breasted suit over the low hump of his belly. The fabric of the gray flannel followed his hand and altered color slightly, as if it were animal fur. The blood had drained from Starling's skin, but he was already so pale that this was not immediately apparent. Marsden Biddle had not mentioned Ellie Furst in a dozen years. Starling had assumed that the doctor had forgotten her. The fact was that he hadn't made Starling suspect that when he'd sent his ailing granddaughter to Biddle: He'd assumed he was a good man, and that was one of the worst assumptions he'd ever made. It was unpleasant, Starling thought, to be so old and still manage to get people so completely wrong.

"You were involved in what happened to Penelope, weren't you?" Starling said.

"Let's let the subject go, shall we?" Biddle said. "More honesty won't help anyone."

"I imagine you'll be at River House for the Deshpandes's luncheon this afternoon," Starling said. "See you there."

"Yes. I'll be there," Biddle said. He gave Starling a curt nod, adjusted his glasses, and walked out of the breakfast room. Starling sat for a moment, staring forward. He fished a cell phone from inside his coat. He dialed Franklin's number. A waiter came toward the table. He raised his hand and pointed at the cell phone and at the other guests.

Starling heard Franklin pick up. He leveled a glance at the waiter, said, "Fuck off," and the waiter backed away.

"Starling? You don't want to start with a hello?" Franklin asked.

"Where is your office, Franklin? I would like to visit you there as soon as is humanly possible."

"Wait here," Starling said to his driver. He got out and went upstairs to Franklin's office. It was just nine in the morning. He rode in the elevator alone and looked at nothing. He went past Ivan Bulgarov's door and moved down the hall swiftly. He knocked hard on Franklin's door and then opened it.

Franklin was inside with Jenny. They'd been quietly drinking their morning coffee together, sharing a pain au chocolat, saying little. When Jenny saw Starling, she went out. He didn't appear to notice her. Starling sat down in a chair across from Franklin.

"I haven't seen you in the flesh in thirteen or fourteen years, but you look awful," Franklin said.

Starling seemed not to hear. "Please put your hands flat on the top of the desk," he said. "If at any time while I am speaking you move your hands, I will stop speaking. And you will not know the entire story or the ensuing plan. I am old. If you attack me, I will have a heart attack and I will die here in your office while my driver waits downstairs. If that occurs, justice will not be served. Do you have any questions before we begin?"

Franklin slowly shook his head. Starling put his pale white hands out in front of him, wiggled his waxy fingers. Franklin followed his example. He placed his hands flat on the desk and stared across at his former father-in-law.

"I suspect that Dr. Marsden Biddle murdered your daughter. I sent Penelope to him so that she would be cured of her drug habit. Incredibly, I believe he thought I'd sacrifice my own grandchild because of my feud with you and my daughter. Of course he was wrong, but he seems . . . unbalanced. He says he's been dealing drugs illegally. Apparently he has some sort of deal with someone at Purdue Pharma. In any case"—and Furst raised his pointer finger because Franklin's hands had begun to jitter—"In any case, Dr. Biddle, who you may remember as Morton Meyrink, will be at a luncheon in a few hours at River House given by the Deshpandes. They're old friends of mine, and now Sunil runs American National Trust. Perhaps you've heard of him. Accompany me. You may do with Biddle whatever you like, but I suggest that you kill him."

"This is the Morton Meyrink who nearly went mad over Ellie, who tried to keep me from marrying her? That lunatic?"

"Yes," Starling said.

"Do you realize what you've done?" Franklin asked.

"Yes. I would like you to take care of Meyrink, or Biddle, or whatever you want to call him, before I leave you all."

"Which will be soon?" Franklin asked.

"You will find my car downstairs at twelve-thirty. Assuredly, any apology I make now will be insufficient. My actions will serve us all better than my words."

Starling got up and walked out of Franklin's office. Franklin watched the door click closed and he remained still. So Marsden Biddle was Morton Meyrink. Franklin put his hands in front of his face and they seemed to float there, shaking slightly, like paper kites in a light wind.

* * *

"I don't want to leave, but my mother needs me," Felix said. He was propped up on one elbow, stroking Lanie's jaw, kissing her chin. She had her eyes closed and she'd just woken up. It had been a long, awful night.

"You're not being ironic?" she asked.

"I wouldn't know how," he said.

"God, that sounds good." She opened her eyes, gazed soberly at him. "If you leave this city I think it'll be the end of me. Why are you bringing leaving up now?"

"It's Thursday. I said I'd be finished by the end of the week, and it seems to me that my work here is just about done."

"But you're not finished with me."

Felix looked away from Lanie. He stretched, but he didn't get out of her bed. Lanie's black cat, Tabitha, appeared at the door to the bathroom, surveyed the scene, and slipped into the closet. The room was unbelievably messy. Felix propped himself up on his side and looked at Lanie.

"I really like you," Felix said. "But I've got family obligations."

"Shut up, dickhead," Lanie said. "It's love. And that changes things."

She pulled the covers over both of them. Felix looked up at the ceiling. He wondered if someone could say that kind of thing and not really mean it. He realized that he didn't know. And that was a good thing. Before coming to New York, he'd just assumed that everyone was like his mother said, untrustworthy and ultimately disappointing. But everybody couldn't be that way. He wondered if maybe he'd bought too much into his mother's vision of the world. But Lanie—she wasn't this new world's most reassuring person, either.

He saw Lanie staring at him and realized she'd been hoping for something, a response of some kind or a confirmation. But he didn't feel ready to speak.

Lanie said, "Let's stay in bed a while longer and readdress this issue when we're fresh."

She pushed her head into the crux of Felix's shoulder and fell asleep there.

Franklin stepped into Starling's black Mercedes. He didn't look at Starling, and they rode on the noisy city streets in near silence. Franklin's cell phone rang. It was Gennardi, returning his call.

"Meet me at the office in two hours," Franklin said. "If I'm not there, call Paul Freid, tell him I'm under arrest and to come down to the Tombs with a check for bail."

Franklin hung up.

"That won't be necessary," Starling said. "Whatever happens will be an accident."

Franklin said, "I was thinking that, too. I didn't bring a gun."

"It's a high floor."

They drove up Sixth Avenue and made a right at 50th Street, headed toward Sutton Place and River House. They stepped out of the car. An iron gate set into an ivy-covered wall clicked open and they passed through it, out of the public street. They walked through a courtyard that looked like an English country garden, complete with a marble boy who peed a high arc of water into a pool filled with brightly colored goldfish. They went into a small chamber with walls made of paneled wood, where there was an elevator. They went up alone, to the eleventh floor, and continued to say nothing. The noise of rich people greeting one another surrounded them as they stepped into the large oval entranceway of the Deshpandes's apartment.

A waiter approached them with a tray of glasses of white wine. Franklin refused the offer. He glanced briefly at the table in the dining room, which was set for twenty.

"Go into the study," Starling said quietly. "I'll deliver him to you." Starling disappeared. Franklin straightened his tie and looked at a painting of two horses running through a field. A short woman in a simple purple dress came up to him. She had large black eyes and a colorful scarf around her neck.

She said, "I'm your host, Rita. This is a celebration for my friend Kofi's new philanthropic organization, Relief. A sort of fund-raiser, if you will. And you are?"

"I'm with Starling," Franklin said. "Would you show me into the study? I need to make a business call before lunch."

"Of course," Rita Deshpande said. They went down the hall and she opened a door on her right.

"Make yourself comfortable," she said, and went away. The rectangular room was entirely filled with bookshelves. It was quite dark, and Franklin went to the far wall, which was partly covered by a brown velvet curtain. He pushed it aside and found a plate glass door, which opened onto a half circle of balcony. He stood there and looked out at the East River and Roosevelt Island. Directly below was the garden that he and Starling had walked through on their way in. He heard a door open behind him, and he turned around.

"Hullo," said Marsden Biddle.

"Morton Meyrink," said Franklin.

"If you like," the doctor said, and shrugged.

Wind whipped at the doctor's light brown hair and he brushed it back.

"You're surprised to see me?" Franklin asked.

"Not terribly. Starling looked a bit panicky this morning. In such a mood one often calls on old acquaintances."

"So the old man's getting soft?"

"You could say that. Let's speed this up, shall we? You've got questions for me? I'll do my best to answer them and we'll say goodbye. I don't want to miss the soup. It's pea with a lobster emulsion. The Deshpandes's cook is famous for it."

Biddle smiled, but there was perspiration on his forehead. He seemed to sniff the room, and then he inched forward. He leaned carefully against a bookcase. He laid his hands against the horizontal surface of the shelves.

"I was sorry to hear about your daughter's death," Biddle said. "Please also send my condolences to your wife."

"I haven't spoken to my wife in twelve years," Franklin said. "But let's talk about something that should concern you. Lem Dawes was arrested last night. He was found with enough OxyContin on him to put the whole city to bed."

"Oh?" Biddle said. He stuck out his tongue, which trembled. He seemed to realize this, and he used it to touch his upper lip.

"He said he got the stuff from you."

"Ridiculous," Biddle said.

"Maybe so. He's a nasty kid, that's for sure. But I'm here to take you in. It's kind of a favor I'm going to do for the police."

"Well, I won't go," Biddle said.

"No. I thought not. If you did, you'd end up on Rikers Island. We've got a mutual acquaintance there. Lionel McTeague. Right now he owes me a favor that he could pay off by killing you."

"You're joking," Biddle said. "Come now, Franklin Novak. Surely you don't think somebody like me could end up on Rikers."

"They'd put you in the Eric Thomas Center with the rest of the celebrities. But McTeague could get to you. Or he'd pay someone to do it. He'd have to, whether I wanted him to or not. With you under arrest, his sentence could grow from two years to twenty."

"You're making rather a lot of threats."

"Sometimes that's a good way to start. Now tell me what happened to my daughter."

Biddle shrugged. "I don't know. I was trying to help Penelope. She was in pain and it was my job to make sure she got a proper dose of medicine to relieve her of that pain. It's what I do. She refused to cooperate. I can't be held responsible for the consequences."

The two men stared at each other. Biddle grinned slightly, and his owlish eyes bulged behind his glasses.

"Were you using Max Udris to distribute OxyContin?"

"I never heard of such a person," Biddle said.

A slight rustle behind them proved to be Starling Furst, who stood in the darkness of the room, watching the two men.

"Udris is under arrest, too. He'll certainly give up your name. He probably already has. Think about it. Everyone's been taken down. They're all sitting in rooms with detectives, talking about their relationship to you."

Starling Furst clicked the door closed behind him. They turned to look at him, but the old man said nothing. The only sound was the wind blowing against the curtains.

"I can't imagine that any of what you've said would bring you all the way here. But I know where this is going, so I'll tell you the truth. Starling delivered Penelope to me," Biddle said suddenly. "He wanted me to murder her. He's mad. Get your vengeance on him, won't you? And leave me alone."

"You think he's as bad as all that?" Franklin asked.

"Of course. I'd never hurt anybody," Biddle said. He was beginning to breathe quickly.

"No city agency is going to buy land from you now, Marsden. They'll simply take it, the same way they'd impound a street dealer's car," Starling said. "And even if you did manage to get off of Rikers Island alive, you'd never practice medicine again. And you'd be bankrupt. Tell us the truth, can't you?"

"Ellie was supposed to be mine." Biddle pointed at Furst. "He promised her to me before she ever knew you. And then he gave me Penelope. It was him—it was some kind of crazy vengeance on his part. Anyway, I didn't kill her. I only saw her twice." Biddle turned to Franklin. "But him, he wanted to destroy you."

Franklin glanced down at the garden. From that distance, the fountain looked like a bull's-eye.

Franklin said, "It's true that Starling doesn't like me. He's proved that. But I can't think of many instances where men like Starling kill their grandchildren. And all to destroy some cheap investigator? You'll have to come up with something better than that."

"He's a psychopath," Biddle said, and he was gasping for breath.

"Is he the one who hired Kenny Price to kill me?" Franklin asked.

"Yes, that's exactly right," Biddle said. "He's the one who did that. It was Starling who did that. I'm amazed that you figured it out."

Franklin shook his head. He frowned at Biddle and said, "Odd, isn't it—that you'd be so quick to remember who Kenny Price is or what he did. You know, Dr. Biddle, my life wasn't perfect a dozen years ago. But you ruined it. And now I know."

Biddle stood against the shelves. He looked from Starling, who blocked the door, to Franklin, who stood at the entrance to the balcony. He was making a noise in his throat, a kind of bubbling sound.

"I've made a tremendous error in judgment," Starling said. "Franklin, you can be assured that no one here will admit to ever having seen you. In fact—" Starling raised an eyebrow. Color rushed into his face. He said, "Get out of my way."

"What?" Biddle said.

Starling rushed at the doctor and pulled him off the bookshelves. The doctor was flung forward, through the door, onto the balcony, where Franklin caught him.

"Ellie was supposed to be mine," Biddle said. "You people have caused me nothing but pain."

"She never liked you," Franklin said.

Biddle held tight to the iron railing. Starling stepped onto the balcony and crouched down. He grabbed Biddle's legs and pulled him free of Franklin, who moved back. Biddle, on the other side of the railing now, found that though he worked with his hands, his stubby red fingers weren't strong enough to help him to hold on, and he let go. He plunged down impossibly quickly, striking the fountain with a flat thud.

Starling and Franklin looked down at his body.

"He didn't yell," Franklin said.

"No," Starling said. "He probably hasn't raised his voice in twenty-five years, so it would not have occurred to him to do so now. Let's skip lunch."

They walked quickly through the apartment's long hallway. They passed the closed door to the dining room, where they could hear happy exclamations about the excellence of the soup. They made their way down in the elevator.

"I was listening at the door. Tell me, can you really reach inside Rikers and make the sort of thing you described happen?" Starling asked.

"I never have. But I suppose I could try. Guys like that do get a lot of protection in there. It's really not a fair system."

"Thanks for not believing him," Starling said. "About me."

"Oh, you're no killer. He was. He could never confess to anything, so he used you. It was time for him to go. I think he knew that."

In the courtyard, they didn't turn to look at the body of Marsden Biddle, which had knocked the head and torso off the marble boy. Water gushed skyward. Several doormen surrounded the mess. One was on the phone to the police.

"Buzz us out, won't you," Starling said. One of the doormen, perhaps out of habit, rushed over and let them through the iron gate onto the street.

Starling said, "You'll forgive me if I don't give you a ride downtown?"

"Of course," Franklin said, and he began to walk west.

"Then I'll see you at my funeral," Starling called after him.

Starling Furst sat in the back of his Mercedes. He turned on his cell phone and listened to a message from Lem Dawes's father, who was desperately pleading for any help Starling might give him with his son, who had been arrested the night before and was now in a hospital, under police custody. Starling frowned. One last favor for an old friend? After all, they'd taken care of the real villain, hadn't they?

He dialed Mike Sharpman's number.

"There's one more thing I'd like you to do for me," he said.

The Mercedes went west until they were on Second Avenue, where they turned south and picked up speed.

"Let me out here," Starling called to his driver. "I want to walk."

The black Mercedes pulled over on Second Avenue and Starling stepped out.

Starling said, "Take the rest of the day off."

The driver sped away then rather than give Starling Furst a chance to reconsider such a terribly rare act of kindness. Starling stood alone between two parked cars on the east side of Second Avenue, between 35th and 36th Streets.

He waited until the light was green. Several city buses picked up speed on the downhill. They were easily going fifty and weighed untold tons. Starling selected one and began to step in front of it. But someone grabbed him at the waist and flung him onto the front of a parked car.

Starling gasped, worked to focus his eyes. Franklin Novak. He was breathing heavily, and his face was covered with sweat. He pulled Starling off the car and stood him upright. People swiveled their heads to watch their awkward embrace, but nobody stopped.

Franklin said, "I caught a cab and followed you. That funeral line had about as much subtlety as the gossip in your newspaper."

"I delivered my granddaughter into the hands of a murderer."

"Yeah," Franklin said: "That is true. But that guy, he's got a history of not doing his own dirty work. Lem Dawes killed Penelope. He must've tricked her with pills. Maybe Lem and Biddle had an agreement between them, maybe they didn't. But when I told Biddle Lem was in custody, he cared, which was enough for me. Lem's the one who was with her when she OD'd. I'm sure of it now."

"Franklin," Starling said. "I just put in a request to set Lem Dawes free."

"You want to wait for another bus and I'll give you a push?"

Starling turned away and bent over suddenly. He leaned on the car and spat ribbons of bile into the gutter. Then he looked back at Franklin.

"I've been a shit," Starling said. "And this is absolution?"

"If you think somebody like me can give it, then sure, that's what it is. Now I've got to get that Lem Dawes character back so I can kill him. Which hospital is he at?"

Starling shook his head. He said, "I don't know."

29

Mike Sharpman went out to Elizabeth Street and got into an unmarked Taurus. He figured this was a five-thousand-dollar favor. After he set the rich fucker free, he planned to stop at that little luncheonette, Chez Brigitte, on Greenwich. He'd have the lamb chop, maybe even some pea soup to start. But nothing with rice. No more rice. It was Thursday and nice out—looked like the bright sun of midday was going to make it a beautiful afternoon.

He drove across town and parked in Saint Vincent's emergency zone and flashed his badge. He walked rapidly up to Lem Dawes's room. The requisite patrol cop sat on a folding chair in front of the door. He was reading the *Spectator* and laughing so hard that his belly jiggled. When Sharpman approached him, the cop nodded. Sharpman showed his shield again.

He said, "Go have a cigarette."

"I don't smoke," the patrolman said.

"Have a candy bar, then, a Mounds," Sharpman said. He handed the cop a twenty-dollar bill, which the cop took between two fingers. He shook the bill at Sharpman.

"Dark chocolate, it gives me a headache. What I'll probably get is a Snickers, you know, that's an old dependable candy, or maybe something classier, a Symphony bar or a mini-Toblerone."

"Uh-huh," Sharpman said. He opened the door and went into Dawes's room. He could hear the cop head down the hall, say a long hello to a nurse.

"Lem Dawes?" Sharpman asked. The kid in the bed nodded. "Can you put your clothes on?"

"Where are we going?" Lem said. His face was badly bruised, but otherwise he was okay. He'd been up for hours, trying to fight through the painkillers and think through to some sort of defense. Mostly he was worried about all that the cops didn't know about him.

"Not we," Sharpman said. "You. Get dressed and get out of here.

Make some calls. Get somebody to meet you at Kennedy with your passport and some cash. Behave like you're important. Go to a country with no extradition," Sharpman continued. "If you can make it to the airport in less than fifty minutes, you should be fine. Were it me, I hear Bolivia is nice."

"You're kidding."

"I'm just the messenger. I don't get paid to have a sense of humor. You got two minutes before the cop comes back—maybe three. You going to eat that apple?"

"Take it," Lem said. He was already into his pants. He was already making a call. "Shit," he said. "I'm in no condition to drive."

"You're rich," Sharpman said. "Call a car service."

Soraya and Gus were in Soraya's tiny bed in her dorm room when Gus's cell phone rang. Gus saw that it was Lem and took the call because he was angry at him for screwing up the permit for the tug the night before. He sat up and figured that he might even call it quits on the whole partnership, considering all the trouble Lem was causing and how much Soraya hated him.

"Yeah," Gus said.

"Listen," Lem said. "I need your help. I'm up on a drug charge and I'm leaving the country right now and I need a ride to the airport. I called Terry, but he said you had his Cadillac. And you know how pissed he gets when people break the law. I need you now, man."

"A drug charge?" Gus said. "Your dad'll get you free of that shit in a minute. Why bother to skip?"

"Look, man. It's serious. I need you to pick me up and get me the fuck out of here."

"I don't know, man. Just now I'm in a bed. . . ." Gus trailed off. He ran his finger down Soraya's cheek and she woke up. They were both still in their clothes. It had been a long, loveless night. He covered the phone, whispered, "Lem." And frowned.

"Okay, okay, it's not the drug charge. I don't give a shit about that.

Dig—Udris and Karoly got taken down last night, and I'm afraid they're going to spill about me and I need to get gone before they do."

"Look, I know they peddle, but if they spill that you're their supplier, so what? They can say whatever—they could say I was involved and it wouldn't be hardly enough to even get me arrested."

"'Cause it's not true for you!" Lem spluttered. "But me, listen. I was there the night that girl died, Penelope Novak."

Gus's eyebrows rose. "So?" he said. He held the phone so Soraya could hear, too. "She overdosed. That's not your fault. Chill out."

"It was my fault and Udris knows it! I crushed the 160s that took her away. I fed her the Oxy and I watched her die. Biddle said he'd pay me to do it, only that fucker hasn't come through with the cash. But Udris doesn't know about Biddle, just me. Udris'll trade his story for leniency. Now come pick my ass up!"

"Biddle paid you to kill Penelope," Gus said. He and Soraya locked eyes.

"Yeah," Lem said. "He's one psycho motherfucker."

"Wait," Gus said. "Slow down. I'll meet you. Tell me where you're at."

He and Soraya listened for a moment. Then Gus said, "Okay," and ended the call. He turned to Soraya and said, "Jesus. There's another thing I forgot to tell you last night. It was Lem who paid for that room. But the night manager didn't know about it. It was Kashmira who took the money from him, and she never entered the information into the computer."

Soraya's voice trembled. She said, "It would've been good if you checked on that a little earlier."

Gus said, "I know that now. I'd call Felix myself, but it'd save time if you do it. You know how he is with me. Tell him Lem got free and I'm going to drive him out to Kennedy. What I'll do is, I'll get him in the car with me and Felix can follow us. Then he can take him from me."

"It'll be me and Felix," Soraya said. She grabbed her sneakers from the floor.

"Good," Gus said. "You can make sure that Felix doesn't get confused about my lack of connection."

Gus drove downtown with Soraya. She called Felix and got him at Lanie's house. She told him that she needed him, now.

"My car's in Clarke's lot. Meet me there," Felix said.

He dressed and ran to the Roadrunner and didn't think to call his father. Gus dropped Soraya at Houston on his way to Saint Vincent's. She caught sight of Felix, running. They grabbed the Roadrunner and Felix keyed the ignition. He looked at Soraya and kissed her once, on the cheek.

"I missed you last night," Felix said. "Now where?"

"Actually," Soraya said, "they'll be by. Let's just wait."

They sat in silence.

"Gus never did anything," Soraya said. "He's innocent."

"Okay," Felix said. "Anyway, I was just thinking about leaving town."

"Where were you when I called?"

"With Lanie."

"Listen," Soraya said. "It's Lem Dawes. He was the one who tricked Penelope into overdosing. It was him. He did it on orders from Marsden Biddle. He said so on the phone just now to Gus."

Soraya watched Felix. He had both of his hands on the wheel. He'd left the car in park and he revved the engine.

She said, "Where's your gun?"

"I threw it away," Felix said.

"Thank God," Soraya said. "There they are."

The Cadillac blew by, going fast on Houston, cutting the light on First Avenue. Felix shot out of the lot, turned right, and followed them toward the Williamsburg Bridge. He moved along the Cadillac's right side and nodded at Gus, who nodded back. Lem hadn't seen them yet. Both cars sped up, dragged along the wide expanse of Houston Street. Felix popped the clutch then and cut in front of the Cadillac. He looked back when they came to Orchard Street. It was only then that Lem Dawes opened his eyes. He looked at the Roadrunner's Plum Crazy paint and he just shook his head. They stopped at the corner of Ludlow and Houston, alongside the neon lights of Katz's Deli. Felix got out of the car and went and looked into the Cadillac.

"I owe you an apology," Felix said to Gus.

"You better deal with this guy first. I don't want him bleeding on Terry's seats."

Felix went and got Lem from the passenger seat. He tried to struggle and all Felix said was, "Don't." He didn't even hit him. He put him in the back of the Roadrunner and Soraya took the wheel.

"He does have mean eyes," Soraya said. "Be careful of him."

"Nobody gets away three times," Felix said.

Felix walked into the Fifth Precinct with Lem. He had him by the elbow, and Lem sagged down, barely able to hold his own weight.

"This man murdered my sister," Felix said. "And he almost got away."

The desk sergeant nodded. Several uniforms approached, took Lem from Felix.

"Yeah, we just had a call from Saint Vincent's. Sharpman is locked down. You're Felix Novak, aren't you?" the desk sergeant said. He reached behind the desk, got a telephone, and handed it to Felix. "Your father's been looking for you. Why don't you give him a call."

30

Ellie Novak sat with Franklin Novak in the bar at the Gramercy Park Hotel. Franklin was drinking a Budweiser and Ellie had a club soda. It was dusk, and the piano player hadn't come in yet. They were bent in toward each other and they were talking about their children.

They looked like tourists, like a middle-aged couple who'd weathered the inherent storms that come with bringing up children but who had stayed together through it all. They looked tired and solemn, as if they'd accepted what they'd become and were satisfied with the course of their lives. Of course, that was not what they were at all.

"I didn't make the decision for Felix," Franklin said.

"I would still prefer it if he would come back with me."

Franklin said nothing. Ellie watched him. Her affair with Billy Navarro really had destroyed their lives. But it wouldn't have ended as badly as it had if Morton Meyrink hadn't hired Kenny Price to kill Franklin. She understood that now.

She looked down into her drink. She had a sense that she was falling, that without the bedrock of distrust she'd used as her center for years, she didn't really know herself. She'd instilled that lack of trust in her son and he would fight for the rest of his life to be free of what she'd put inside him. She realized that it was only right that he should stay here, with his father.

She said, "I thought you tried to kill Billy."

"I didn't," Franklin said. "I didn't even know you were having an affair."

Ellie glanced away from the table. Then she said, "Morton Meyrink hired Kenny Price to kill you. And Billy Navarro saved your life."

"You'd had an affair with Meyrink," Franklin said. "Too?"

"Not an affair. I was with him years earlier, in college. He was controlling."

"Must've been brief."

"Yes," Ellie said. "It was. I'm sorry, Franklin. I know he was complicit in Penelope's death."

"Complicit? I guess you could put it that way. Have you seen your father?"

Ellie nodded. "I saw him. He's very grateful to you. He seems destroyed now, dangerously depressed. But I believe he'll come out of it."

Franklin said, "He's a tough old man. I'm sure he'll get better."

He sipped his beer. The piano player came in and sat down behind the piano. But he was reading that day's *Spectator,* and he didn't begin to play.

"I didn't understand everything about the day Billy Navarro died until now," Ellie said.

Franklin didn't smile, only stared at his ex-wife.

"You really loved Billy," he said.

Ellie hesitated. Then she said, "I was furious at you for how much of a cop you'd become. You promised me you wouldn't get that way. And you broke that promise."

The waiter stopped at their table and refilled their wooden bowl with goldfish. Franklin nodded for the check.

"I'm going to stay here for a little while," Ellie said. "I'll take care of my father and spend time with Nancy. My farm can get along without me for a few months, I'm sure. I believe I can trust the people who are taking care of it."

"I'm happy to hear that," Franklin said.

Franklin took Felix and Soraya back up to his office after lunch at Zitto's with Gennardi and Philip. It'd been a long lunch, punctuated by somber moments and interrupted by people coming over to pay their respects. Everyone had read Lanie's story in the *Spectator* by then and the buzz in New York on that Friday belonged to their table. Even Richard, the waiter, was nice to Franklin.

Now Felix and Soraya sat across from Franklin in the silence of his office. The place was unchanged, except that when they came in, Franklin had put the Raging Bull in a drawer. Gennardi and Philip had gone off to close out the Edelstein case and collect a much-needed check. Franklin had left his suit jacket on. He was leaning back in his big chair.

Franklin bit his lips for a moment. Then he said, "Lem Dawes murdered Penelope. Biddle said he'd pay him and that he needed it done to get Udris off his back so he could make more money. But Biddle didn't know that Lem was still distributing through Udris. Lem was looking for whatever money he could get. And all Lem had to do was do nothing when she overdosed. But it's still murder."

"It was unfortunate that Penelope's grandfather introduced her to the most evil man in the world," Soraya said.

"That's how it happened," Franklin said. "But I don't believe he knew what he was doing. In fact, I know he didn't. Biddle was just the name that came to him when Penelope went to see him."

Felix leveled his gaze at Franklin.

"Why do you think Starling's not guilty?" Felix asked. "He seemed pretty ashamed, wouldn't you say? After all, you're the one who said he tried to throw himself in front of a bus."

"When Biddle went over that balcony . . . let's just say Starling Furst was with me when that happened. I'm not saying I'm a fan of that old man, but he paid his dues."

Felix and Soraya were quiet. Neither asked whether the official explanation for Biddle's suicide was not, in fact, the truth. The timing for suicide made sense and there would be no investigation. He wasn't the sort of man who would go to jail, and there were several people informing against him. People wouldn't think of his suicide as acquiescence. Rather, because of its venue, it appeared to be an act of defiance.

Franklin said, "I want to believe that Penelope really did go to Starling for help. I'd like to believe that she wanted to kick the Oxy and she couldn't. These guys, they kept her in pills while they forced her into a situation that was way beyond her control. There's no evidence that she ever actually dealt drugs or did anything but use them."

Felix nodded at his father. He said, "Her suppliers were scaring her. That was all. And there was Lem in the room with her, feeding her Oxy. She stopped breathing. He watched."

No one spoke. It was apparent that Felix had been saying this to himself over and over again for quite some time. Then Franklin nodded. Felix had his cowboy hat on and he tipped it back on his head. He scratched his nose and looked over at Soraya. She raised an eyebrow at him. Half a minute passed.

"You still seeing that girl, the one who wrote the article?" Franklin asked.

"Lanie Salisbury. Well, she's been busy these last couple of days. I guess the *Post* is trying to hire her away from the *Spectator.* She wants the crime beat, and they're offering it. So she's pretty excited about her career. She hasn't called."

"God, I really can't stand her," Soraya said.

"Not everybody can be as lucky in love as you," Felix said.

Soraya looked away.

"Sorry about that," Felix said. "But I never did have good feelings about that guy."

"Have you told her the truth about what happened to her father?" Franklin asked Felix.

"No," Felix said. "But she must have learned it."

Soraya gazed at the two men. Then she looked up at the ceiling. There was light gray particleboard up there. Soundproofing.

She said, "Do I know that my father almost killed Franklin over Ellie and at the last second he couldn't do it and saved Franklin's life instead? Yes, I know that. Do I know that Marsden Biddle hired the gunman who shot my father to death? Yes, I know that."

"And you're still sitting here?" Franklin asked.

Soraya kept looking up at the ceiling. She'd shifted back in her chair and then she dropped forward, o the front legs thumping on the carpet.

She said, "Where else would I go? You're both good men. You've proved that. I'm not finished with the two of you."

"I'm going to stay here and work with Franklin," Felix said.

Soraya stood up and took a step toward the door. She gestured at the paper bag with the Cookie Monster drawing on it. She said, "That's a pretty good portrait, Franklin. It looks just like you."

Franklin nodded a thank-you. He'd put the drawing in a large wooden frame and hung it on the side wall so he could see it from behind his desk. Franklin clasped his hands behind his head and smiled at the drawing.

9 780743 463317

Printed in the United States
By Bookmasters